FOR MY MOM

FOR HELPING ME
LEARN THE
GREATEST LESSON:
TO BE MYSELF

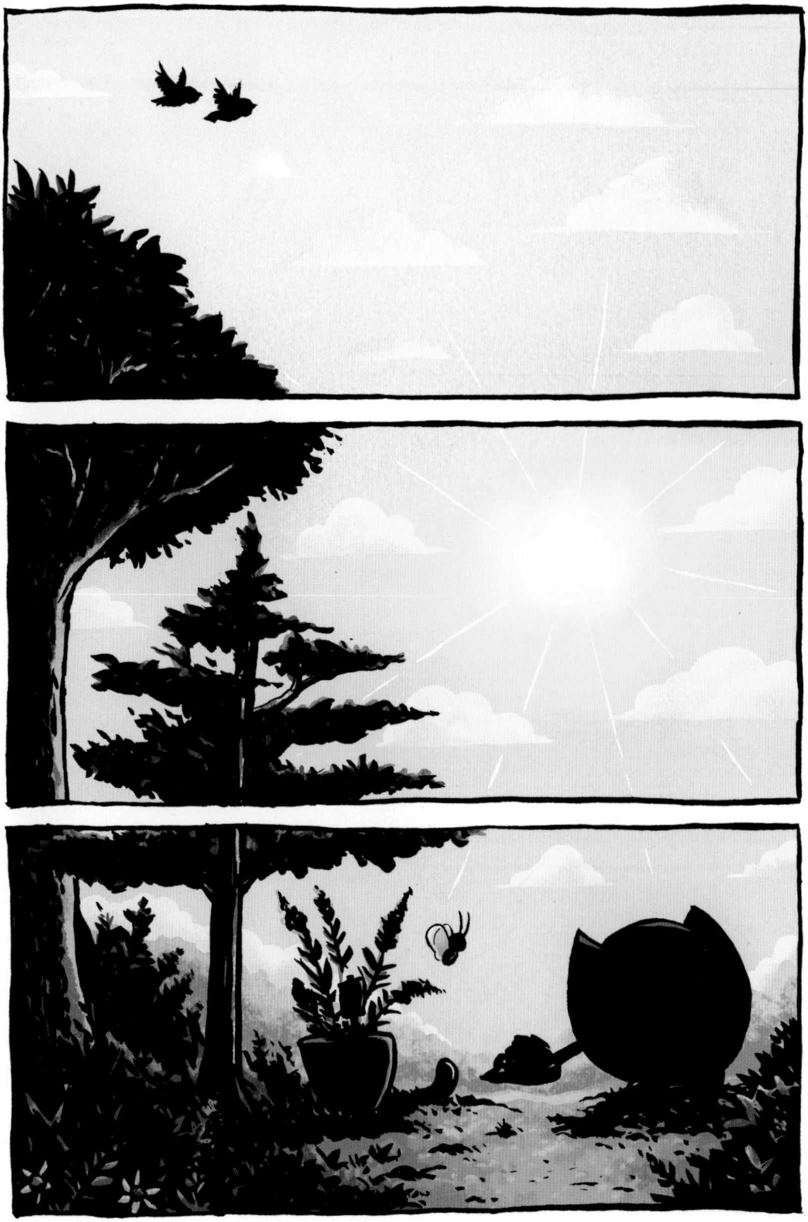

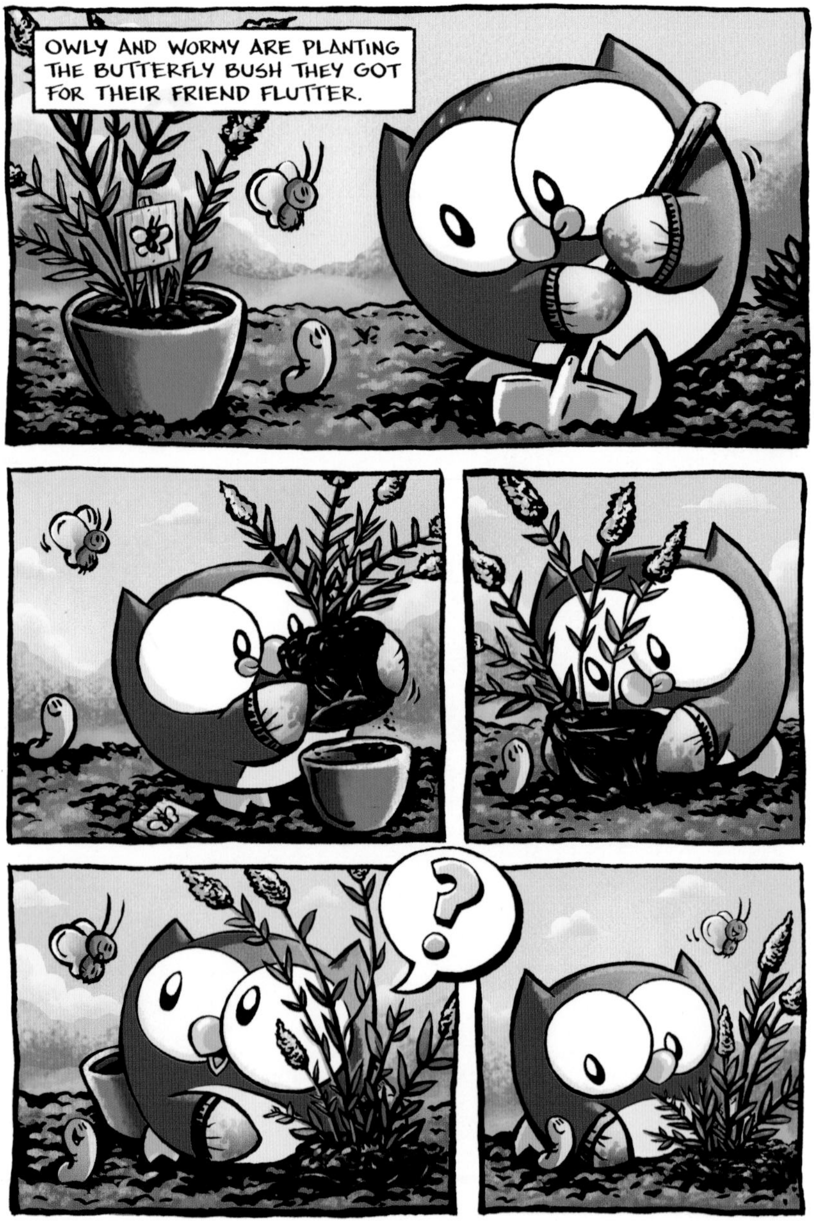
OWLY AND WORMY ARE PLANTING THE BUTTERFLY BUSH THEY GOT FOR THEIR FRIEND FLUTTER.
?

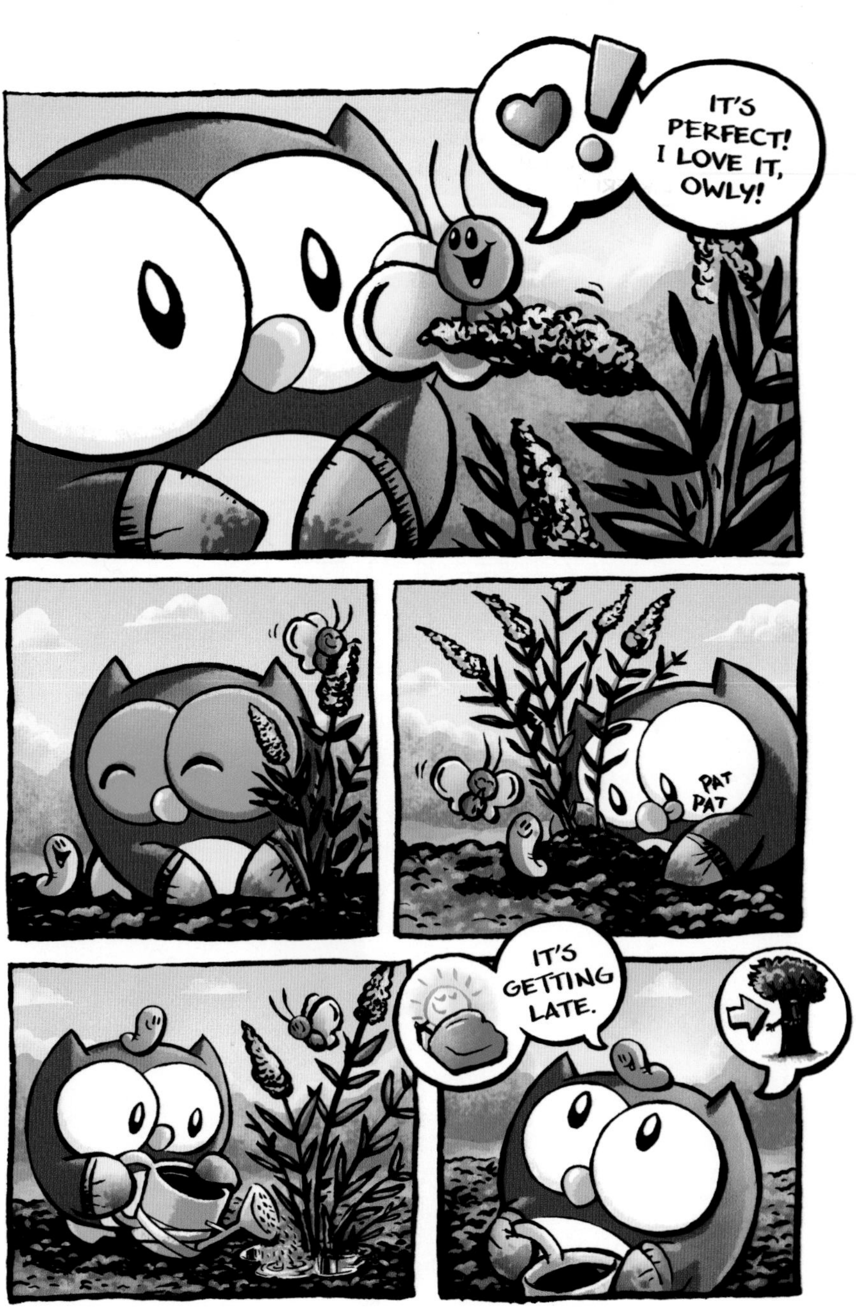
IT'S PERFECT! I LOVE IT, OWLY!
PAT PAT
IT'S GETTING LATE.

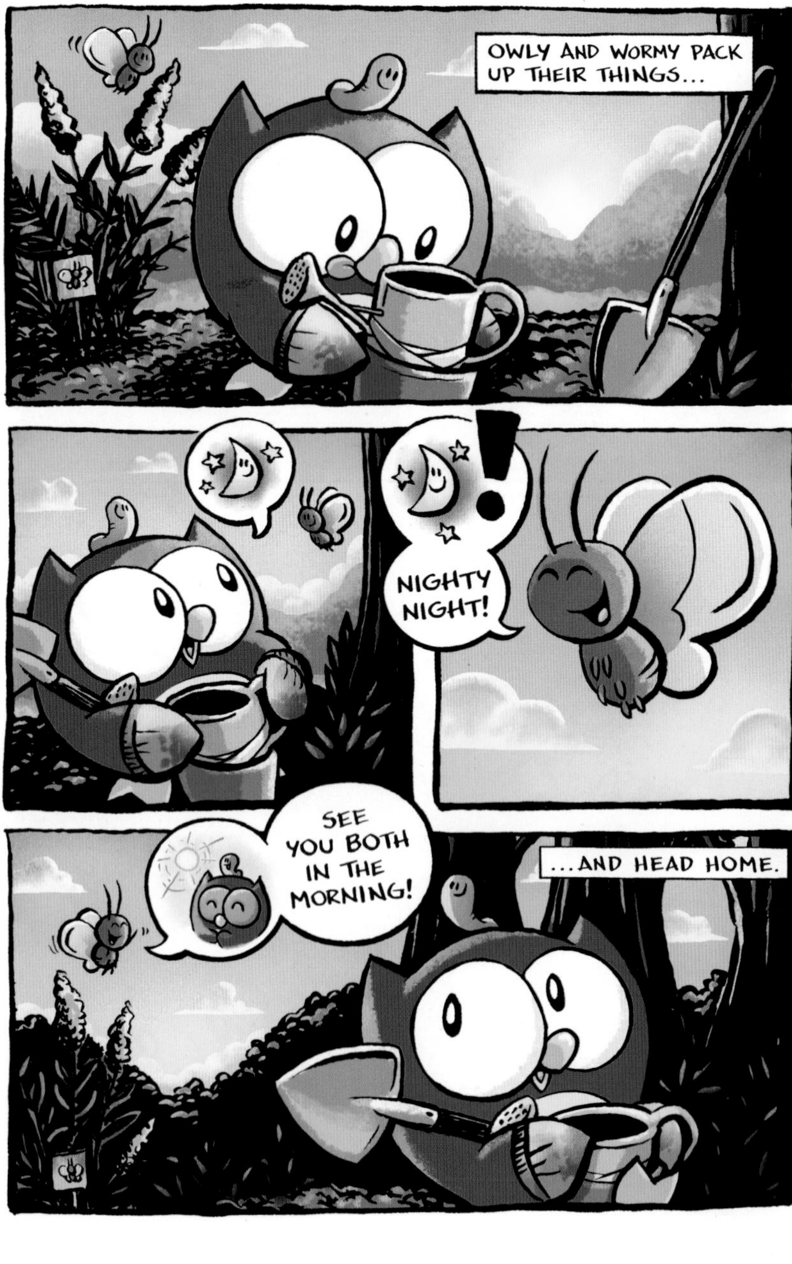
OWLY AND WORMY PACK UP THEIR THINGS...
NIGHTY NIGHT!
!
SEE YOU BOTH IN THE MORNING!
...AND HEAD HOME.

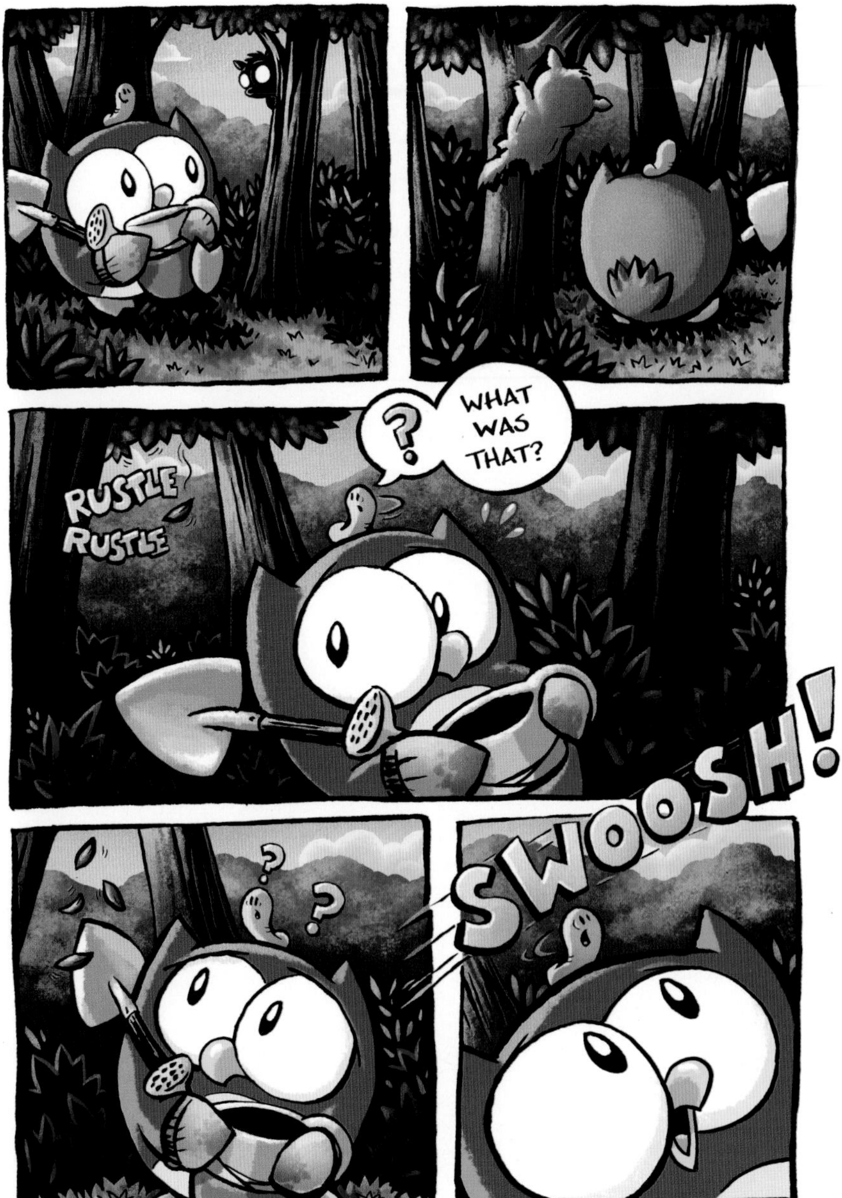
RUSTLE
RUSTLE
?
WHAT WAS THAT?
?
?
SWOOSH!

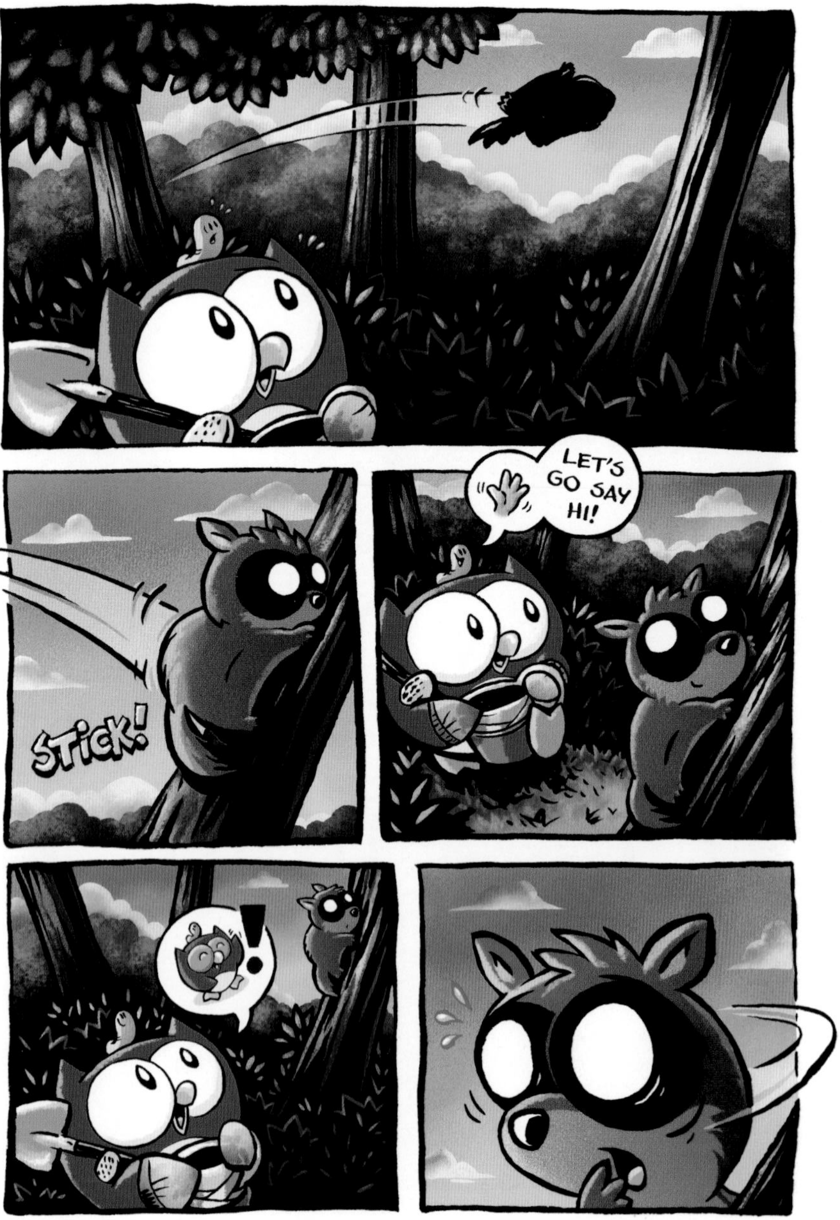
STICK!
LET'S GO SAY HI!
!

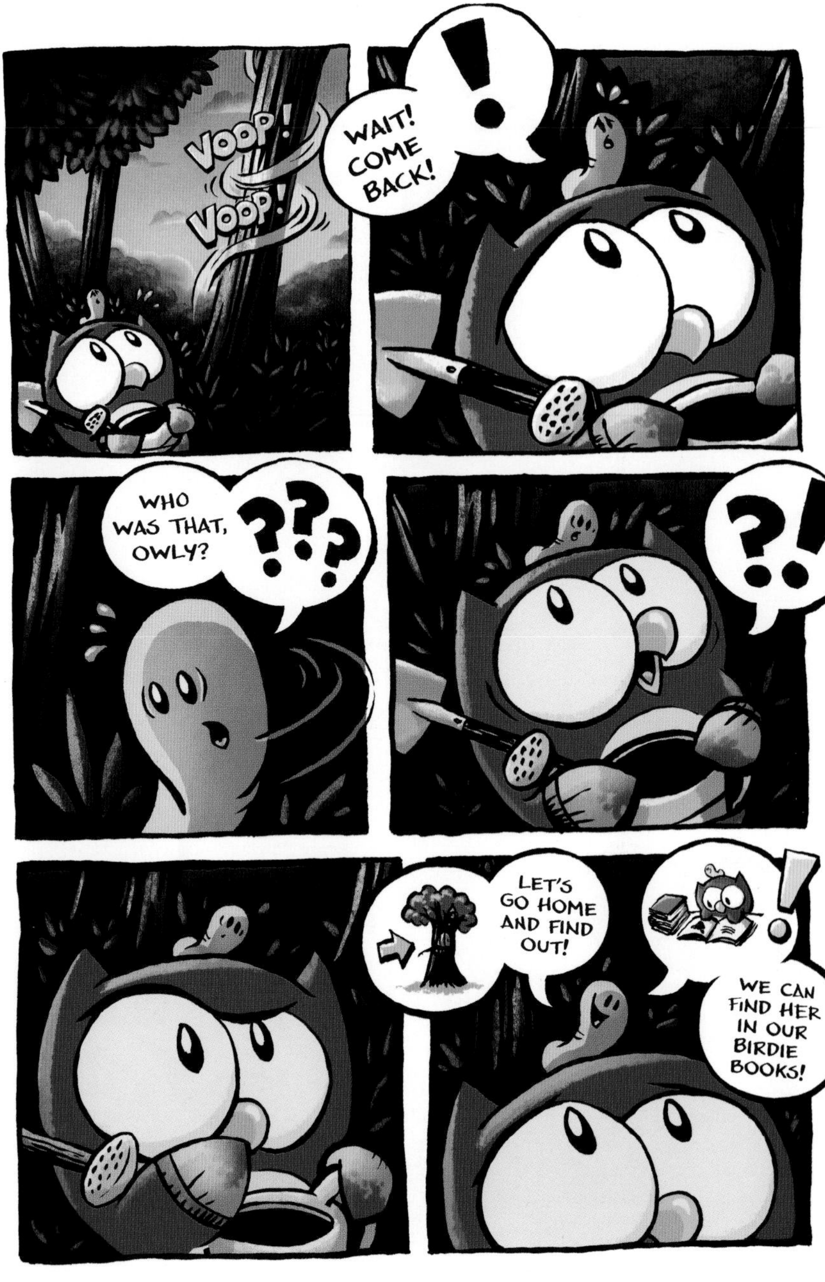
VOOP! VOOP!
!
WAIT! COME BACK!
WHO WAS THAT, OWLY?
???
?!
LET'S GO HOME AND FIND OUT!
!
WE CAN FIND HER IN OUR BIRDIE BOOKS!

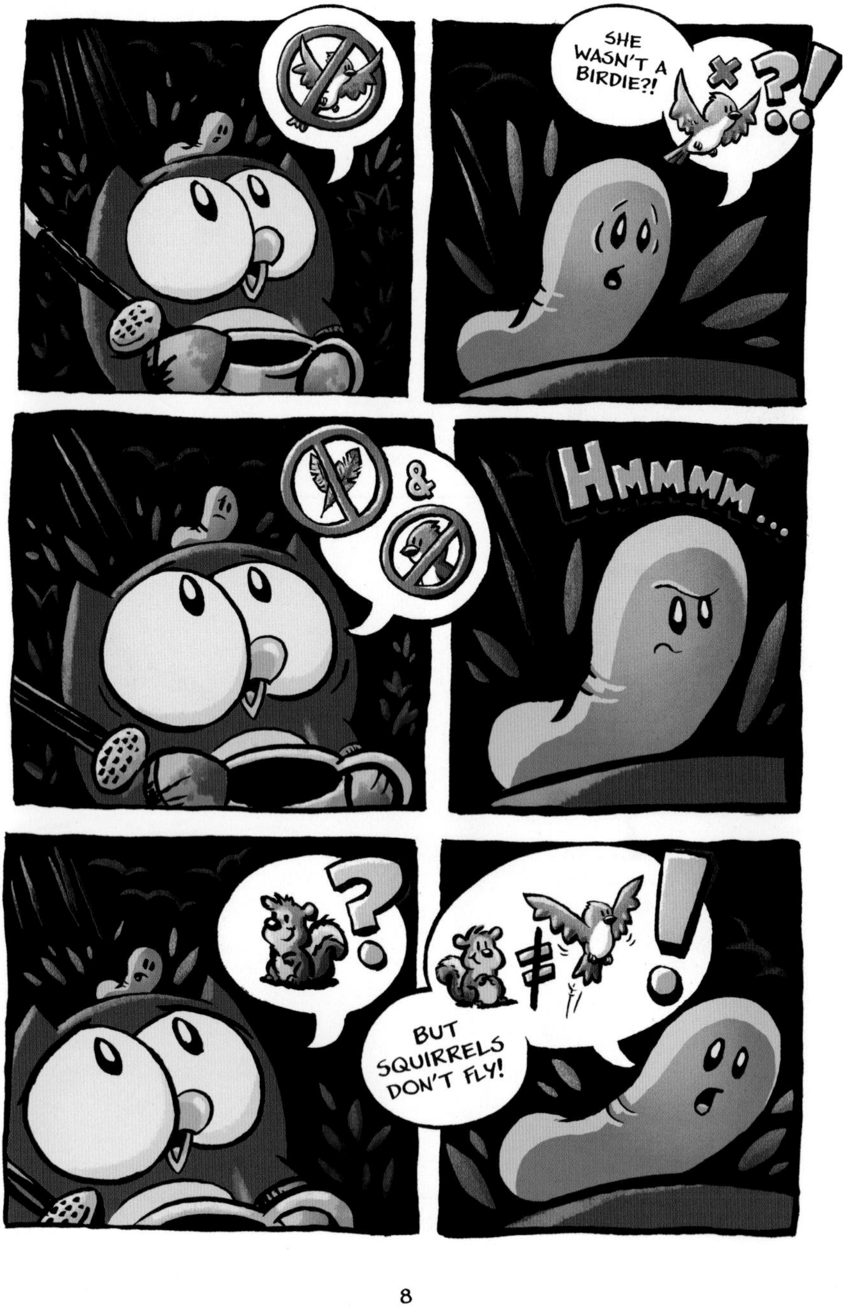
SHE WASN'T A BIRDIE?!
HMMMM...
BUT SQUIRRELS DON'T FLY!

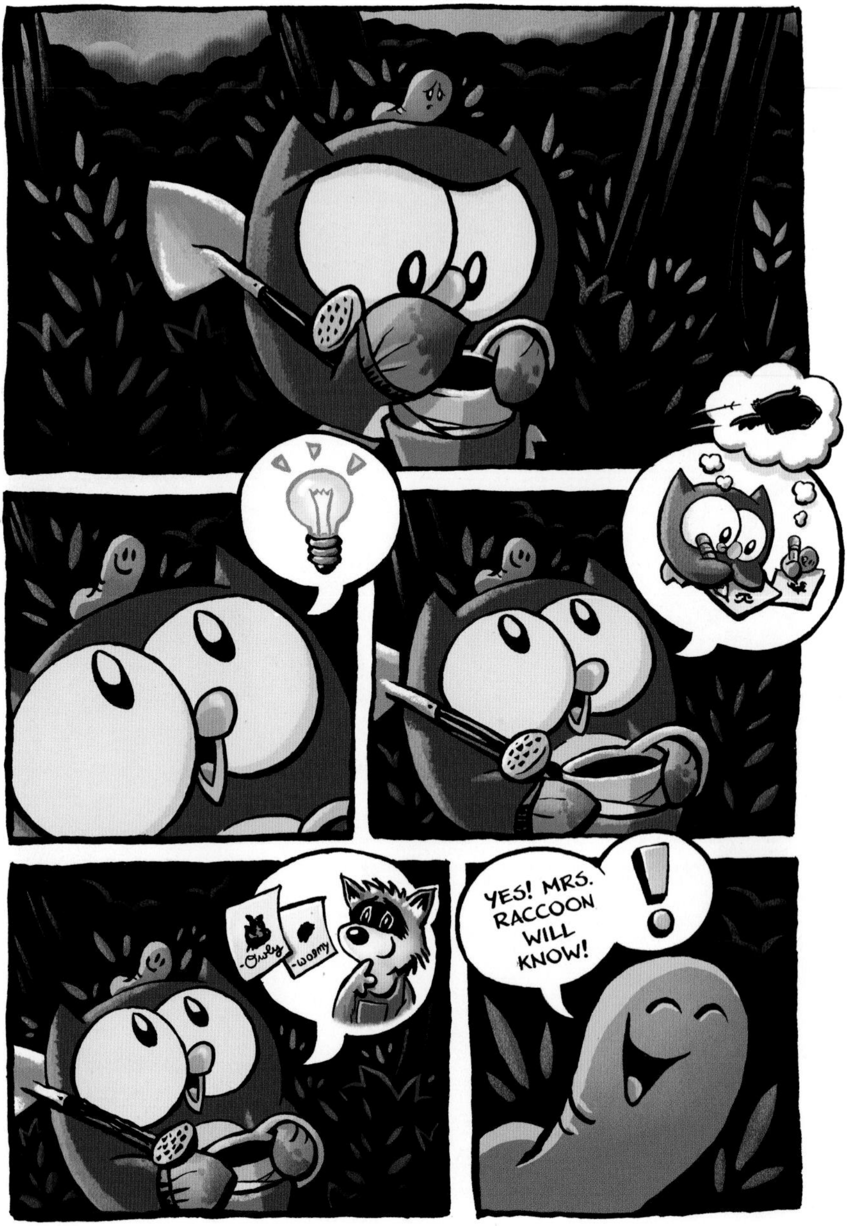
-Owly
-Wormy
YES! MRS. RACCOON WILL KNOW!
!

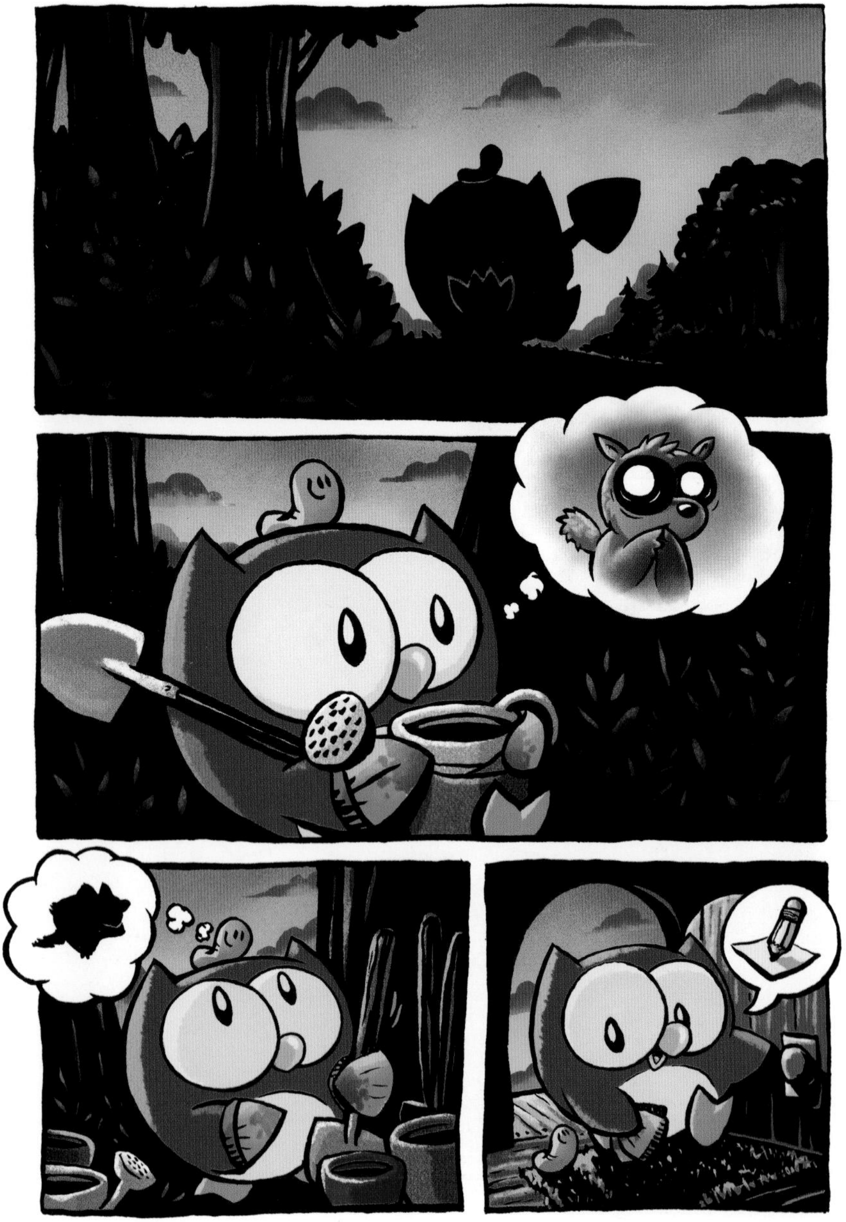

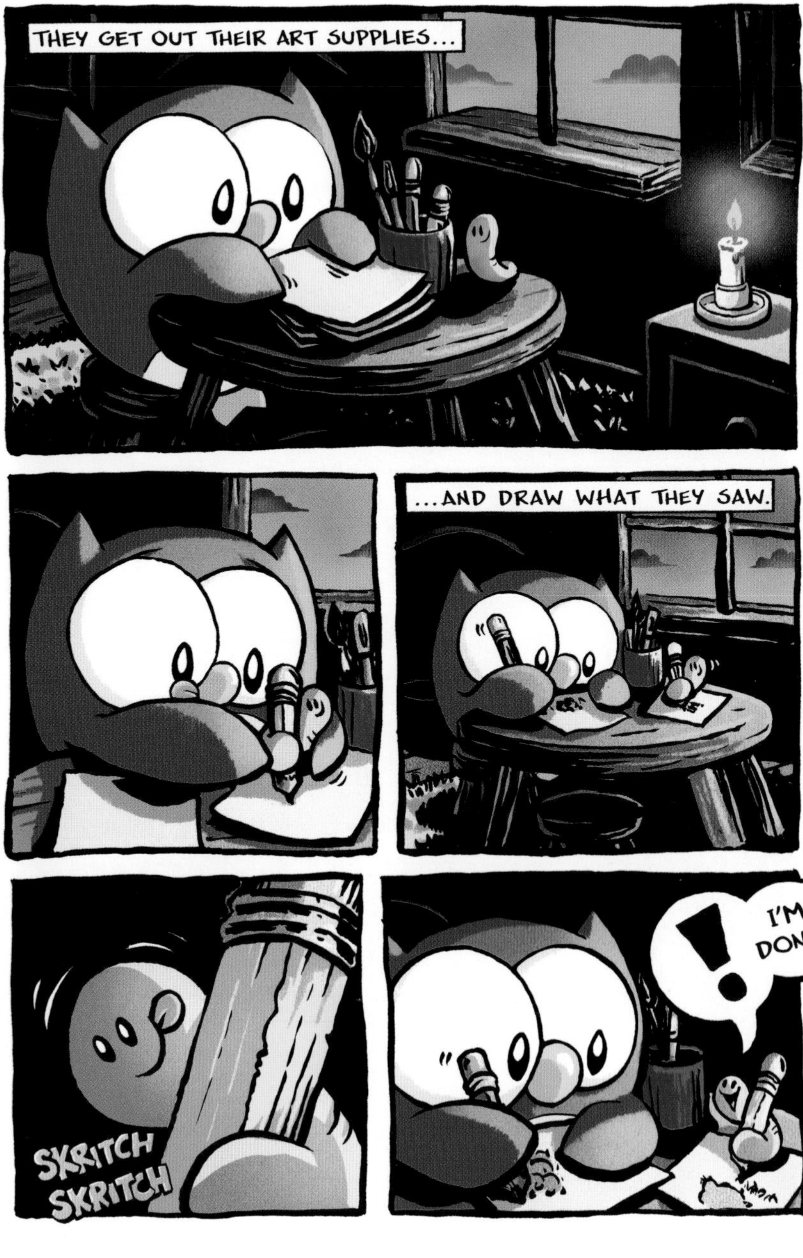
THEY GET OUT THEIR ART SUPPLIES...
...AND DRAW WHAT THEY SAW.
SKRITCH SKRITCH
I'M DONE!

CAN I SEE YOUR DRAWING, OWLY?

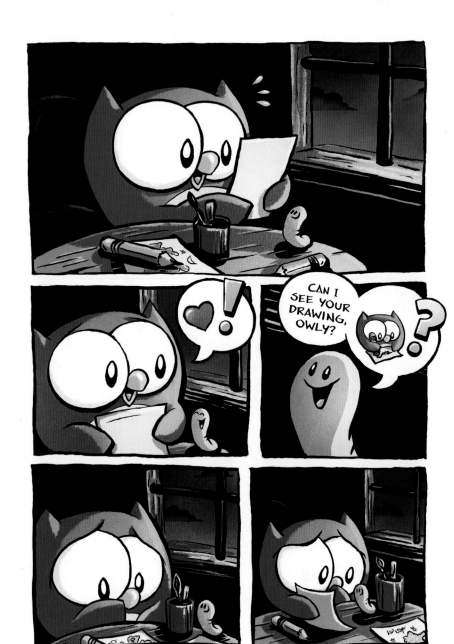

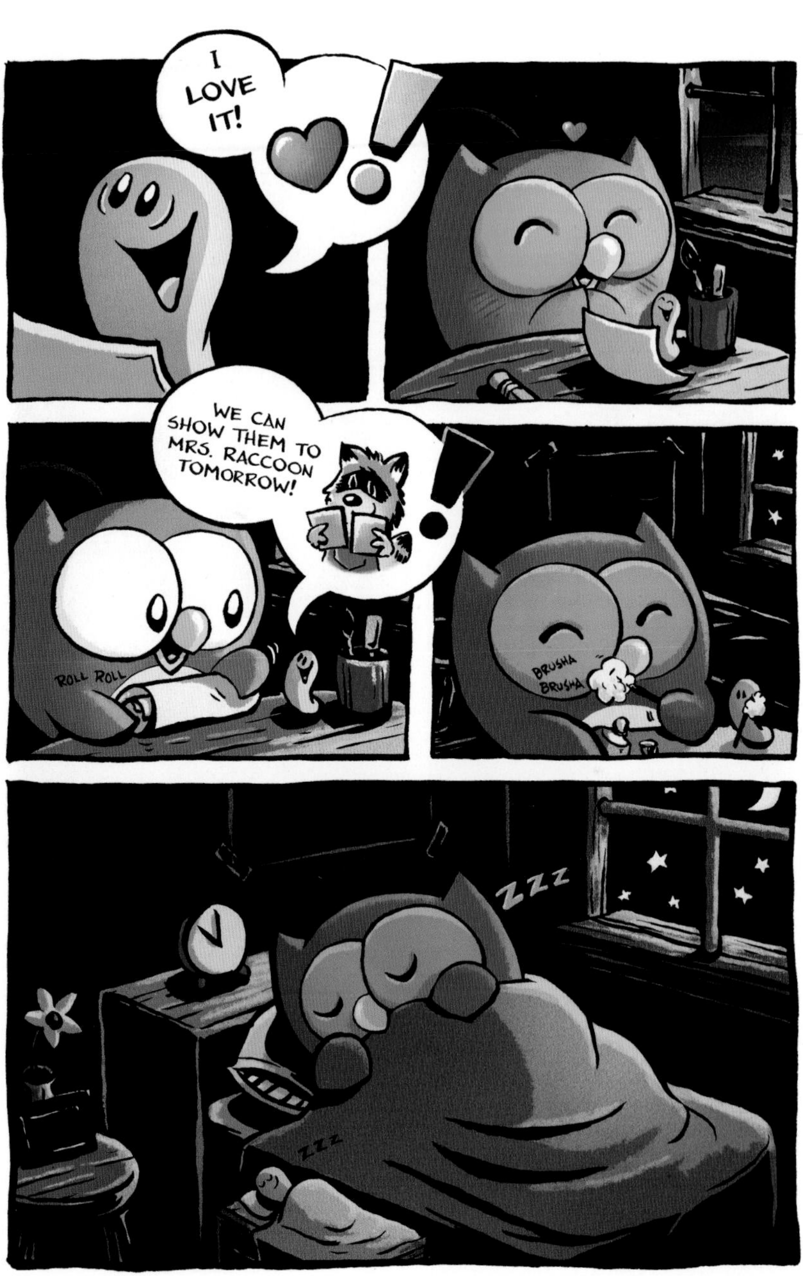
I LOVE IT!
WE CAN SHOW THEM TO MRS. RACCOON TOMORROW!
ROLL ROLL
BRUSHA BRUSHA
ZZZ
ZZZ

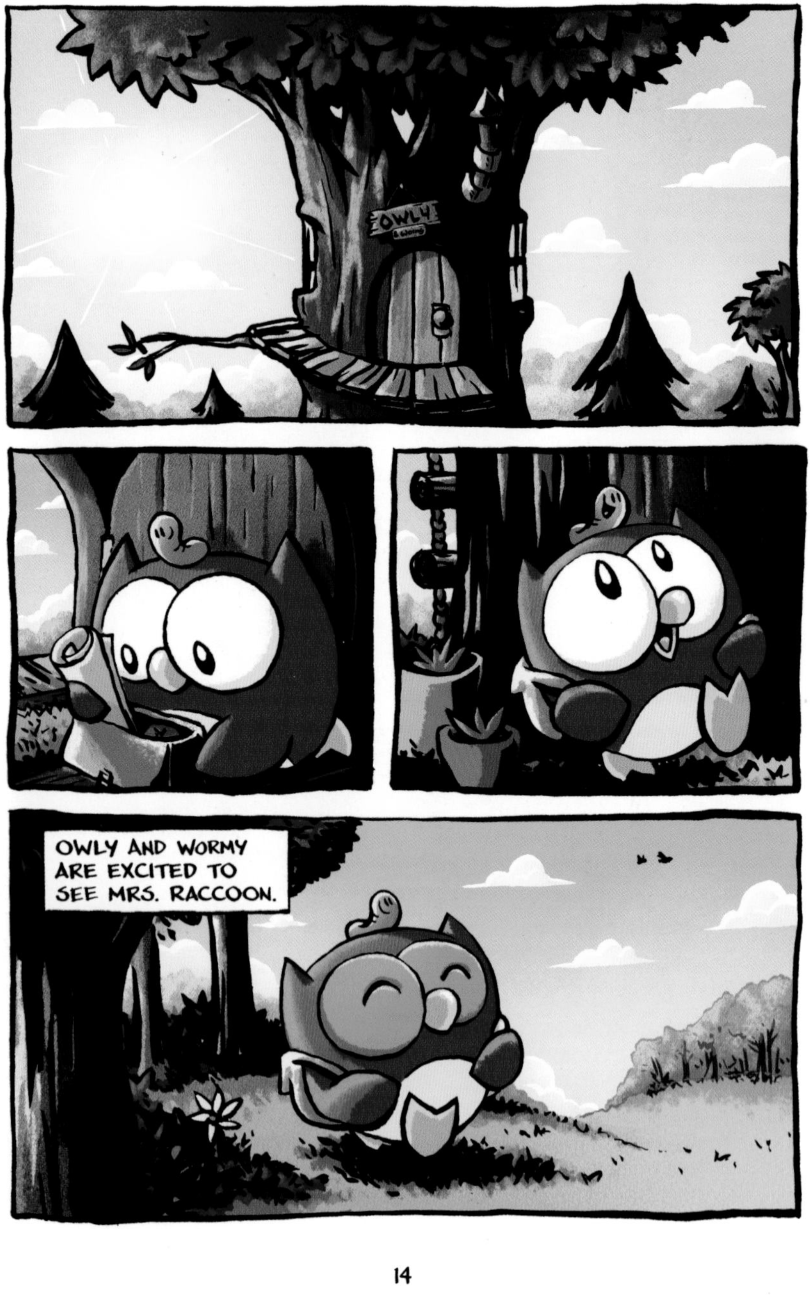
OWLY
OWLY AND WORMY ARE EXCITED TO SEE MRS. RACCOON.

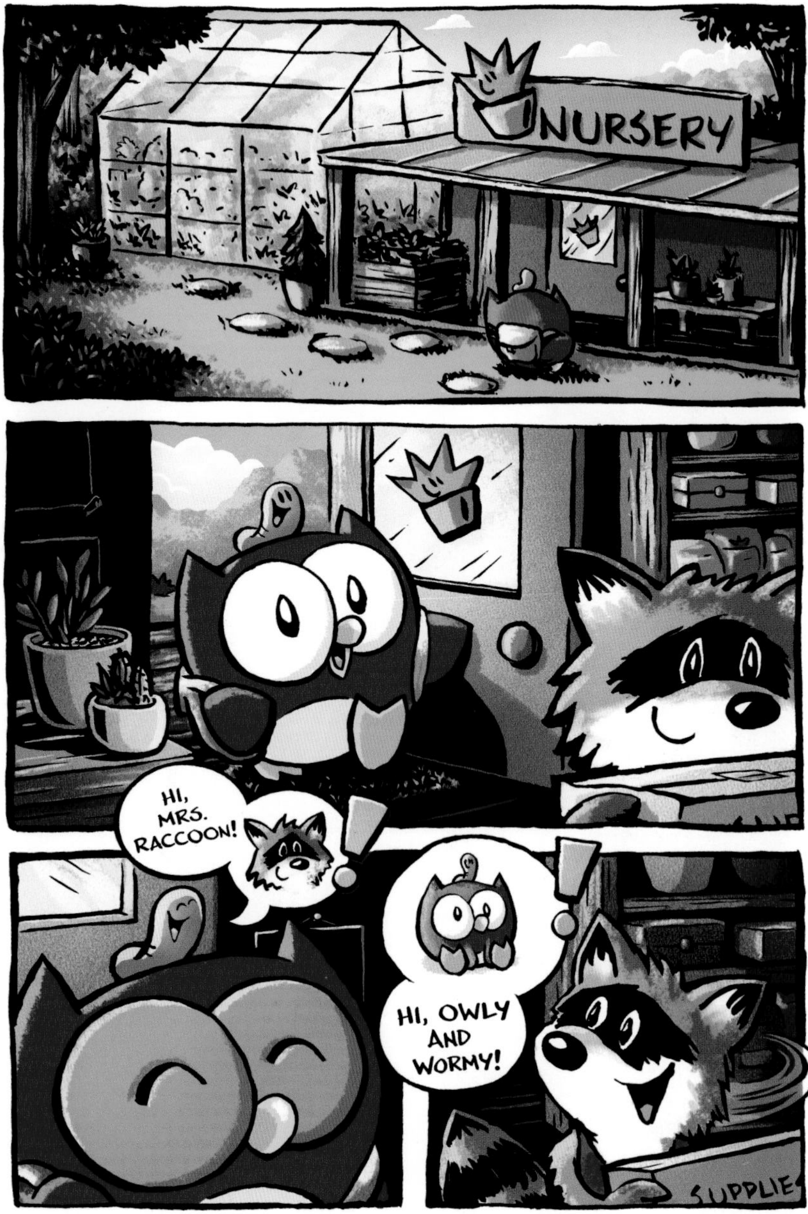
NURSERY
HI, MRS. RACCOON!
HI, OWLY AND WORMY!
SUPPLIE

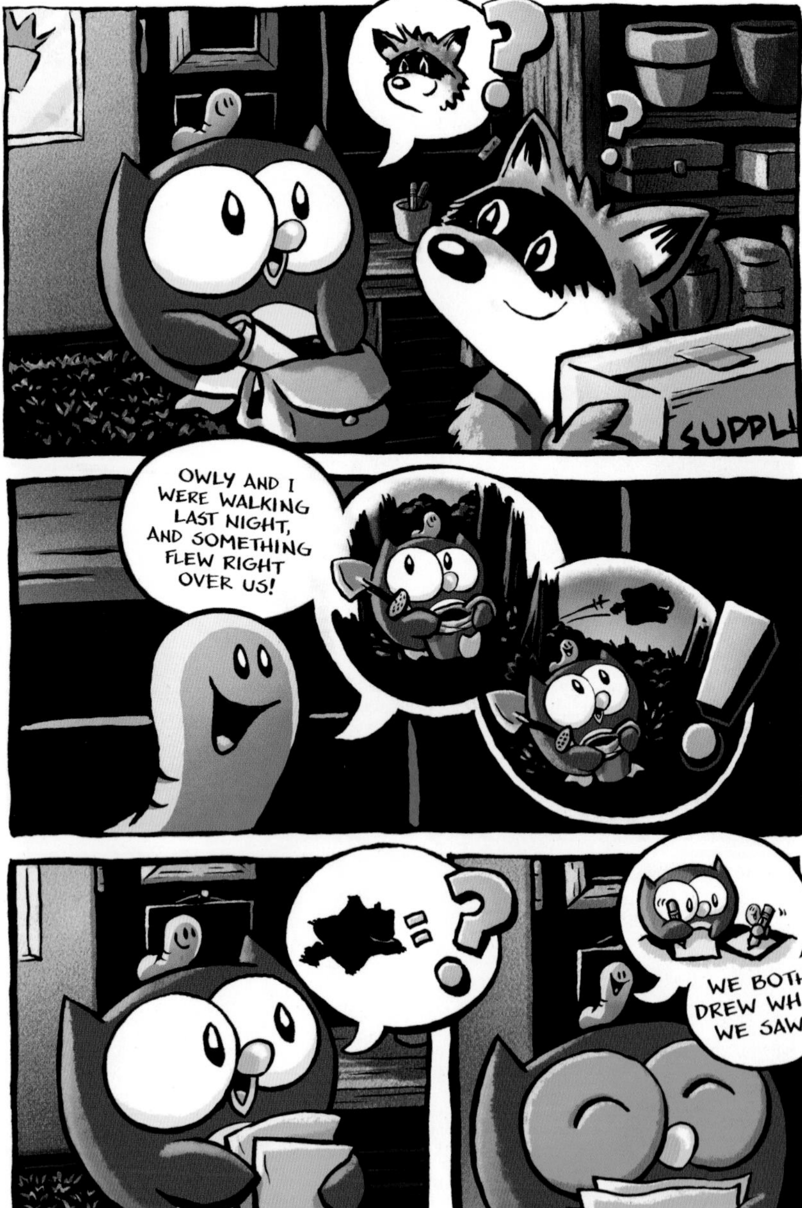
SUPPL
OWLY AND I WERE WALKING LAST NIGHT, AND SOMETHING FLEW RIGHT OVER US!
WE BOTH DREW WHAT WE SAW!

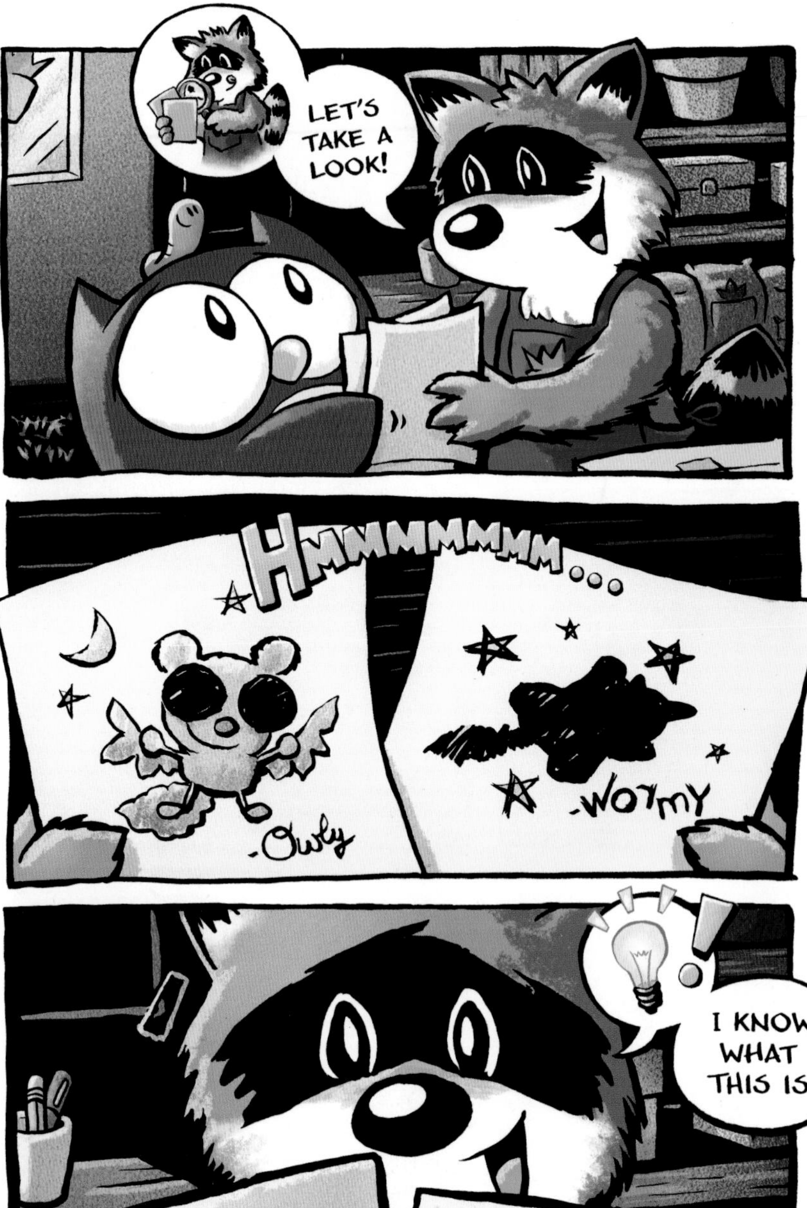
LET'S TAKE A LOOK!
HMMMMMMMM...
-Owly
-WORMY
I KNOW WHAT THIS IS!

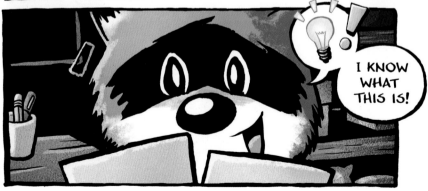

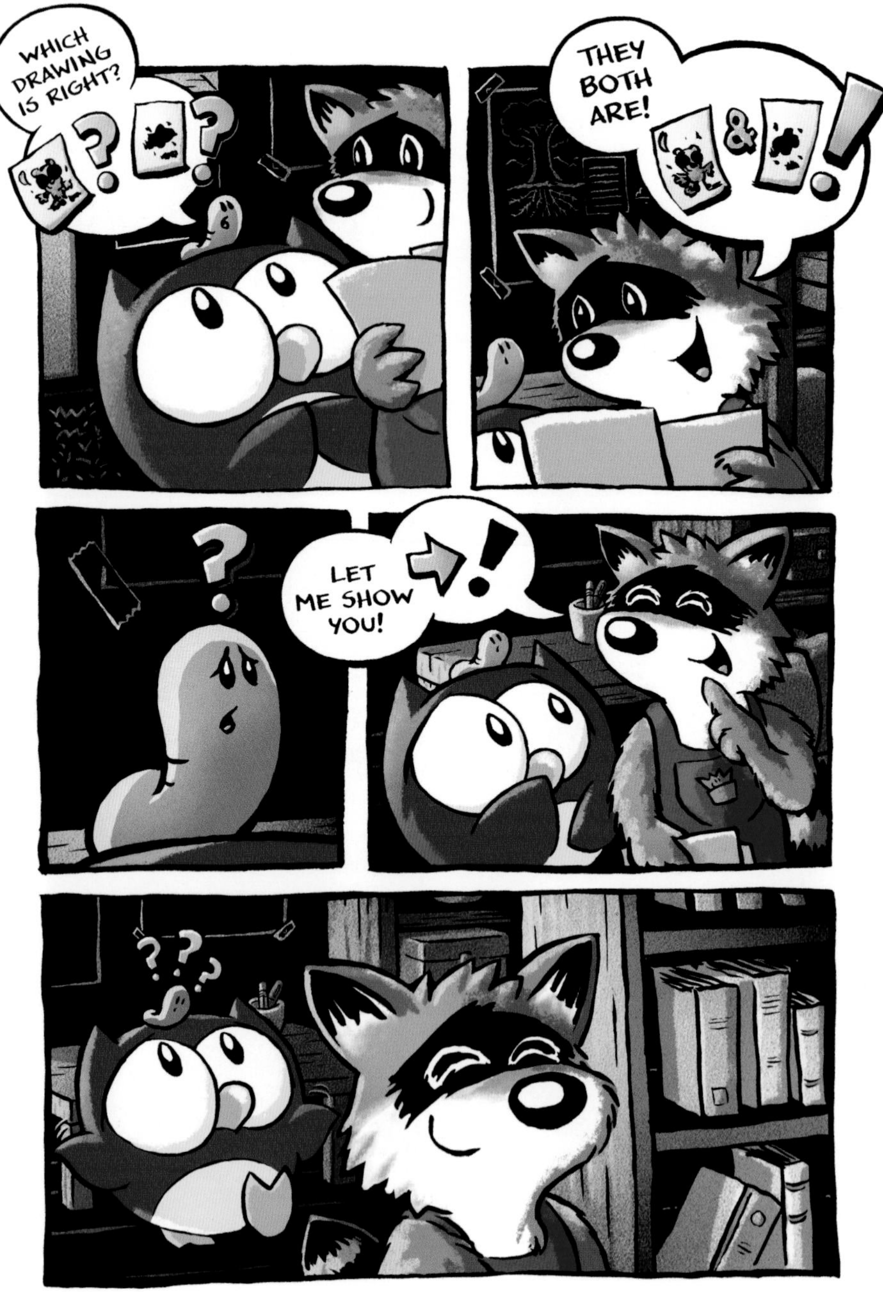
WHICH DRAWING IS RIGHT?
THEY BOTH ARE!
LET ME SHOW YOU!

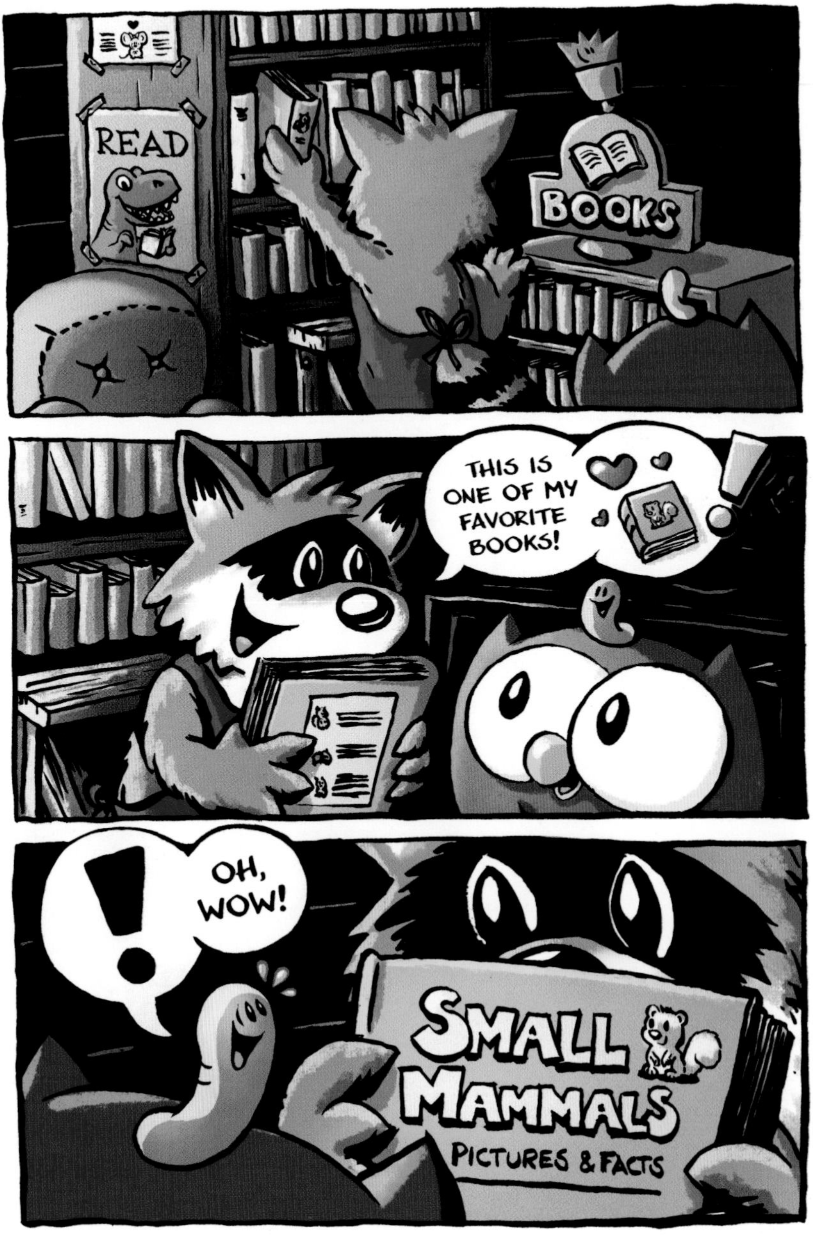
READ
BOOKS
THIS IS ONE OF MY FAVORITE BOOKS!
OH, WOW!
SMALL MAMMALS
PICTURES & FACTS

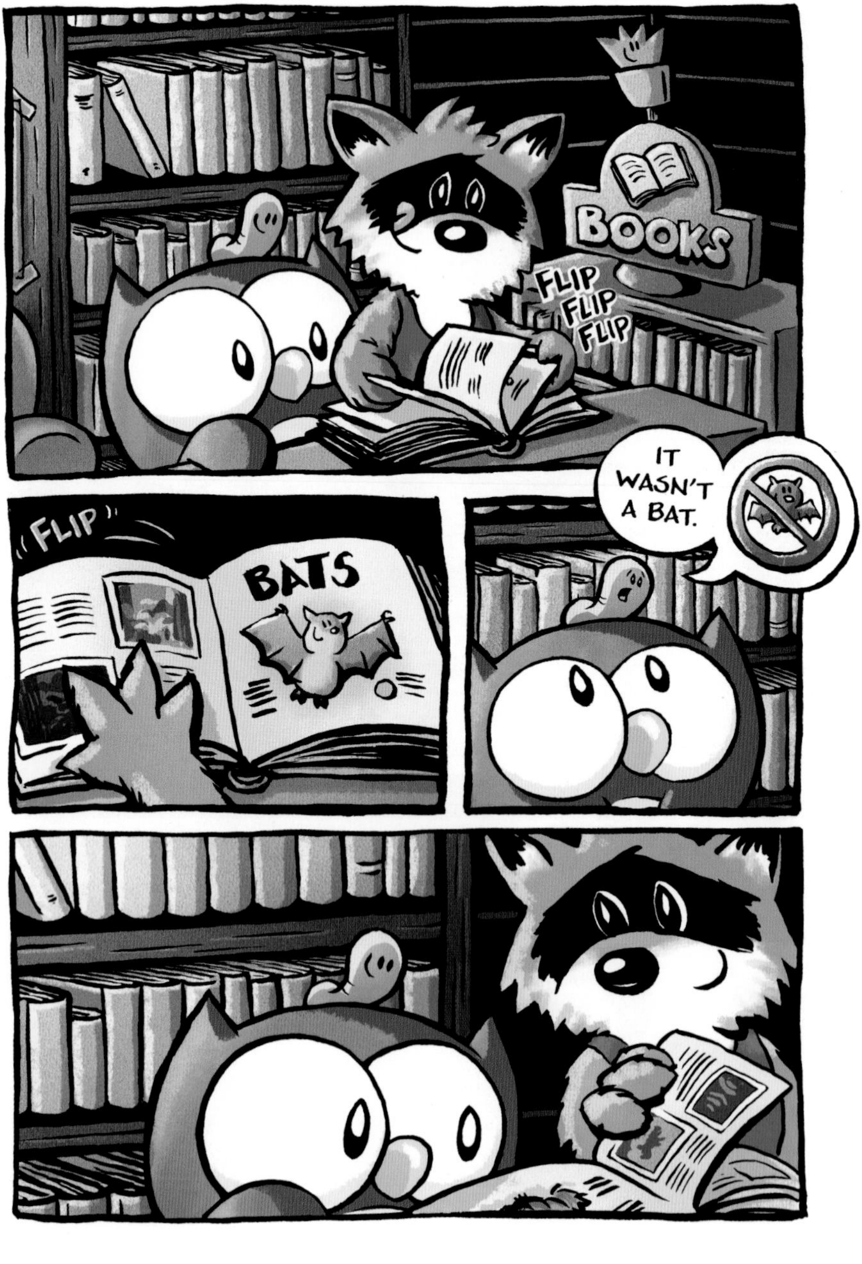
BOOKS
FLIP FLIP FLIP
FLIP
BATS
IT WASN'T A BAT.

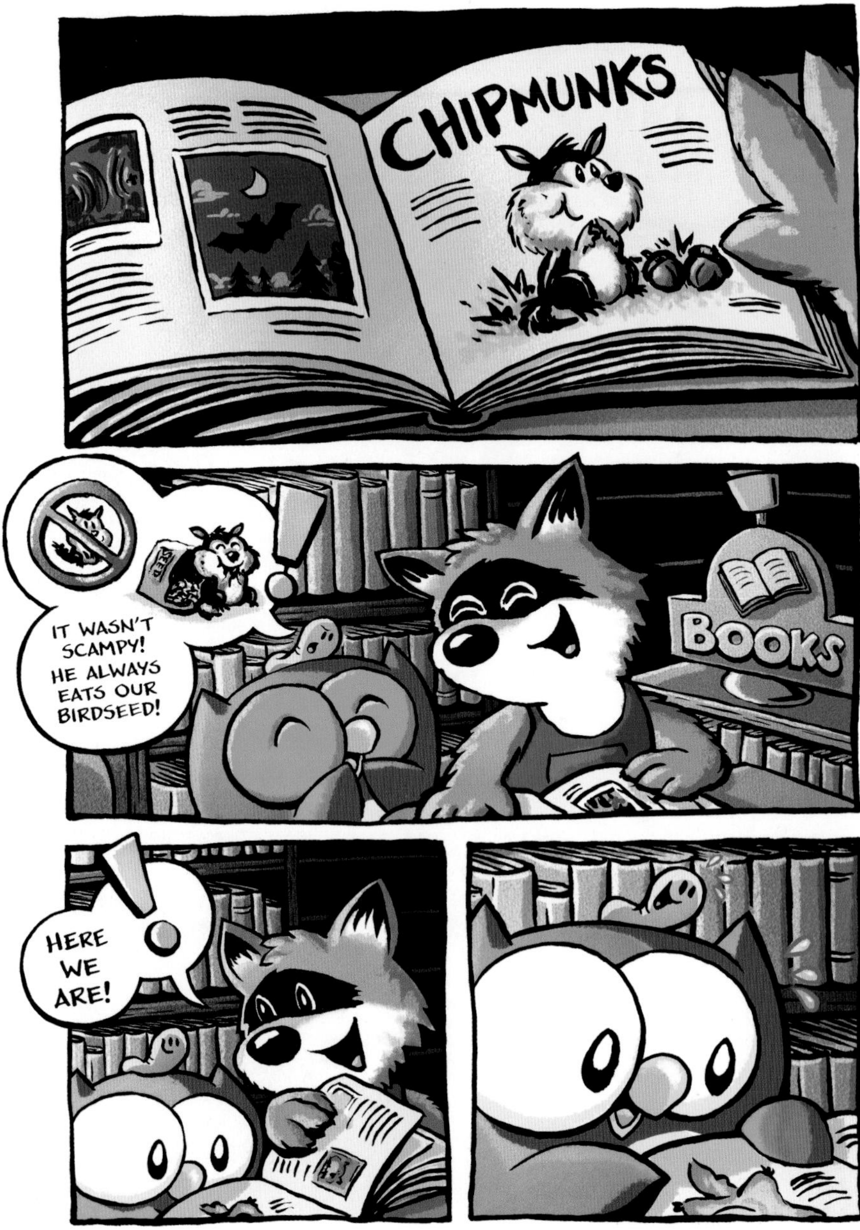
CHIPMUNKS
IT WASN'T SCAMPY! HE ALWAYS EATS OUR BIRDSEED!
SEED
BOOKS
HERE WE ARE!

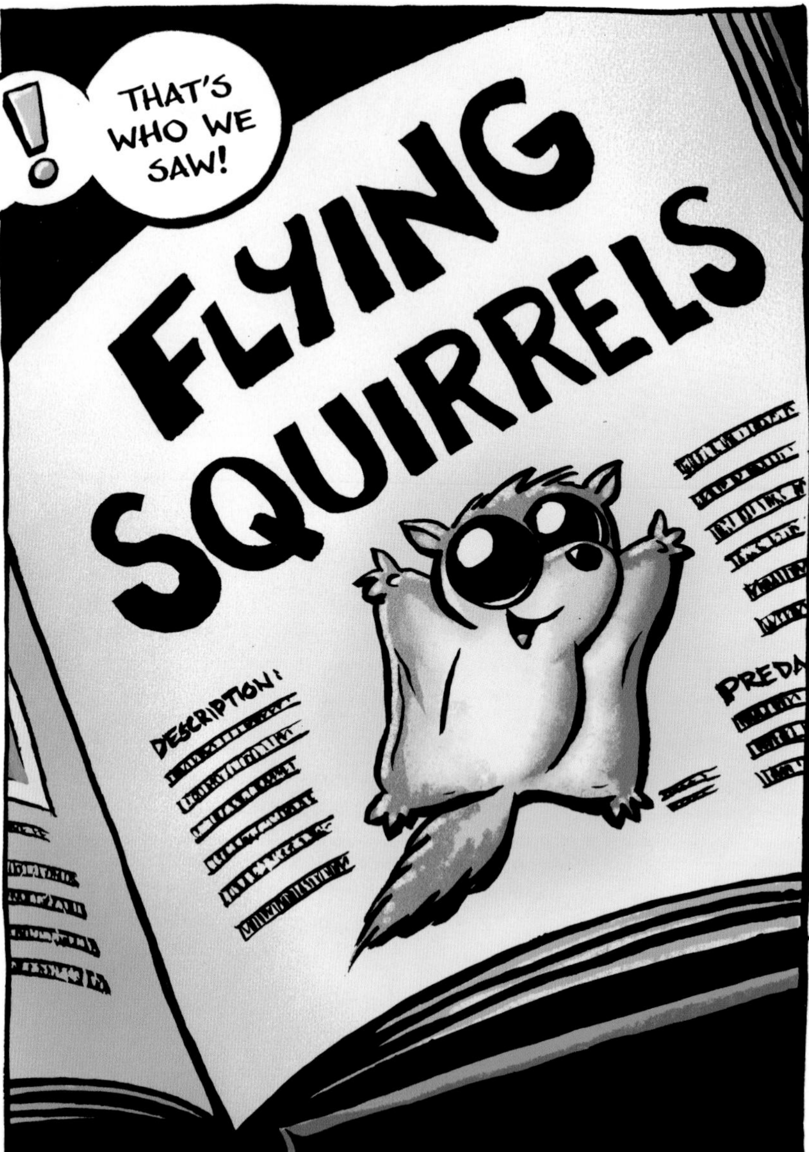
!
THAT'S WHO WE SAW!
FLYING SQUIRRELS
DESCRIPTION:
PREDA

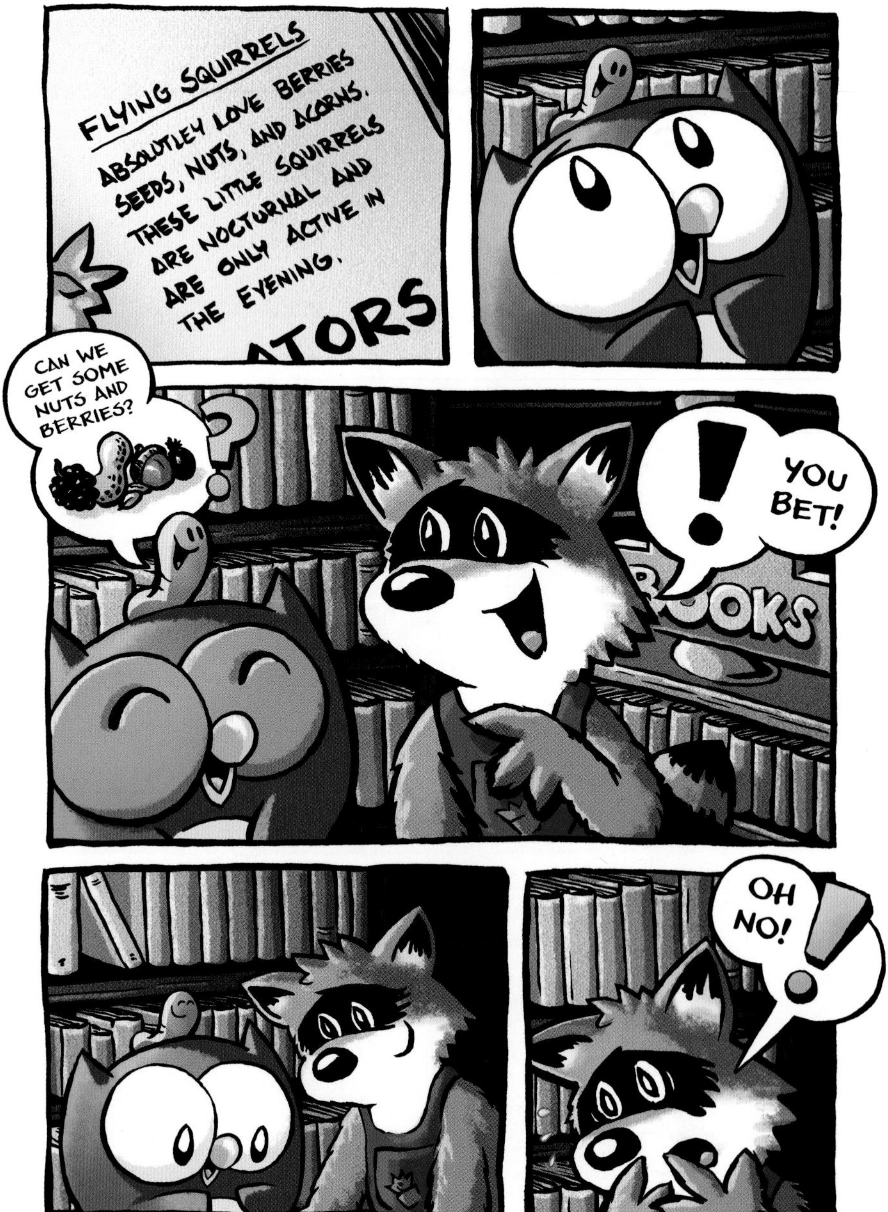
FLYING SQUIRRELS
ABSOLUTLEY LOVE BERRIES SEEDS, NUTS, AND ACORNS. THESE LITTLE SQUIRRELS ARE NOCTURNAL AND ARE ONLY ACTIVE IN THE EVENING.
ATORS
CAN WE GET SOME NUTS AND BERRIES?
?
!
YOU BET!
BOOKS
OH NO!
!

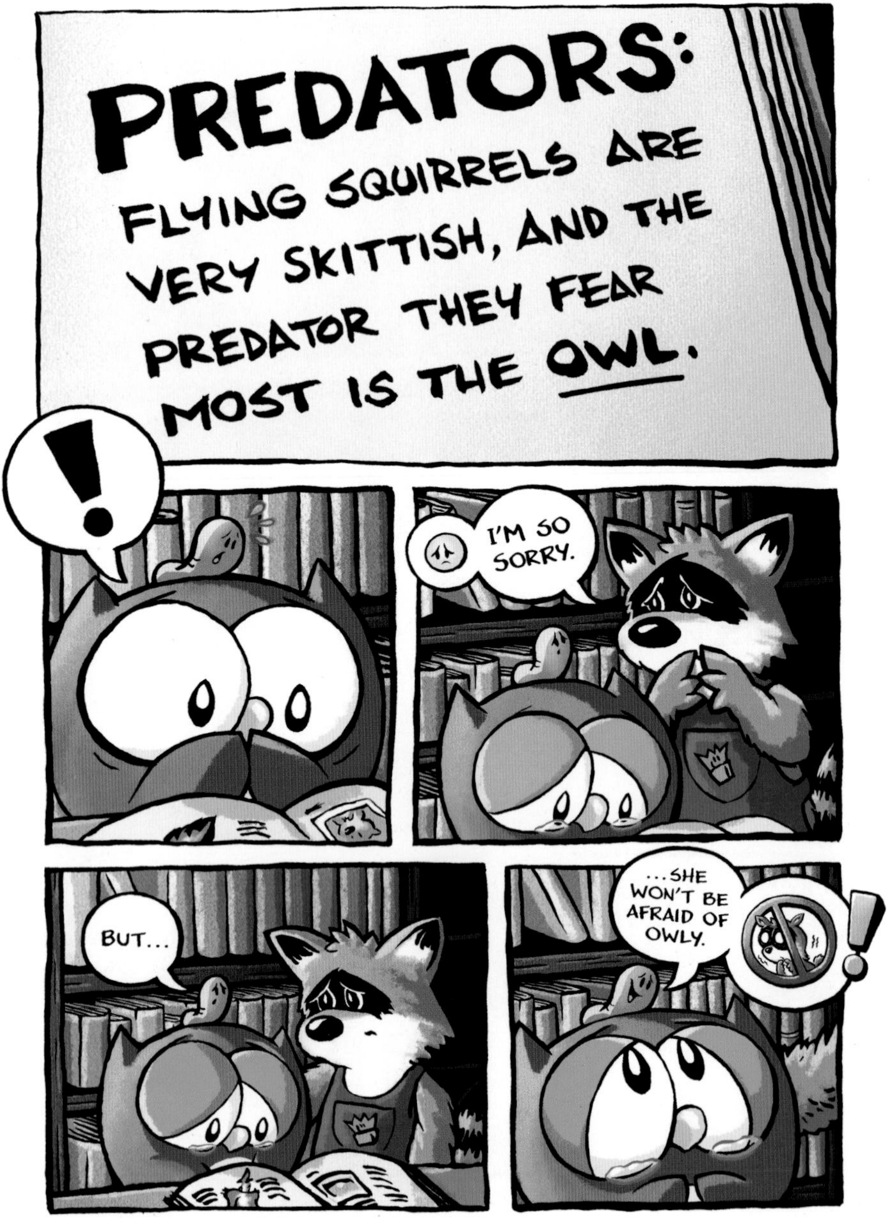
PREDATORS:
FLYING SQUIRRELS ARE VERY SKITTISH, AND THE PREDATOR THEY FEAR MOST IS THE OWL.
!
I'M SO SORRY.
BUT...
...SHE WON'T BE AFRAID OF OWLY.
!

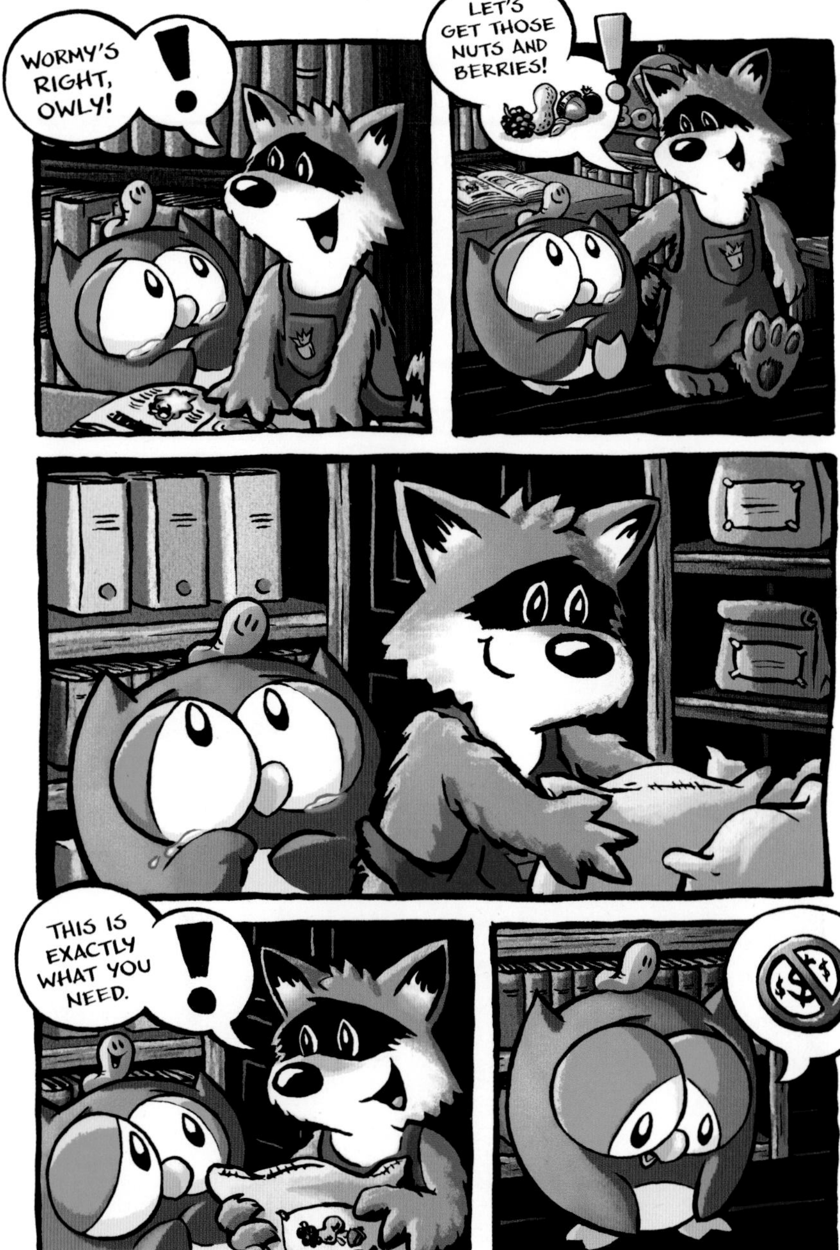
WORMY'S RIGHT, OWLY!
!
LET'S GET THOSE NUTS AND BERRIES!
THIS IS EXACTLY WHAT YOU NEED.
!

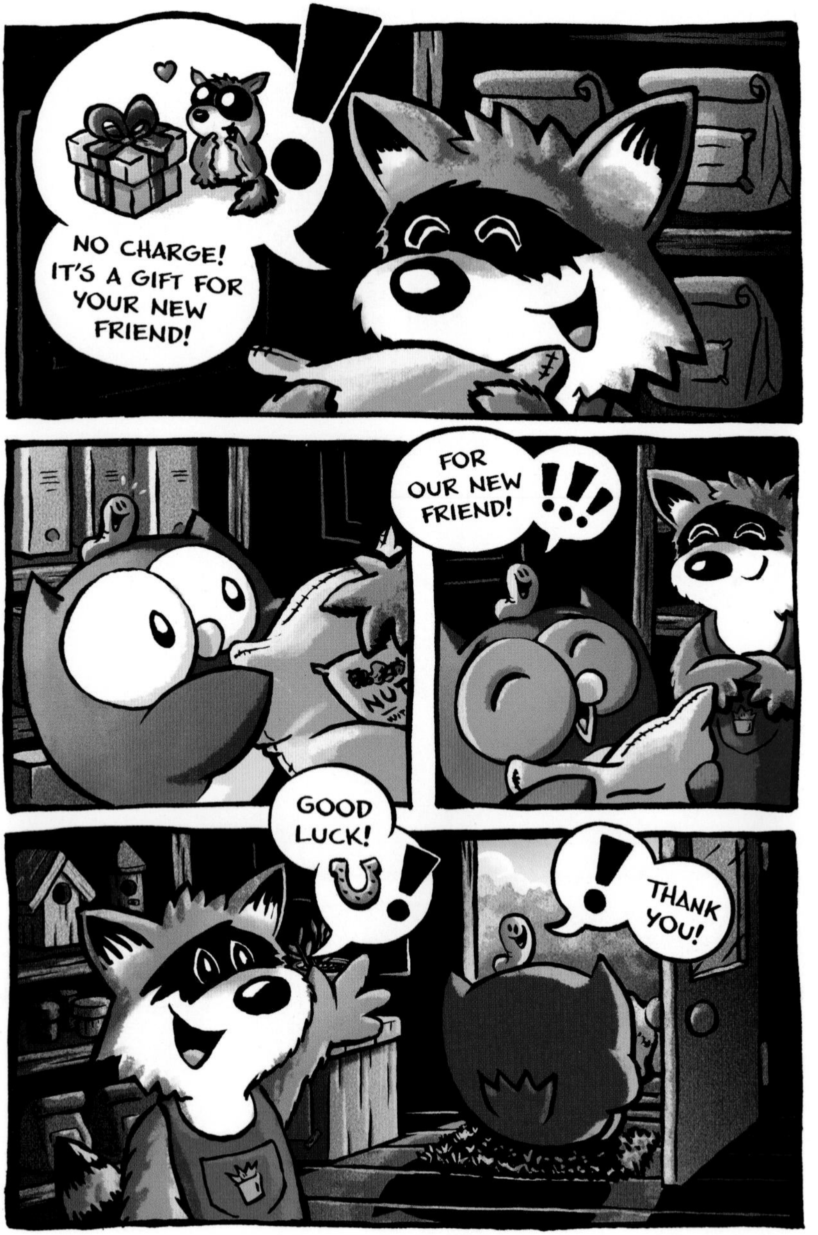
NO CHARGE! IT'S A GIFT FOR YOUR NEW FRIEND!
!
FOR OUR NEW FRIEND!
!!!
GOOD LUCK!
!
!
THANK YOU!

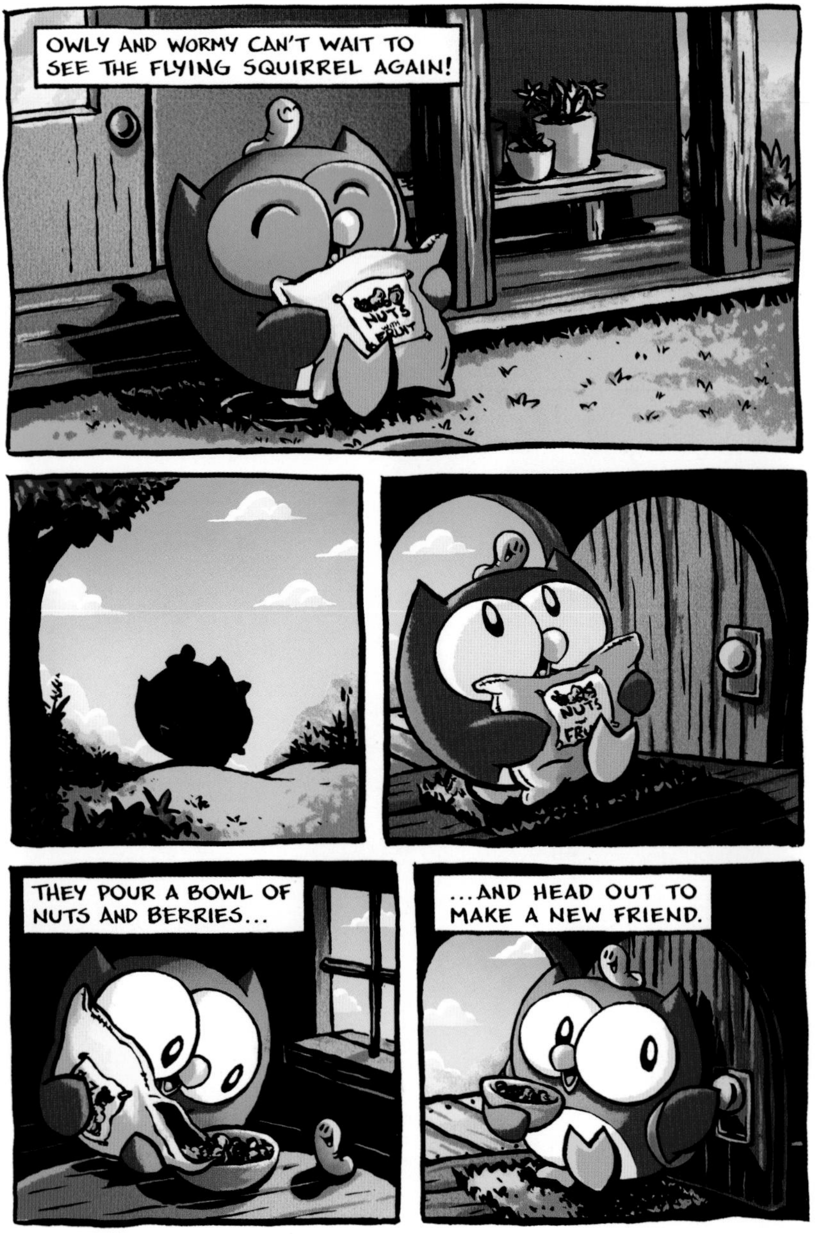
OWLY AND WORMY CAN'T WAIT TO SEE THE FLYING SQUIRREL AGAIN!
NUTS WITH FRUIT
NUTS FRUIT
THEY POUR A BOWL OF NUTS AND BERRIES...
...AND HEAD OUT TO MAKE A NEW FRIEND.

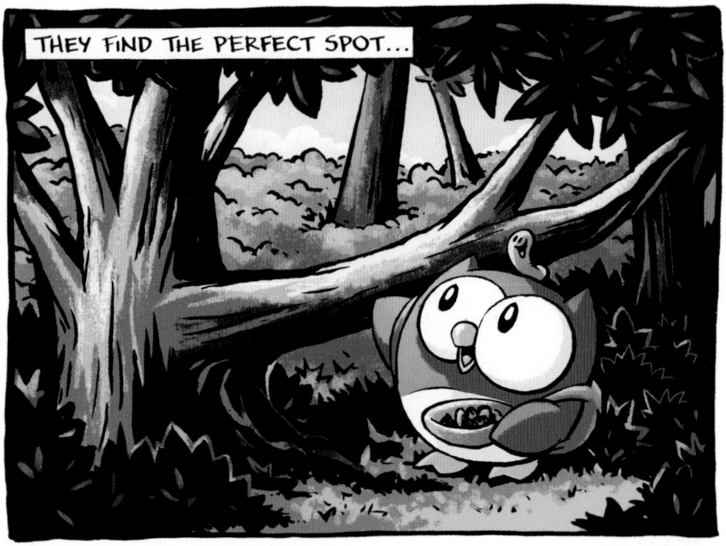
THEY FIND THE PERFECT SPOT...

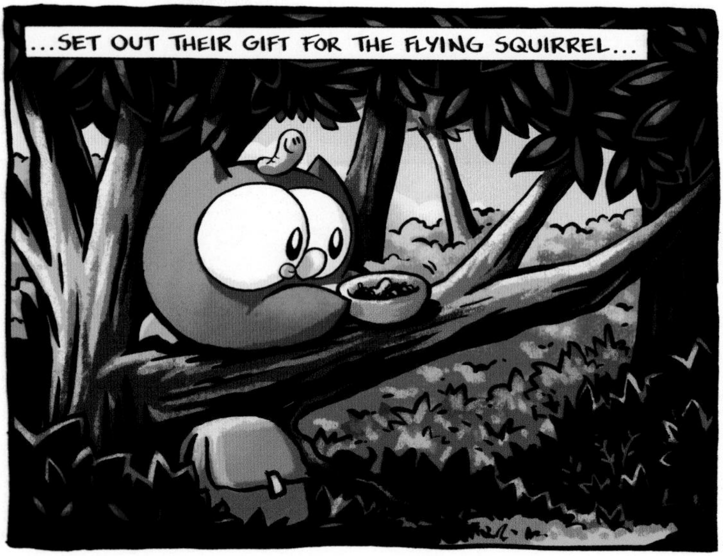
...SET OUT THEIR GIFT FOR THE FLYING SQUIRREL...

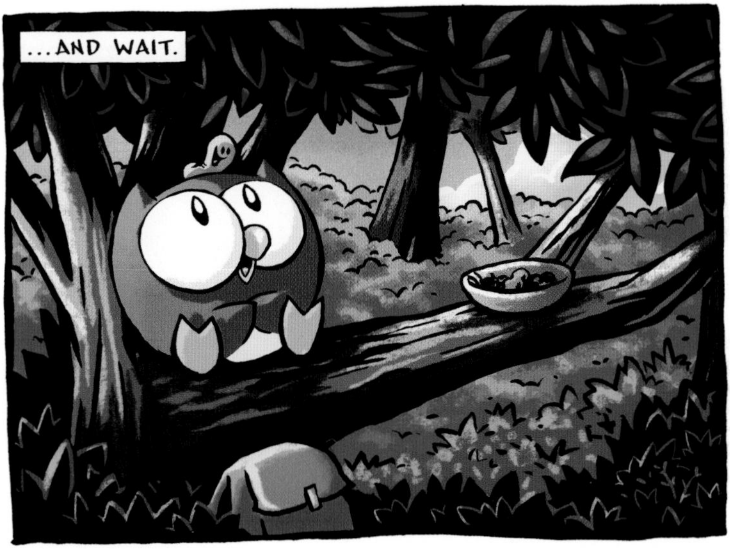
...AND WAIT.

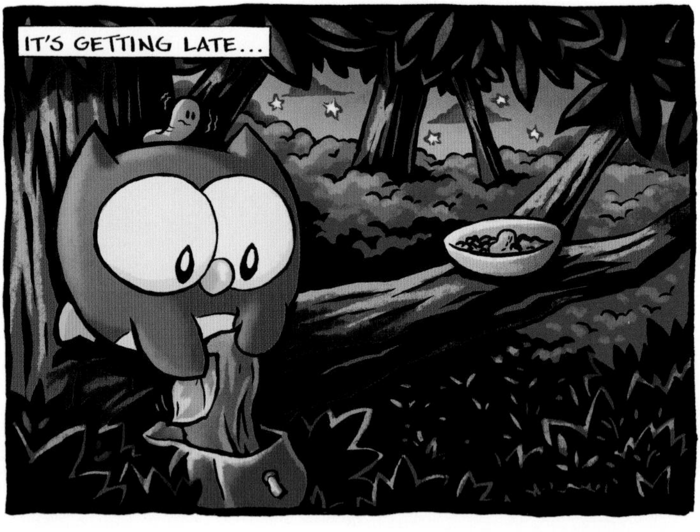
IT'S GETTING LATE...

THEY KEEP WAITING...

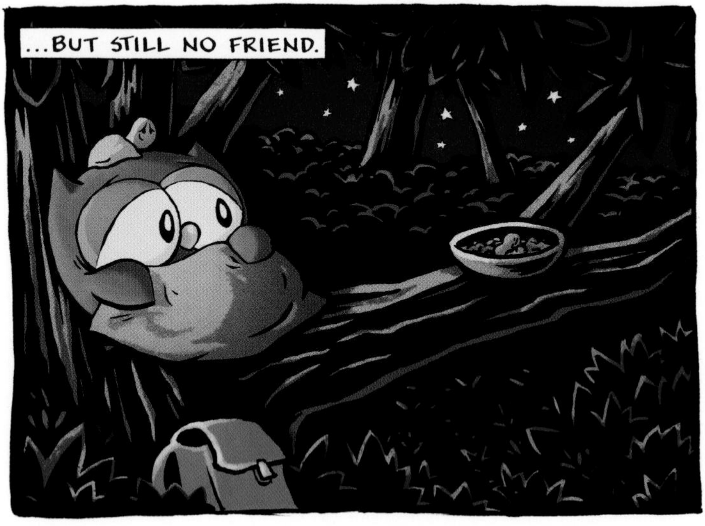
...BUT STILL NO FRIEND.

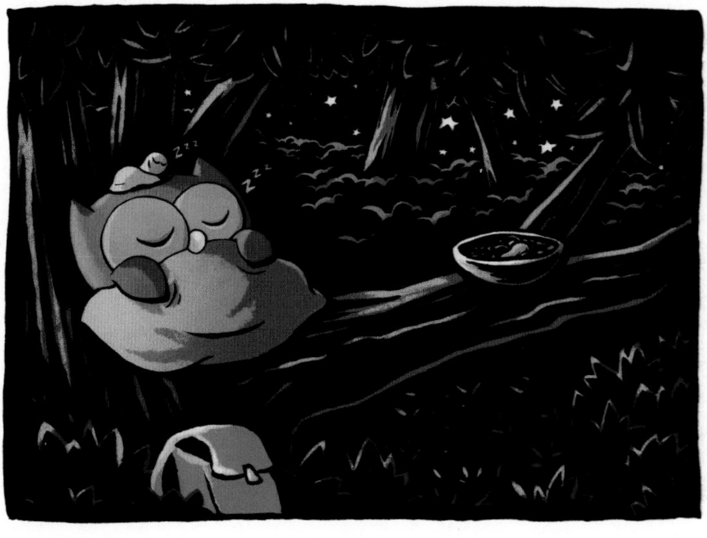
zzz
zzz

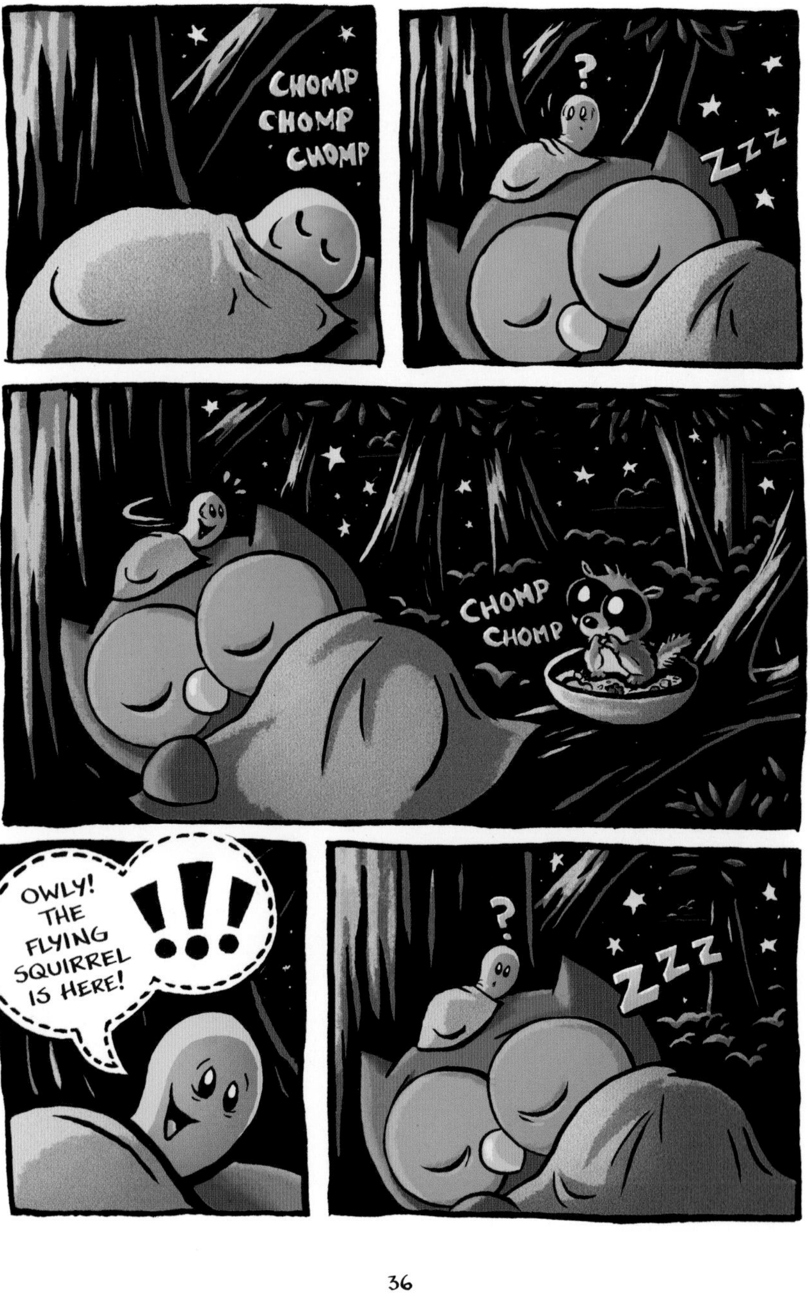
CHOMP
CHOMP
CHOMP
?
ZZZ
CHOMP
CHOMP
OWLY! THE FLYING SQUIRREL IS HERE!
!!!
?
ZZZ

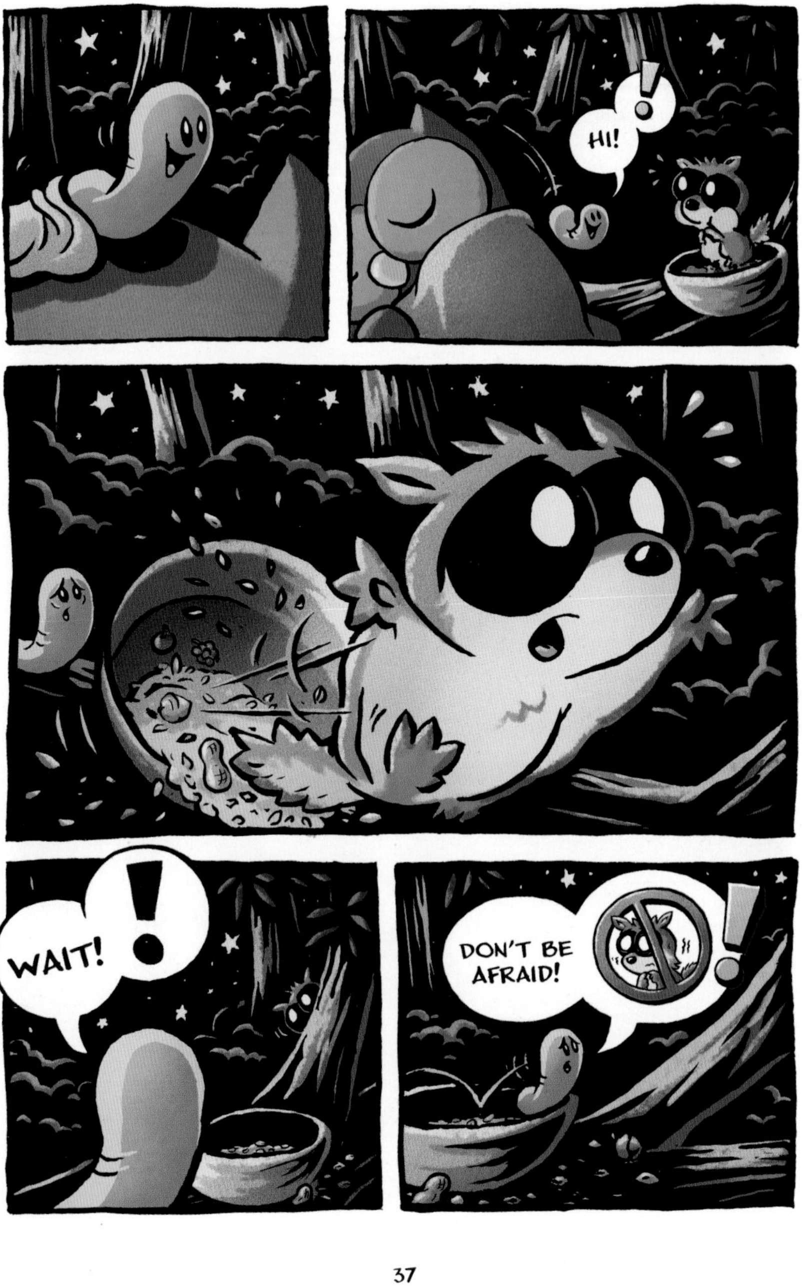

HI!
!
WAIT!
!
DON'T BE AFRAID!
!

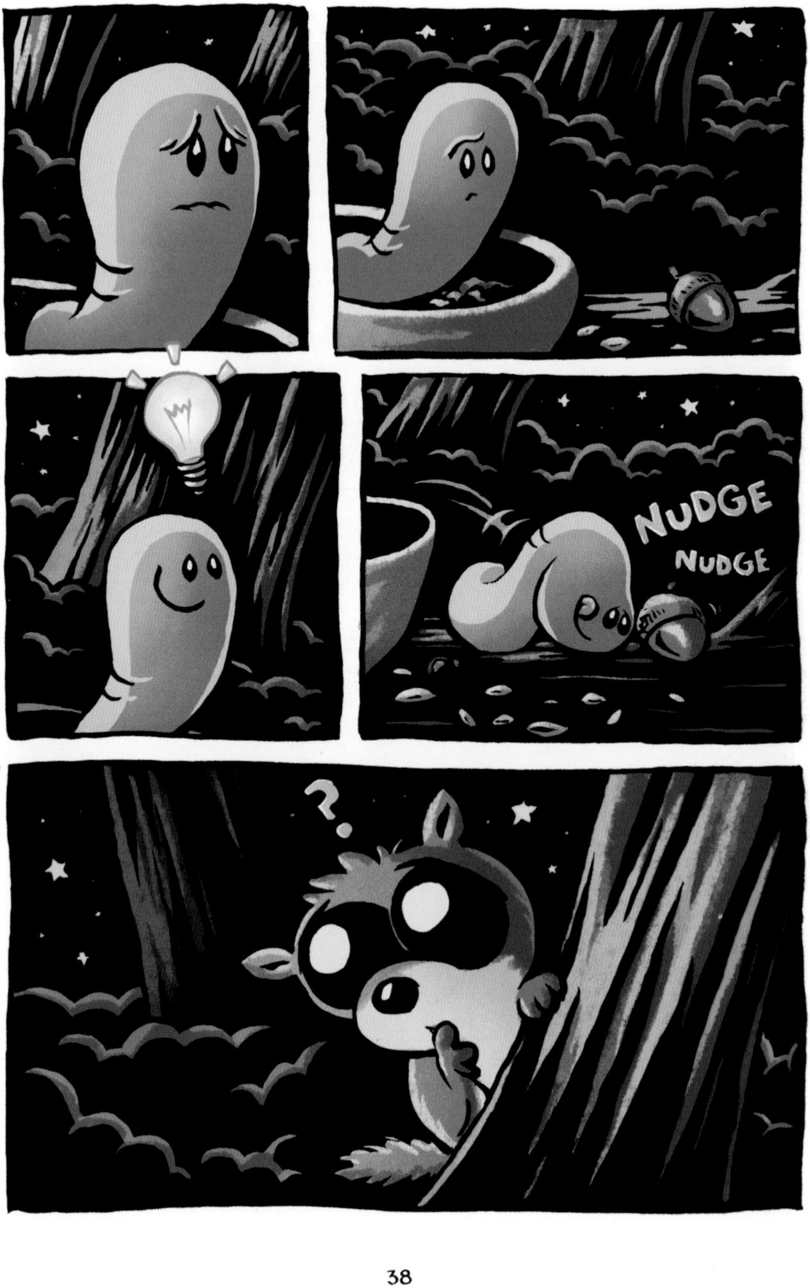
NUDGE
NUDGE
?

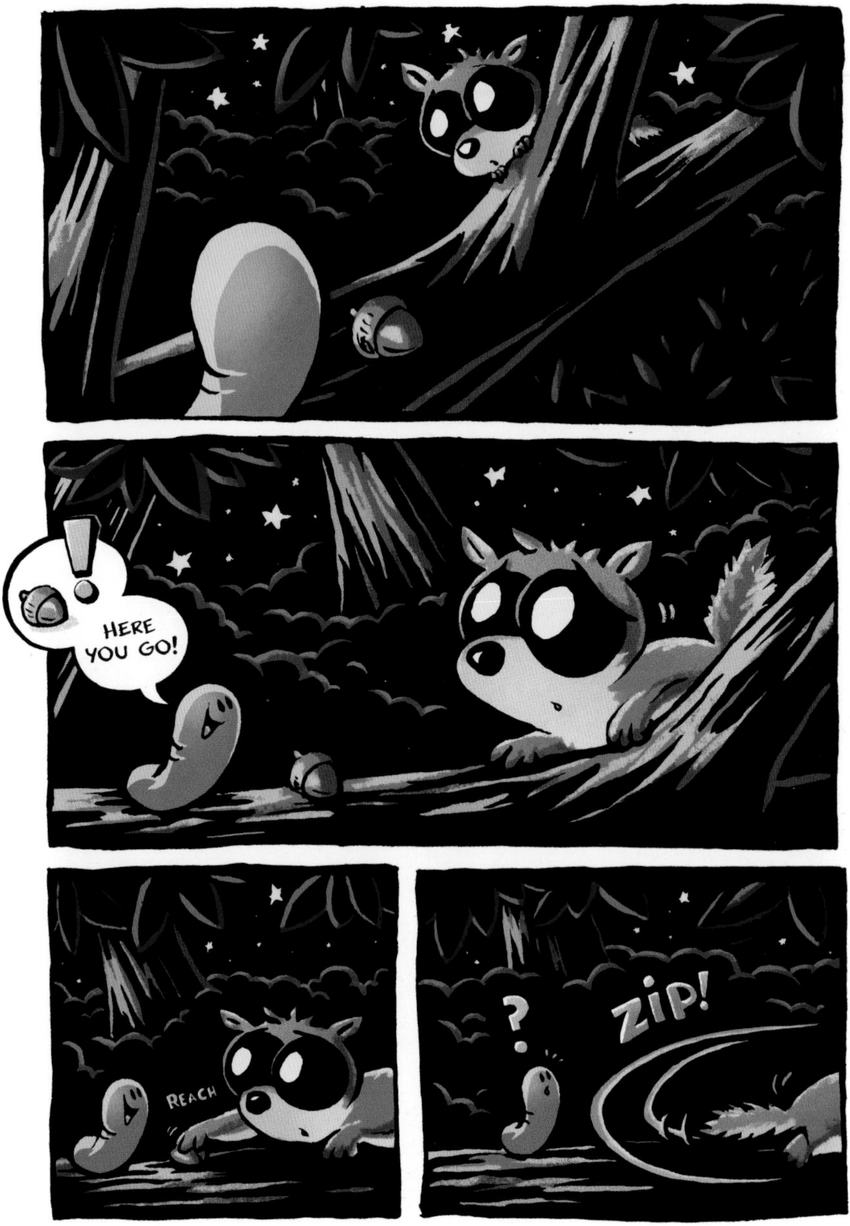
!
HERE YOU GO!
REACH
?
ZIP!

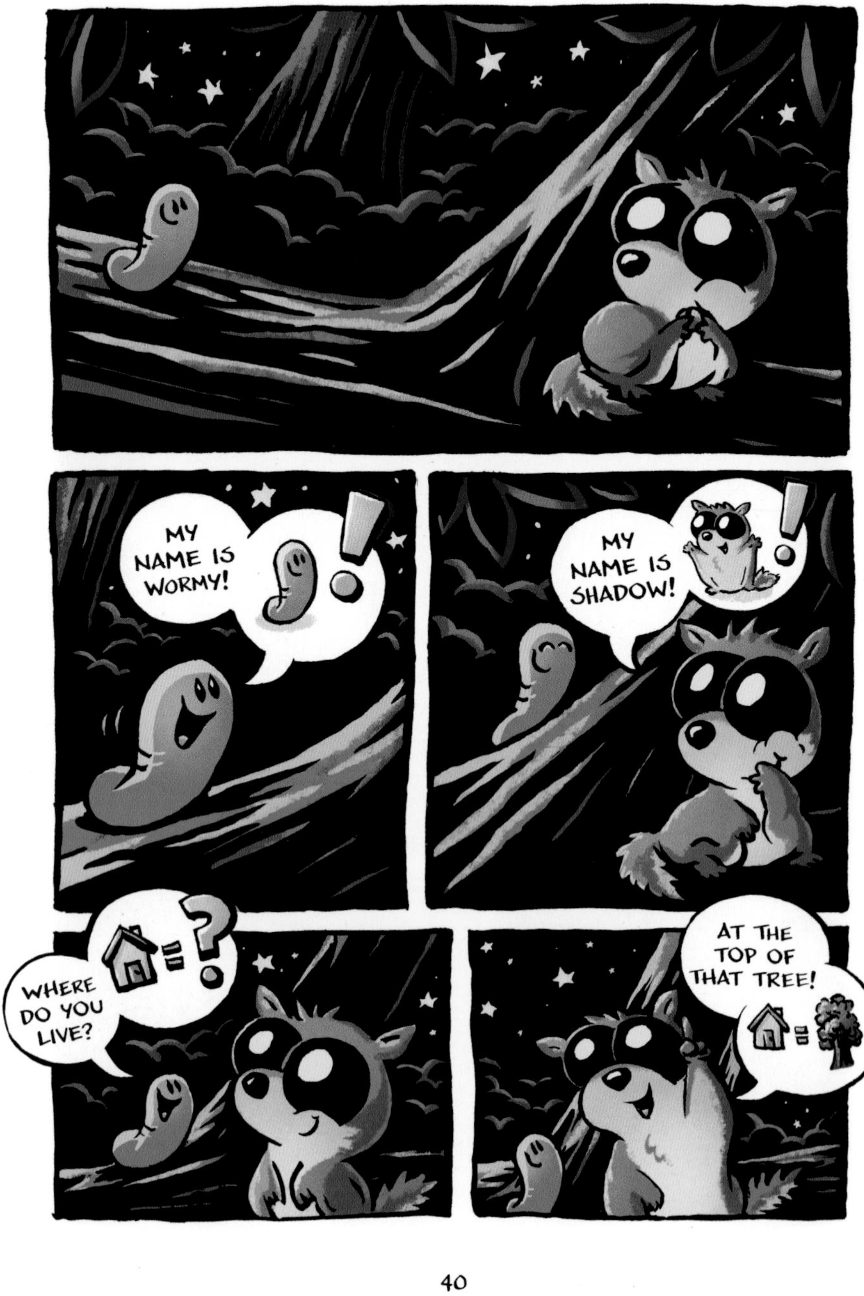
MY NAME IS WORMY!
MY NAME IS SHADOW!
WHERE DO YOU LIVE?
AT THE TOP OF THAT TREE!

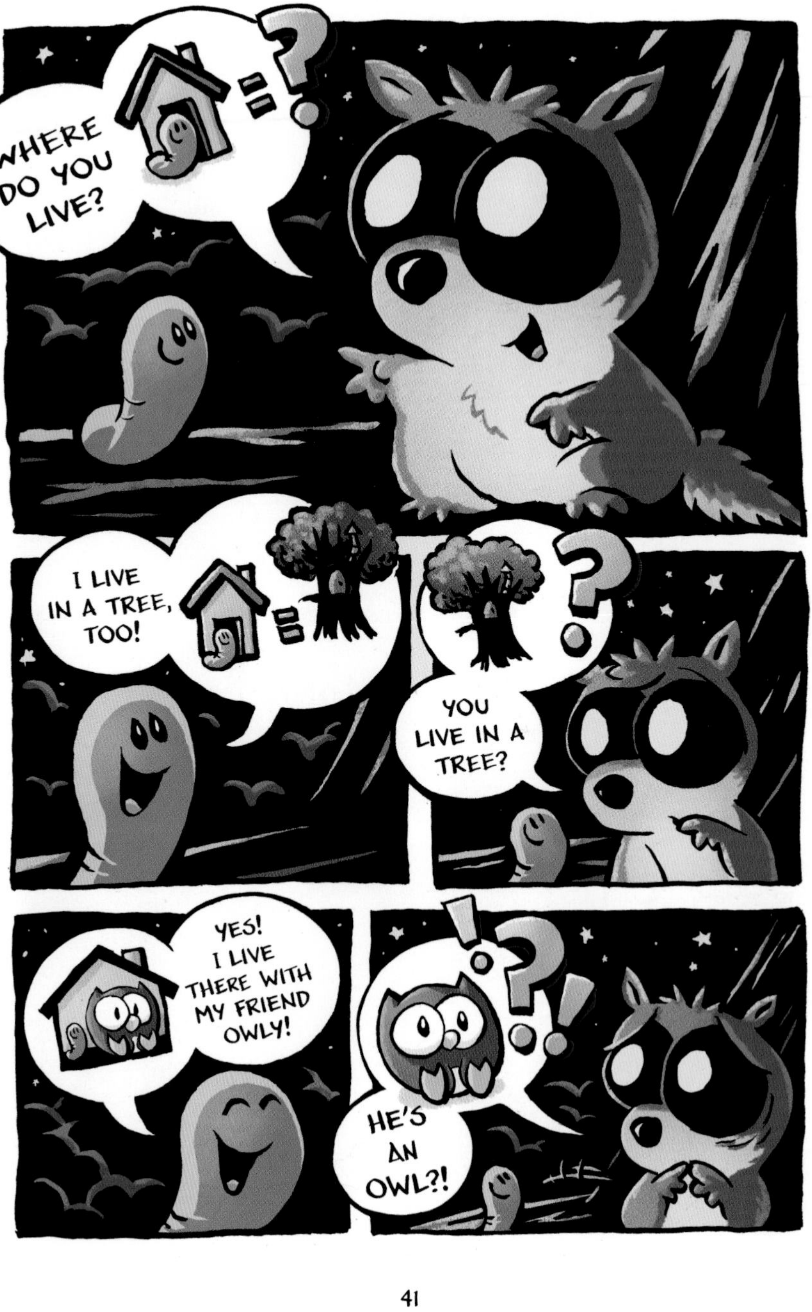
WHERE DO YOU LIVE?
I LIVE IN A TREE, TOO!
YOU LIVE IN A TREE?
YES! I LIVE THERE WITH MY FRIEND OWLY!
HE'S AN OWL?!

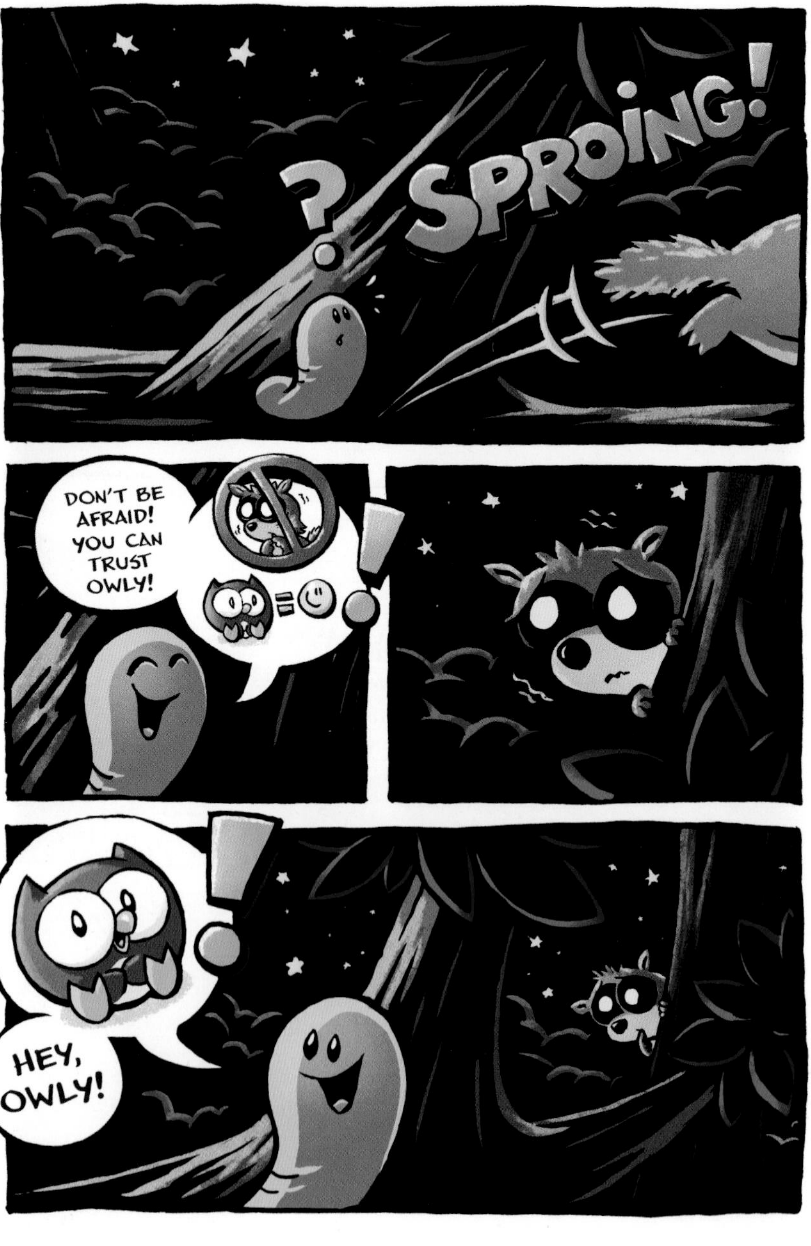
?
SPROING!
DON'T BE AFRAID! YOU CAN TRUST OWLY!
!
!
HEY, OWLY!

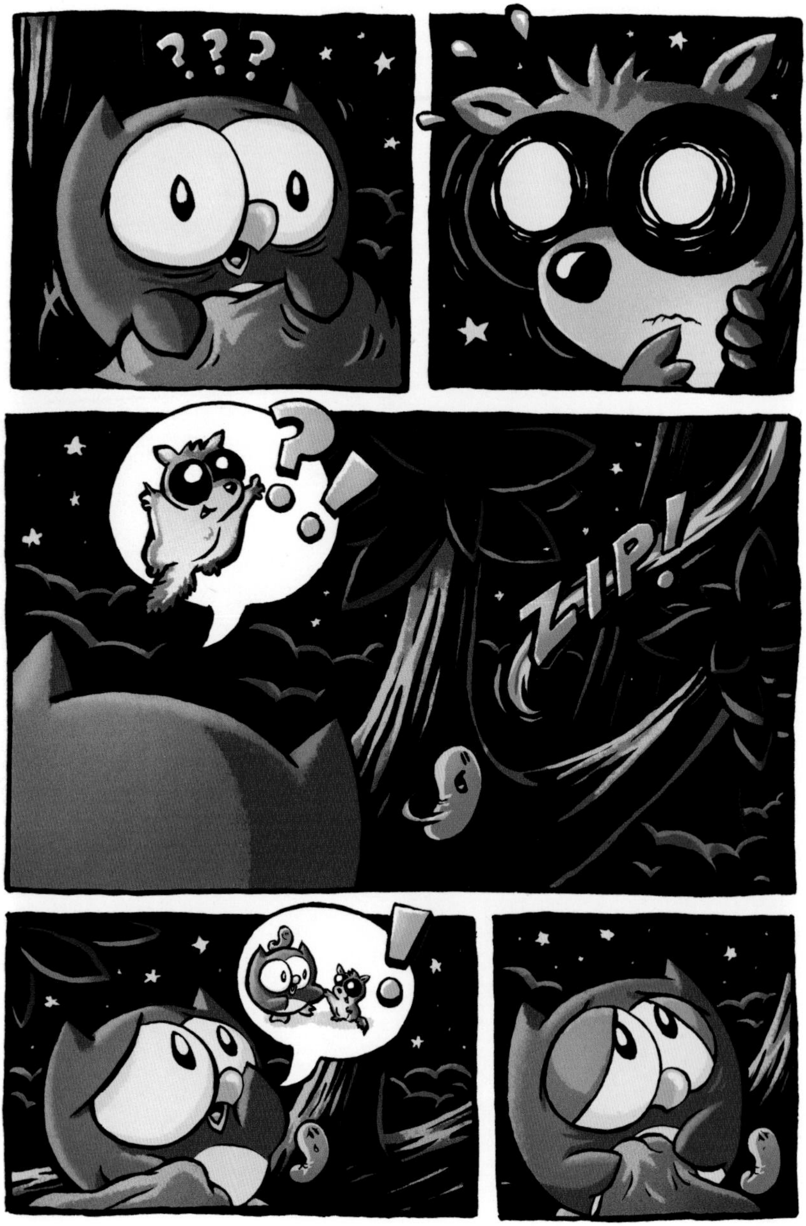
???
?!
Z-I-P!
!

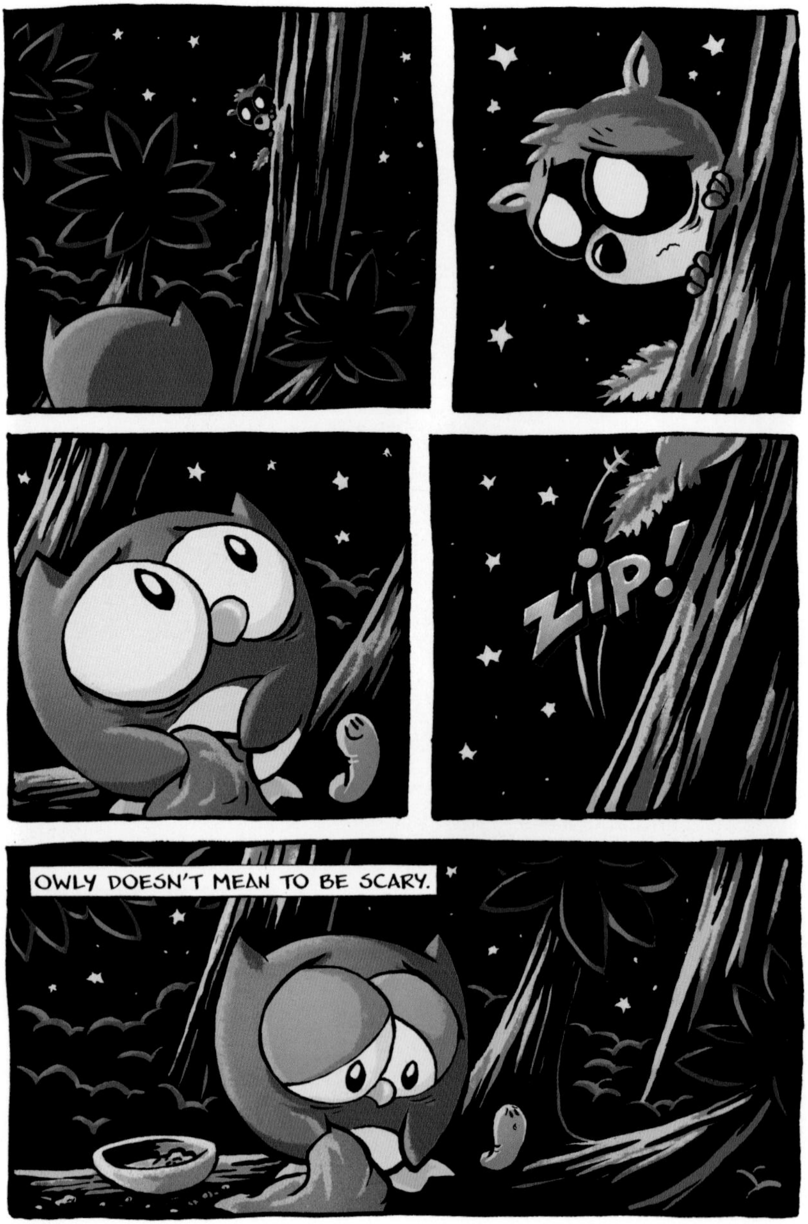
ZIP!
OWLY DOESN'T MEAN TO BE SCARY.

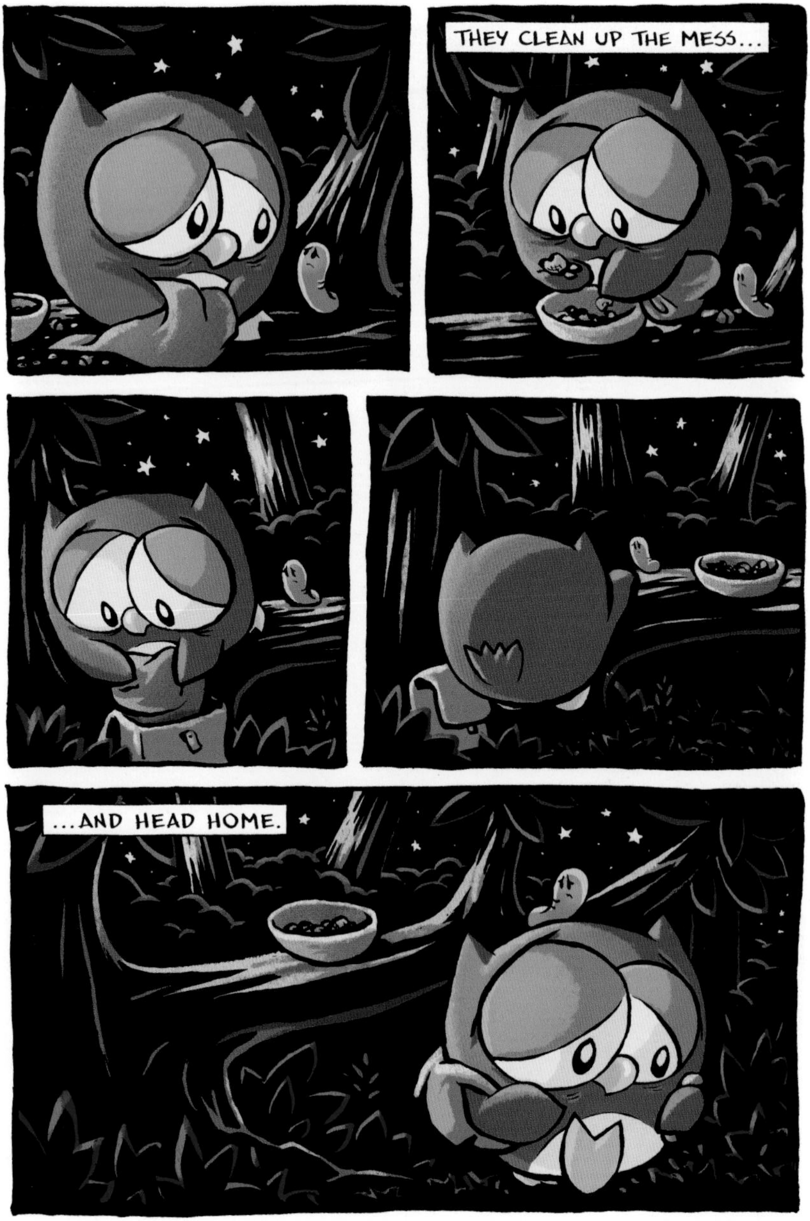
THEY CLEAN UP THE MESS...
...AND HEAD HOME.

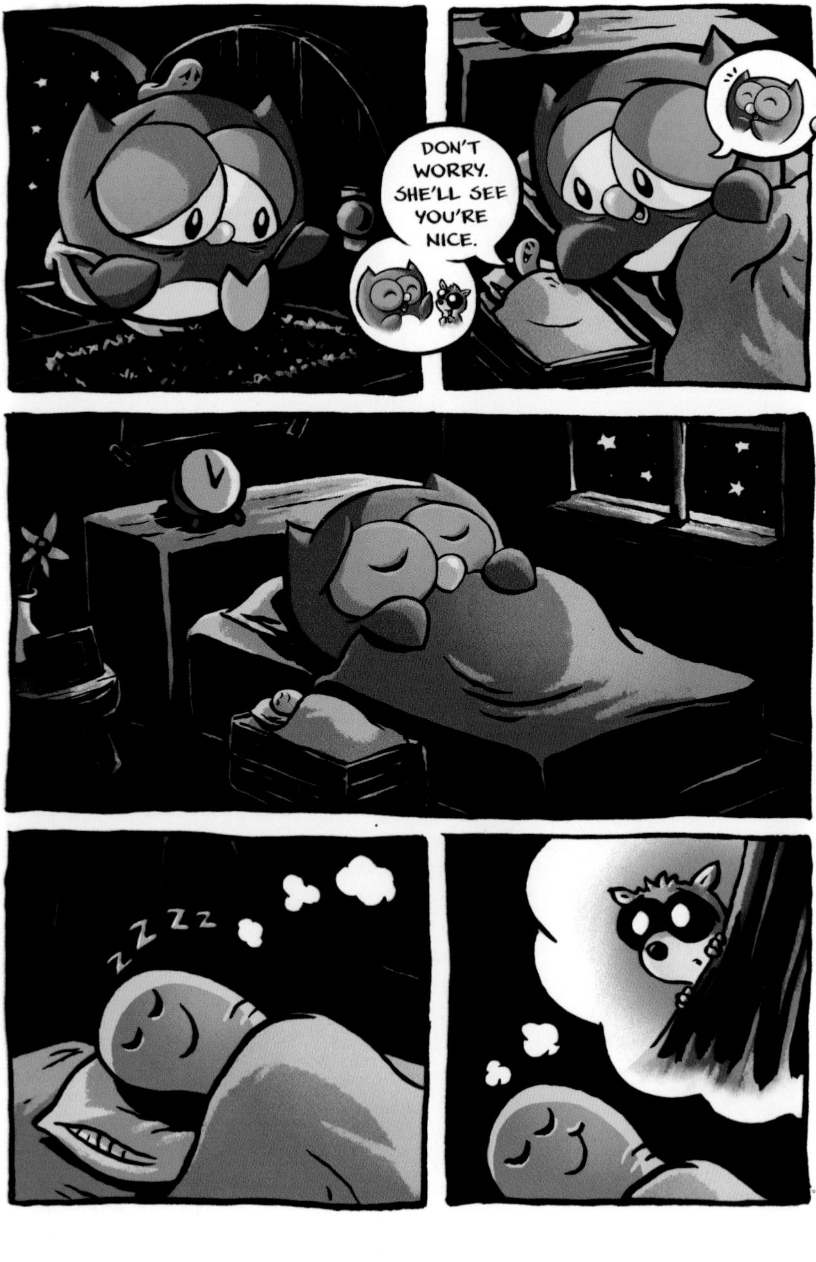
DON'T WORRY. SHE'LL SEE YOU'RE NICE.
!
Z Z Z Z Z

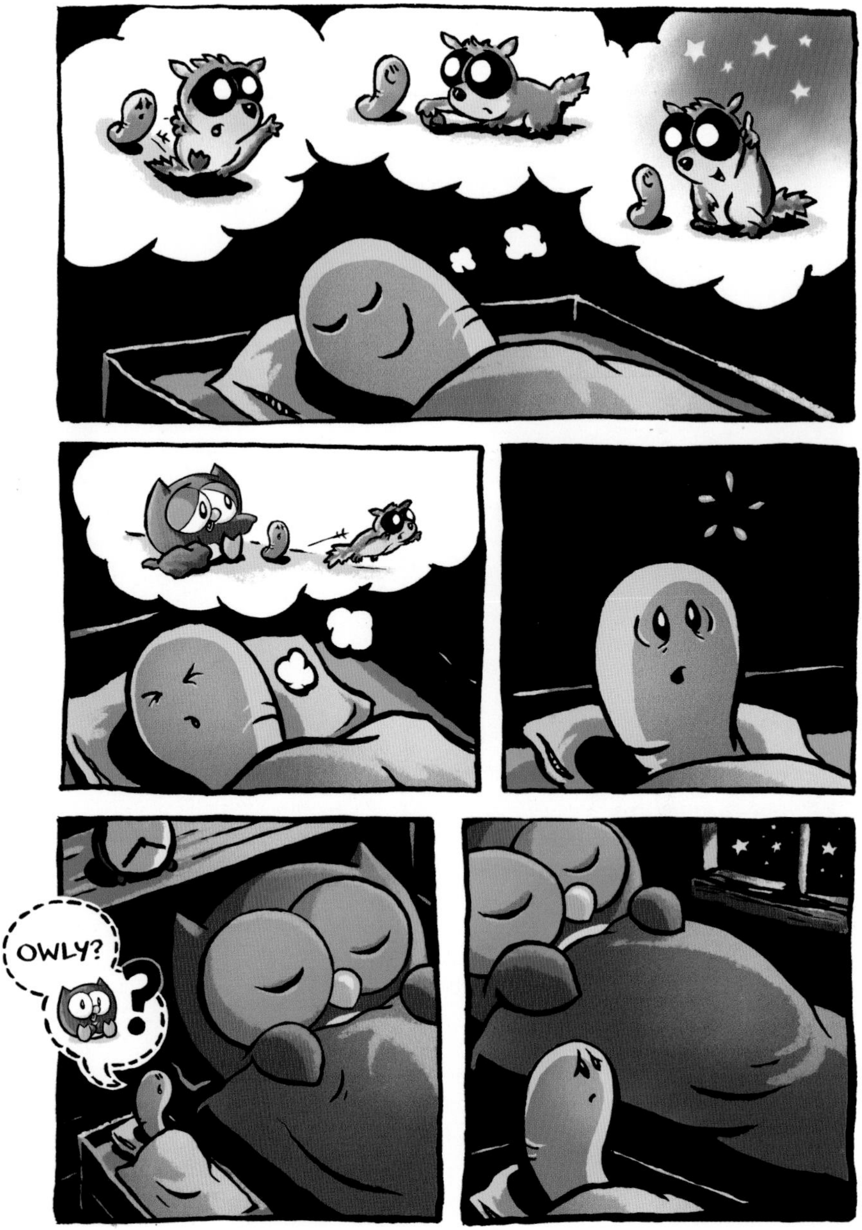
OWLY?

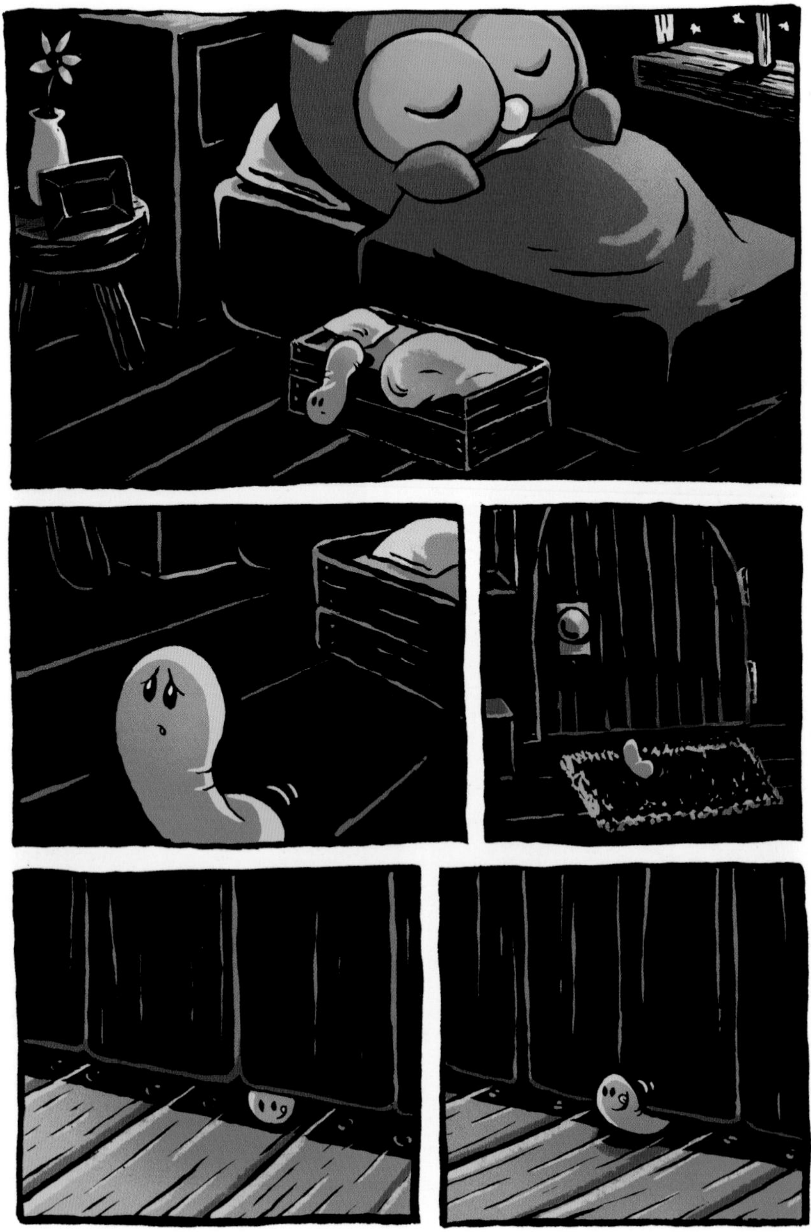

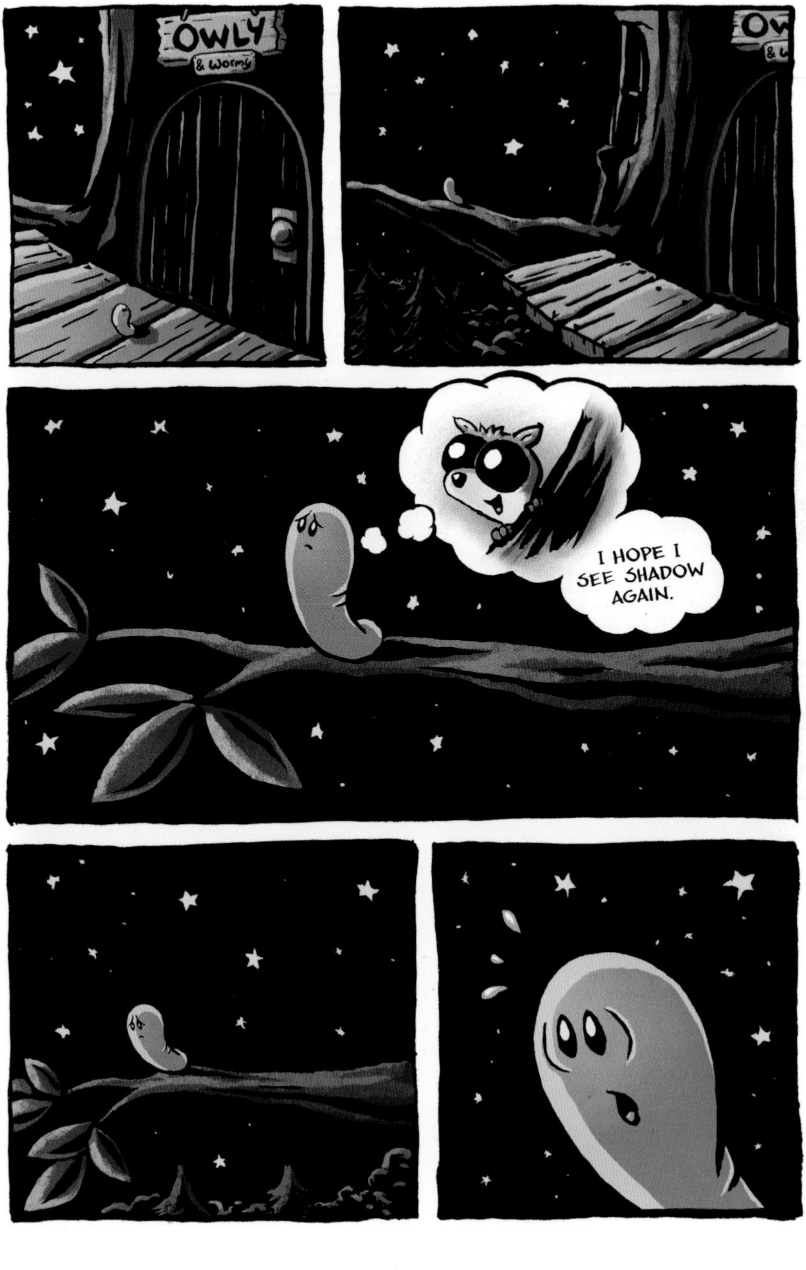
OWLY
& Wormy
I HOPE I SEE SHADOW AGAIN.

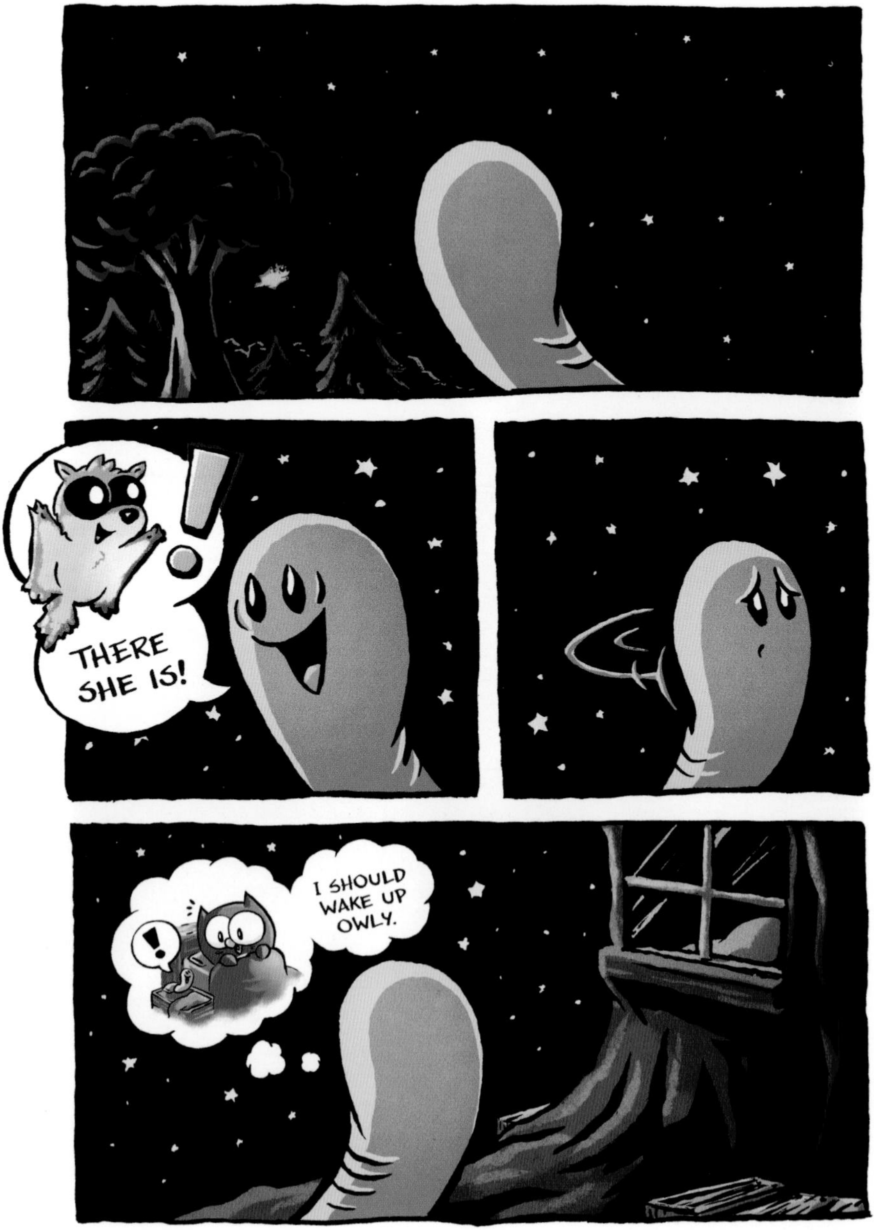
THERE SHE IS!
I SHOULD WAKE UP OWLY.

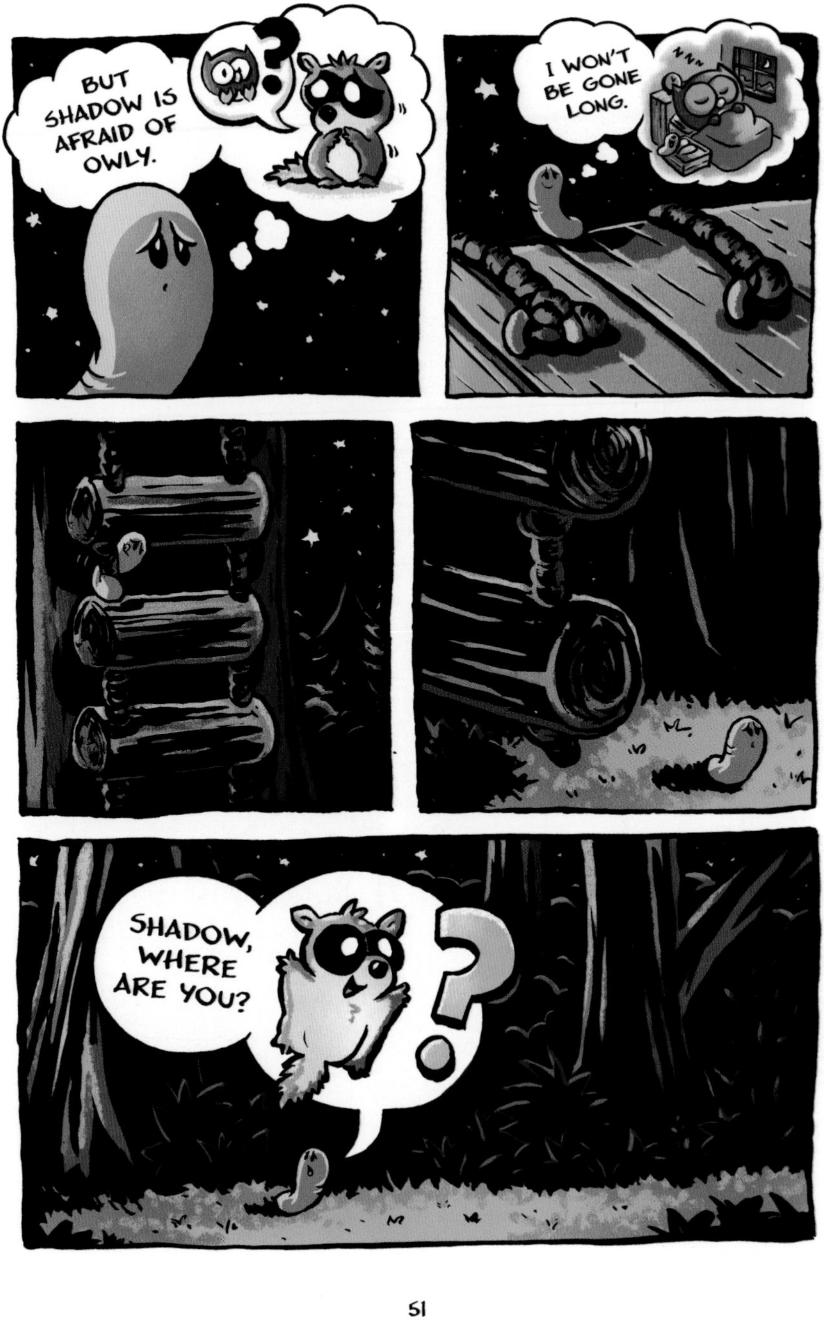
BUT SHADOW IS AFRAID OF OWLY.
?
I WON'T BE GONE LONG.
Z Z Z
SHADOW, WHERE ARE YOU?
?

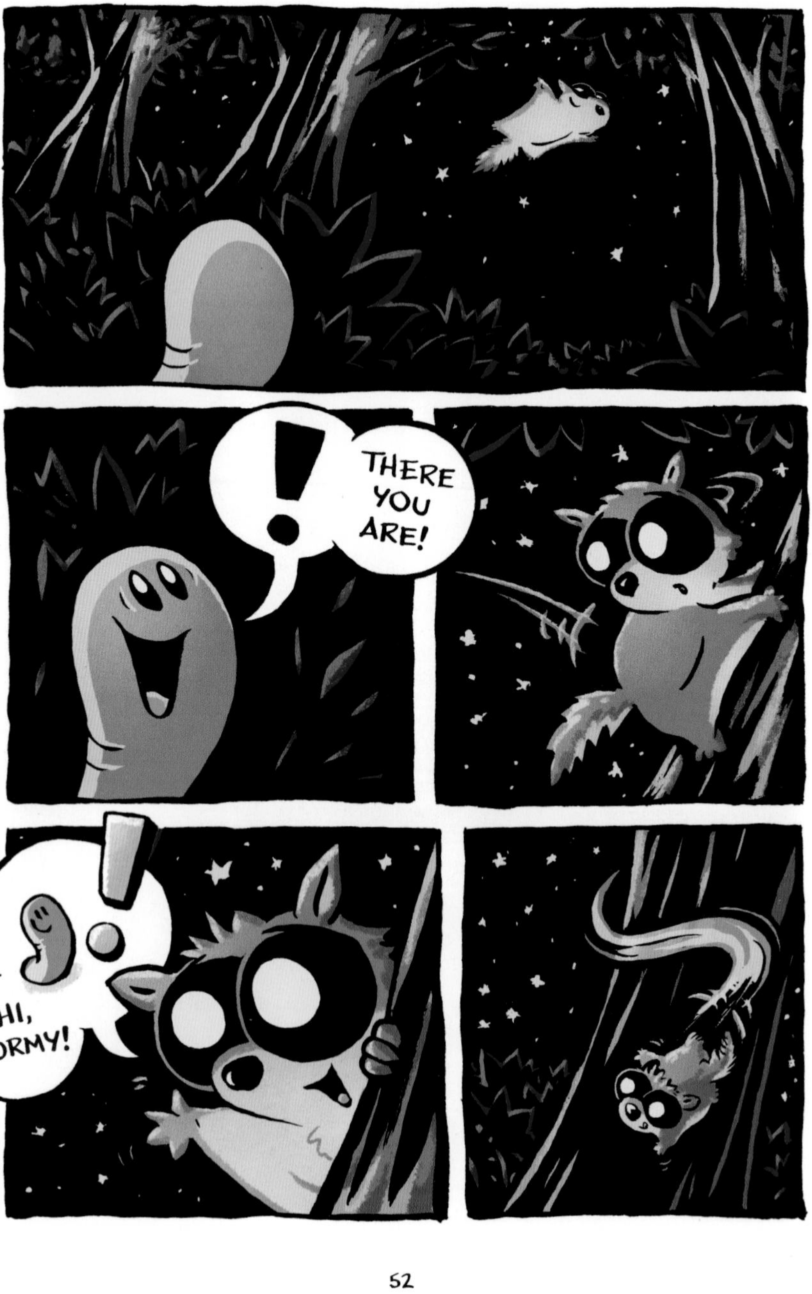
!
THERE YOU ARE!
!
?
HI, WORMY!

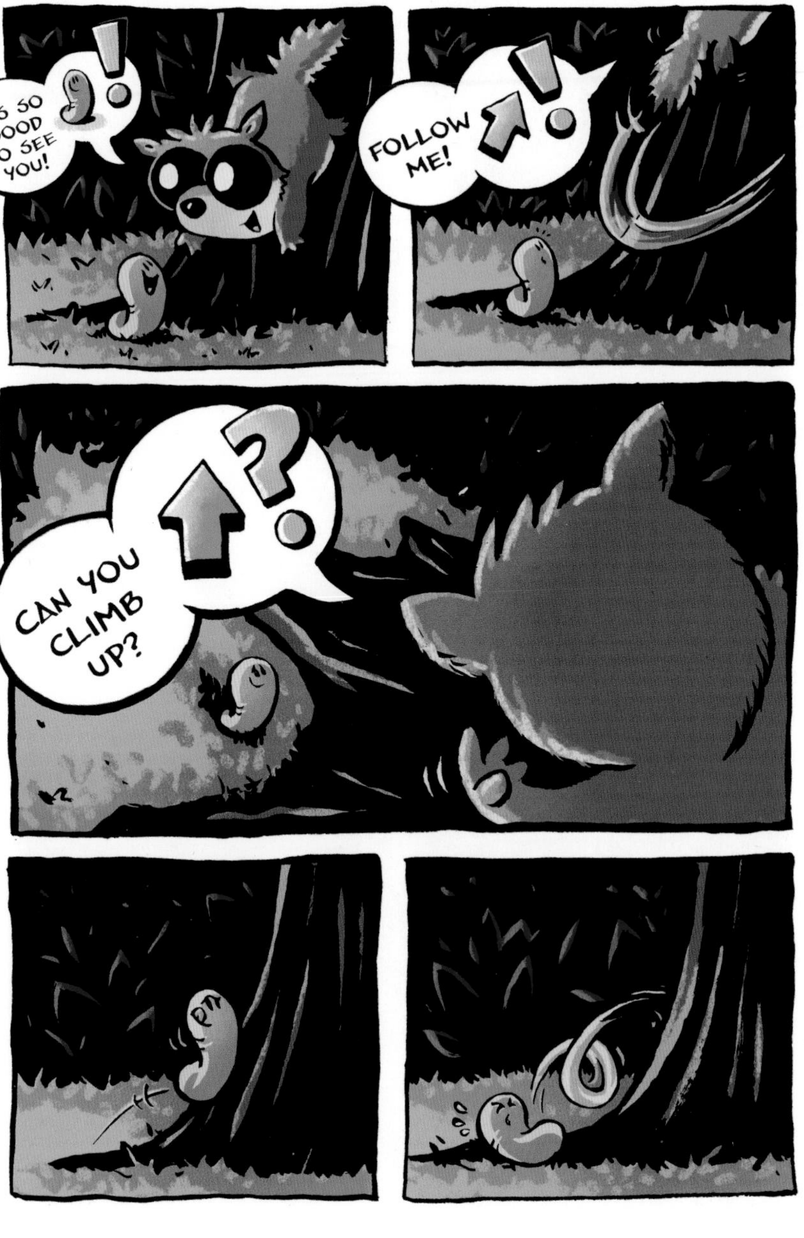
IT'S SO GOOD TO SEE YOU!
FOLLOW ME!
CAN YOU CLIMB UP?

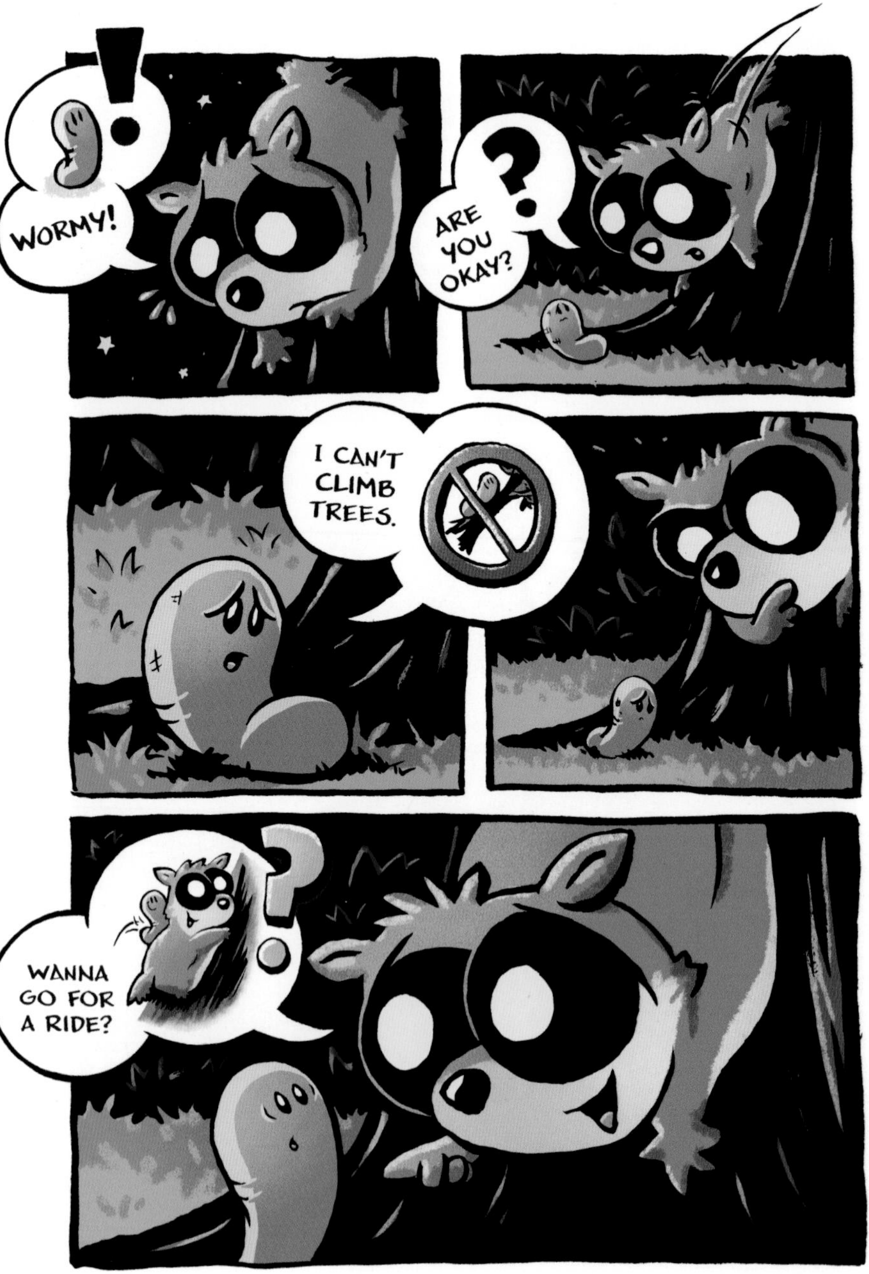
!
WORMY!
?
ARE YOU OKAY?
I CAN'T CLIMB TREES.
?
WANNA GO FOR A RIDE?

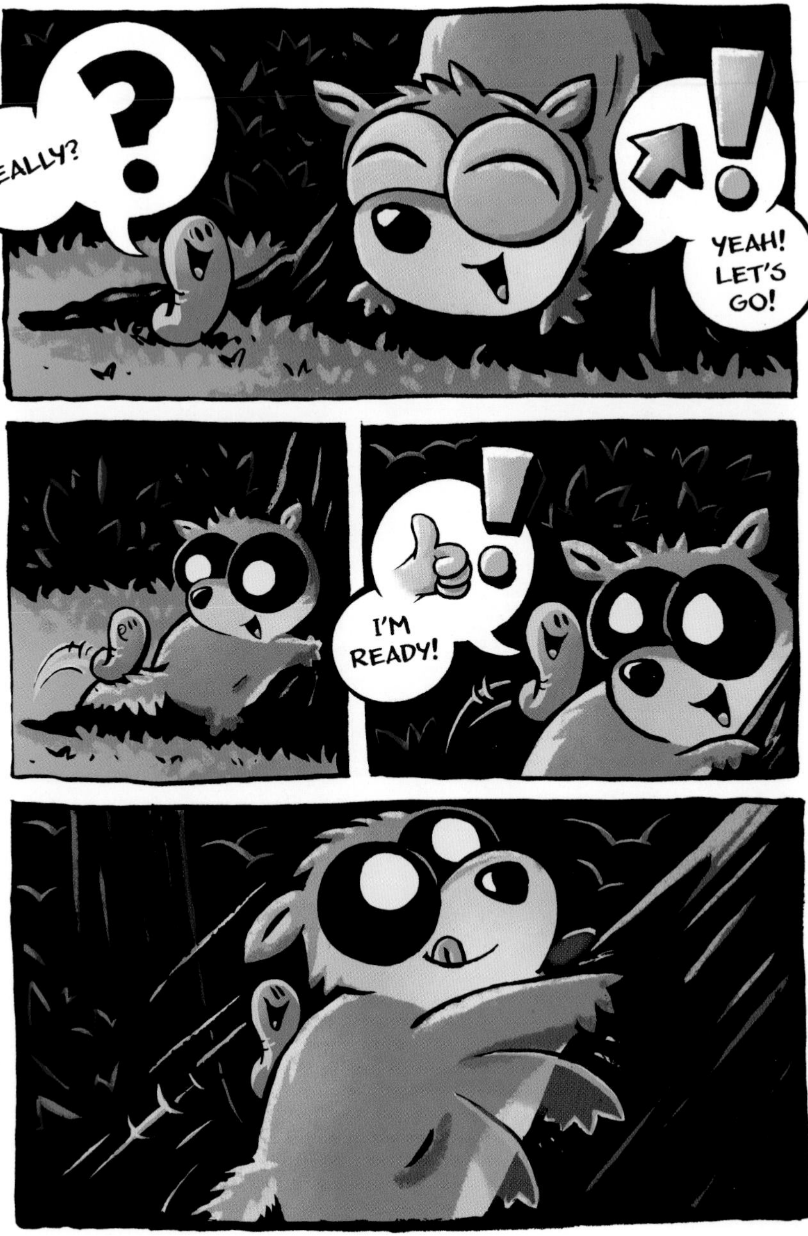
REALLY?
YEAH! LET'S GO!
I'M READY!

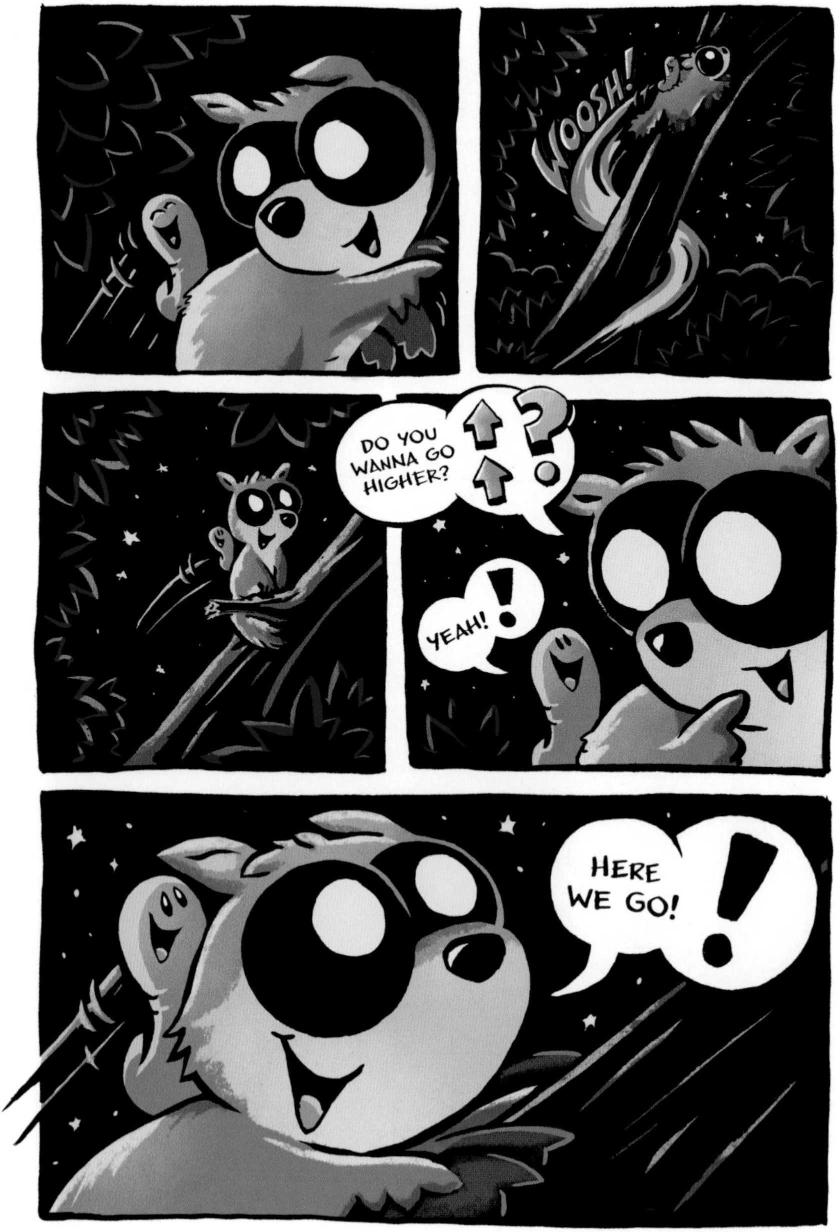
WOOSH!
DO YOU WANNA GO HIGHER?
YEAH!
HERE WE GO!

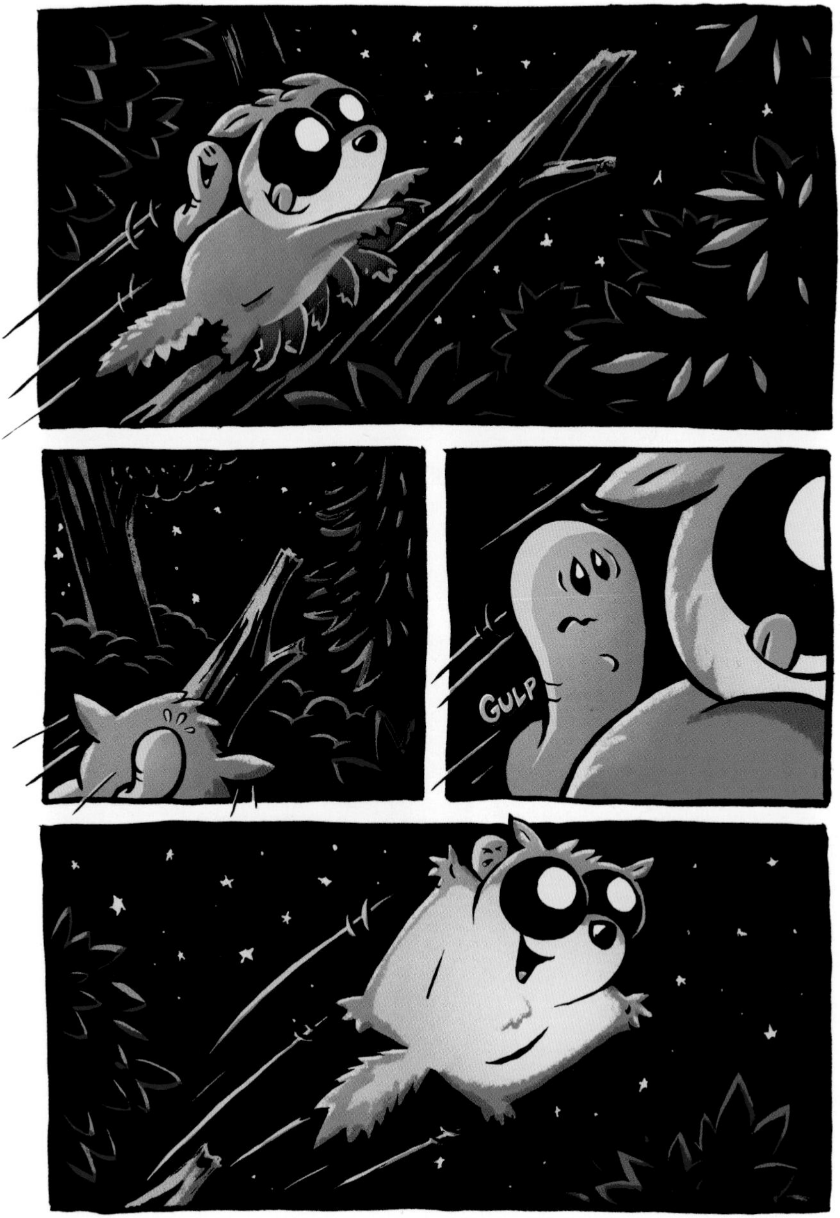
GULP

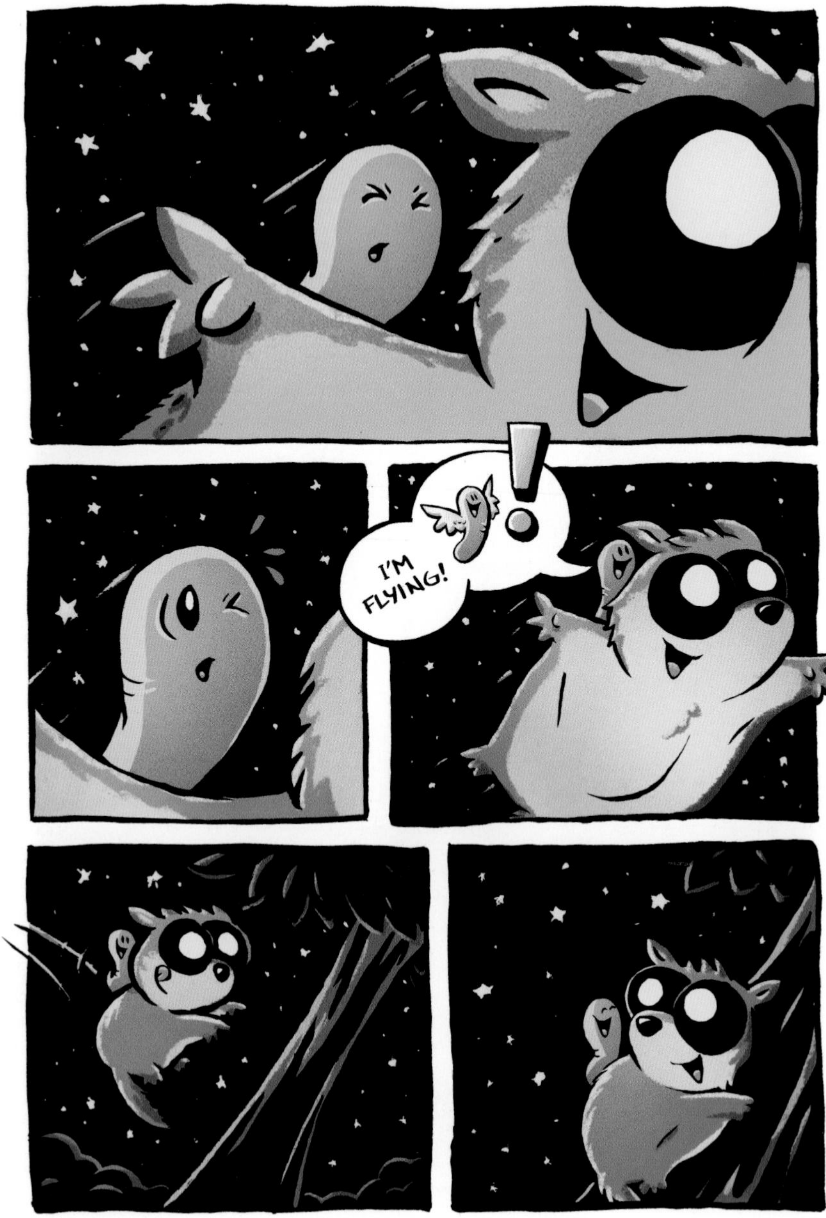

I'M FLYING!
!

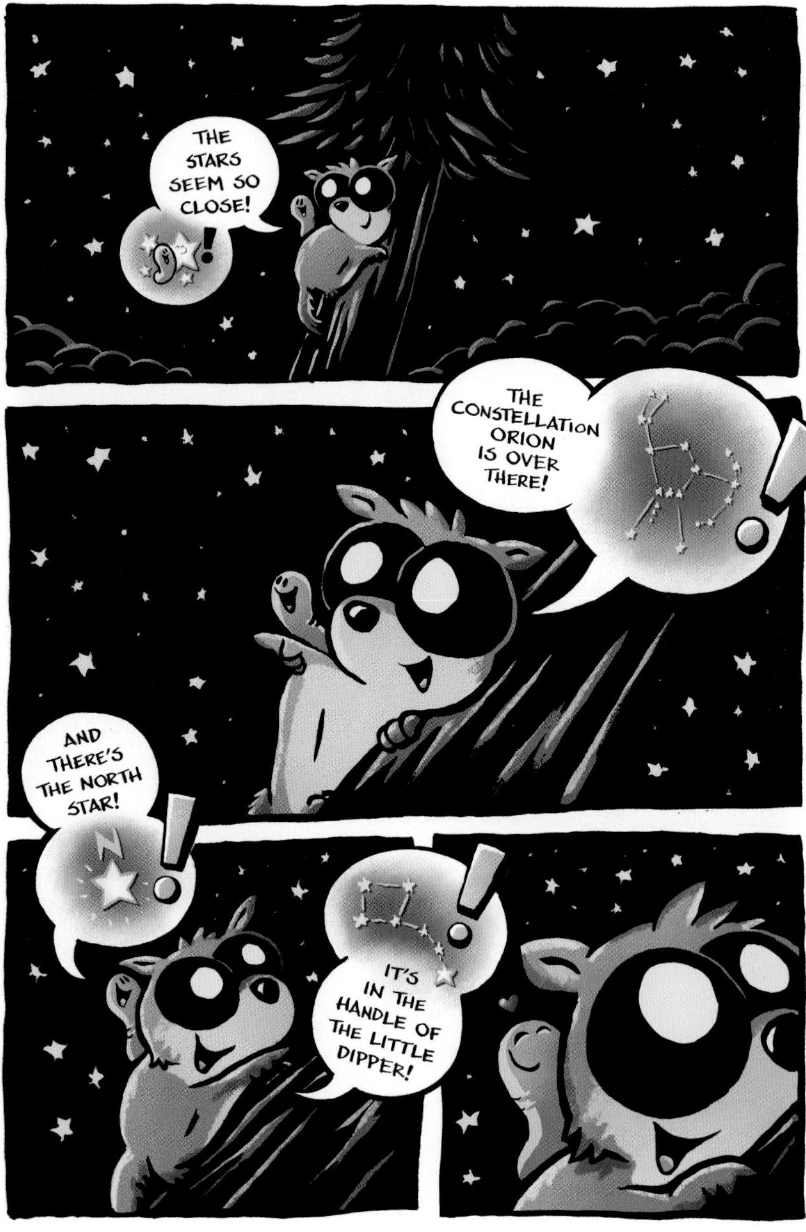
THE STARS SEEM SO CLOSE!
THE CONSTELLATION ORION IS OVER THERE!
AND THERE'S THE NORTH STAR!
IT'S IN THE HANDLE OF THE LITTLE DIPPER!

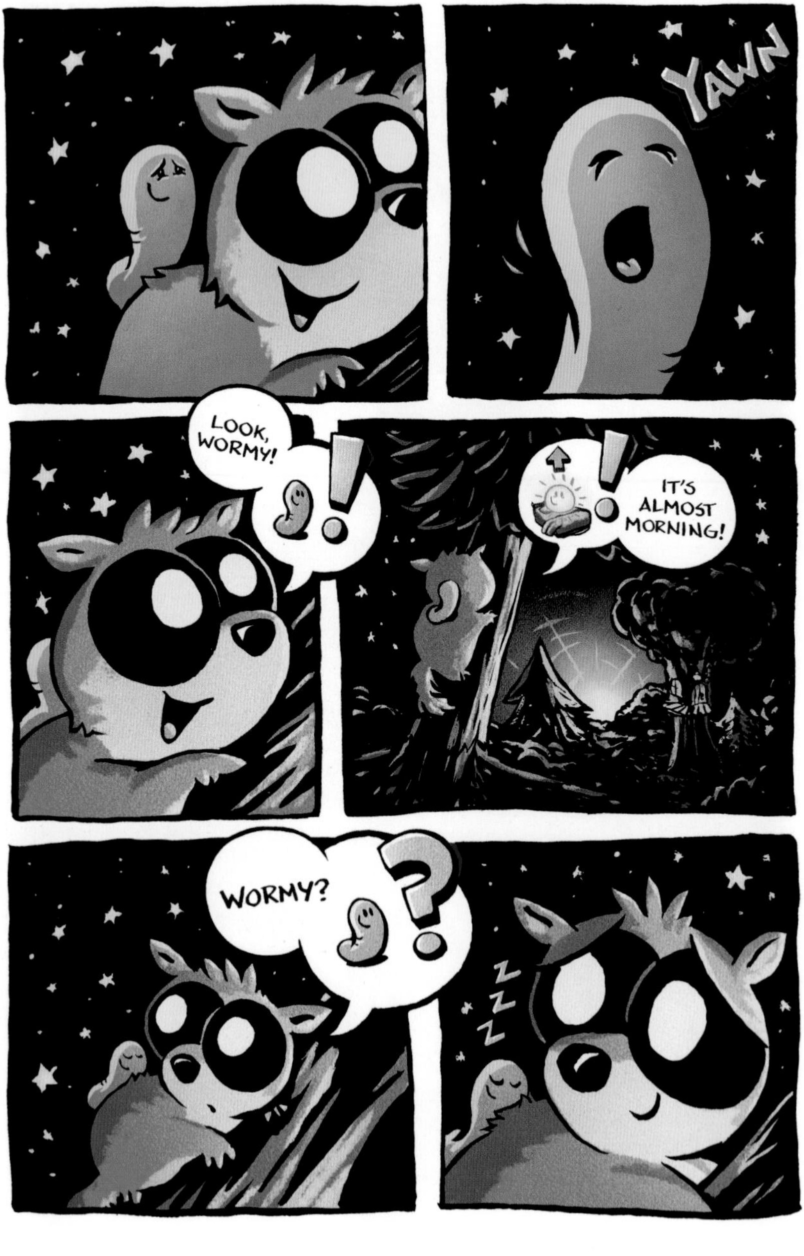
YAWN
LOOK, WORMY!
IT'S ALMOST MORNING!
WORMY?
Z Z Z

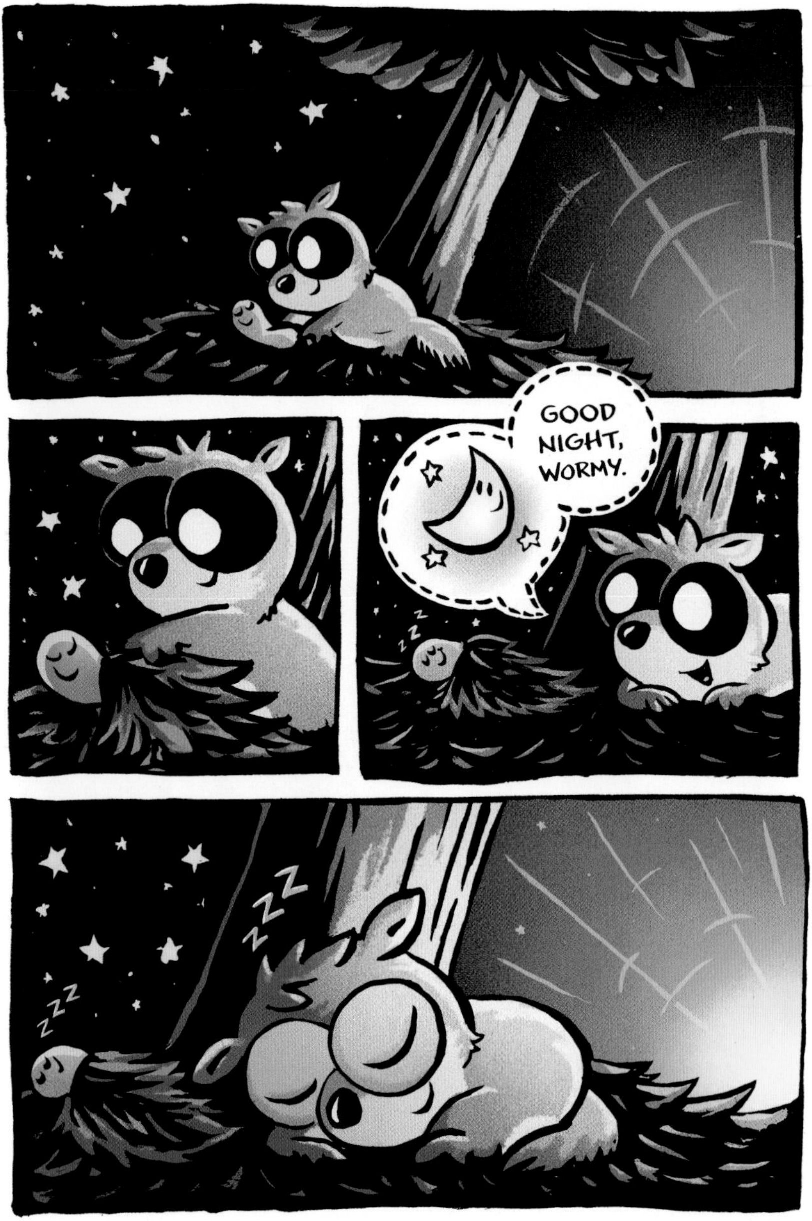
GOOD NIGHT, WORMY.

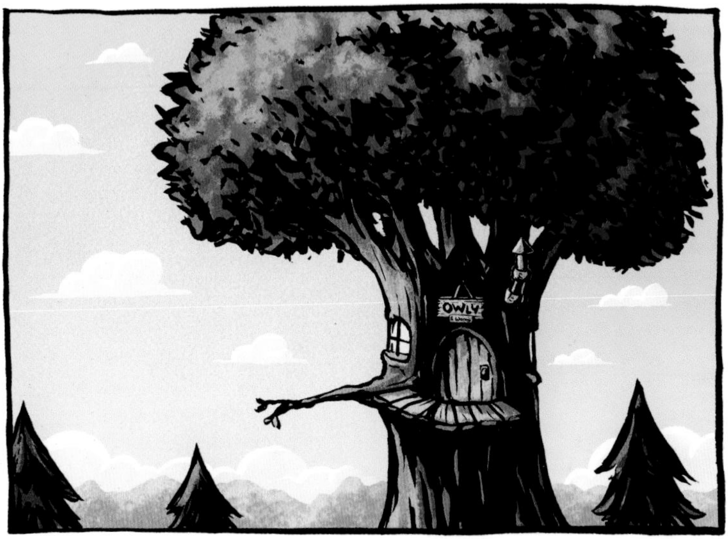
OWLY

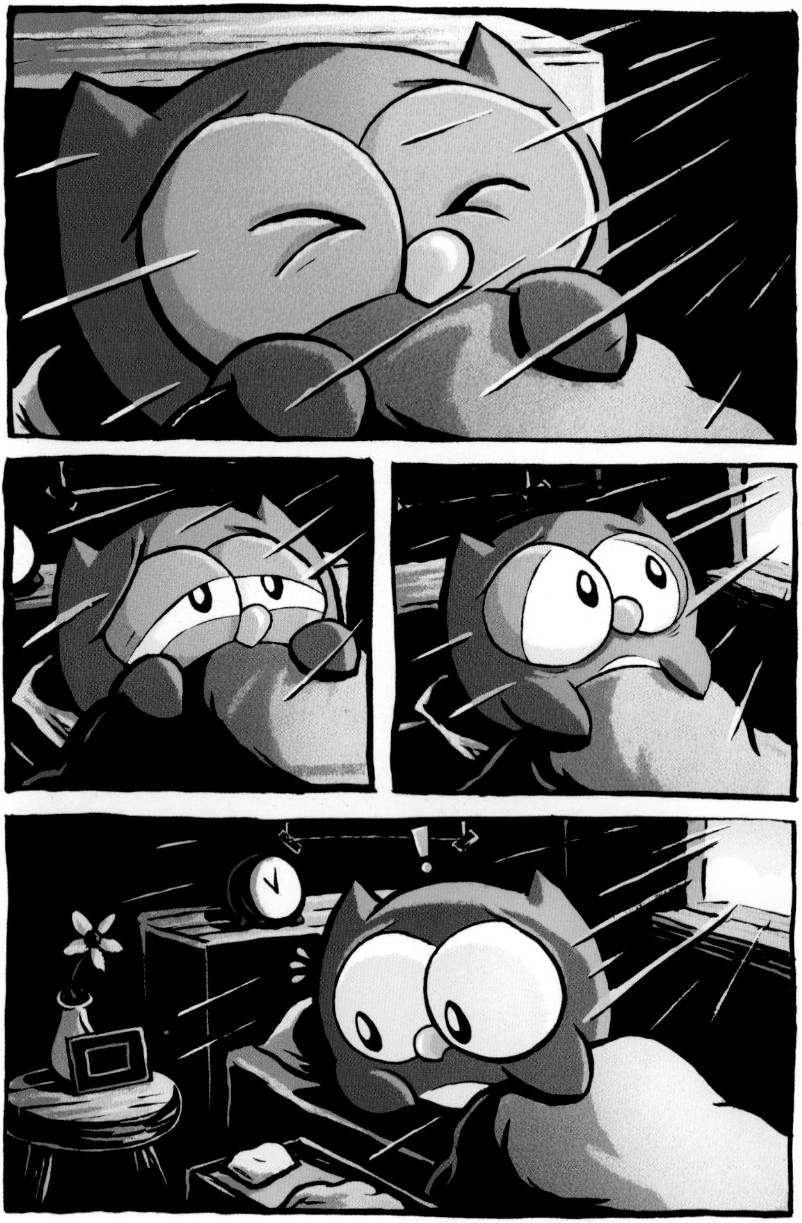

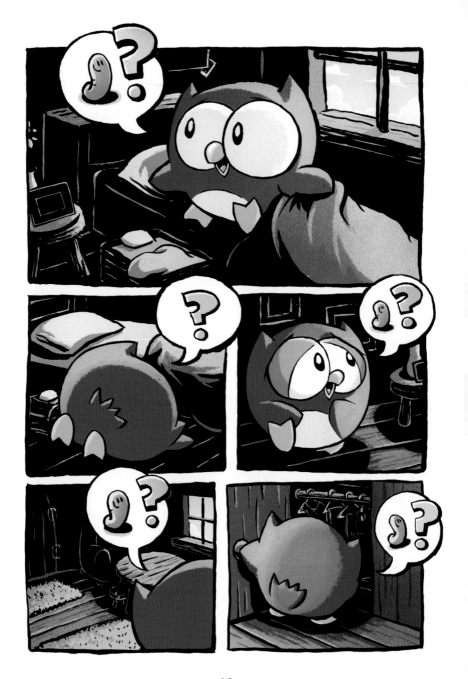

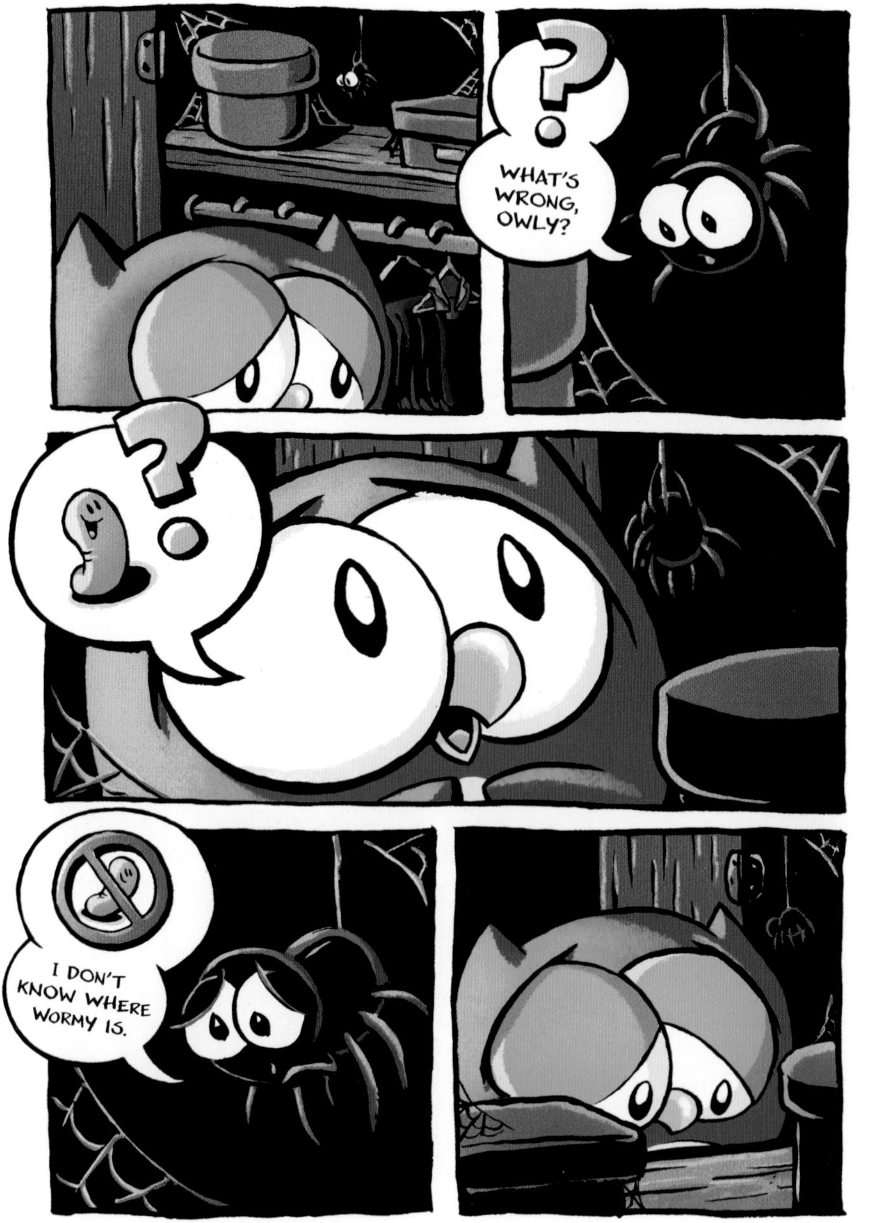
?
WHAT'S WRONG, OWLY?
?
I DON'T KNOW WHERE WORMY IS.

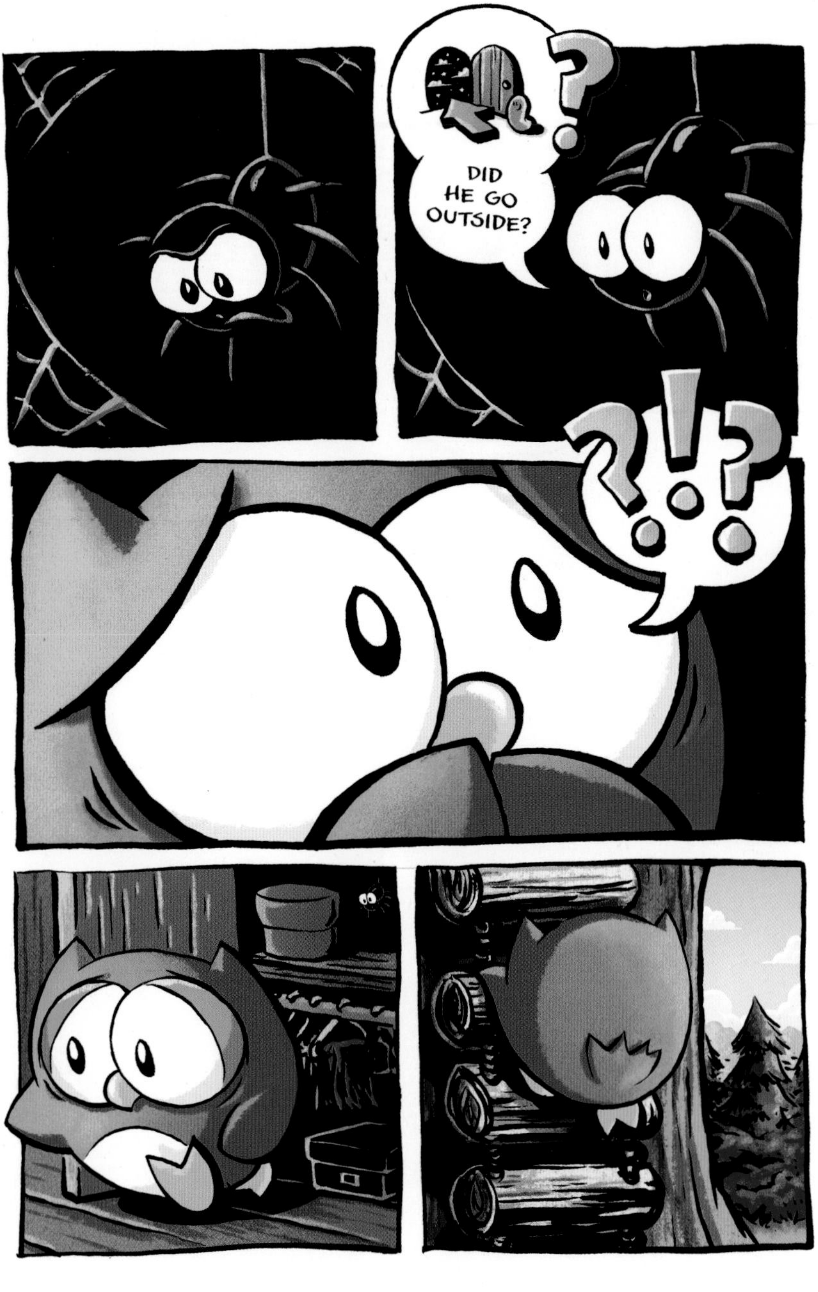
DID HE GO OUTSIDE?

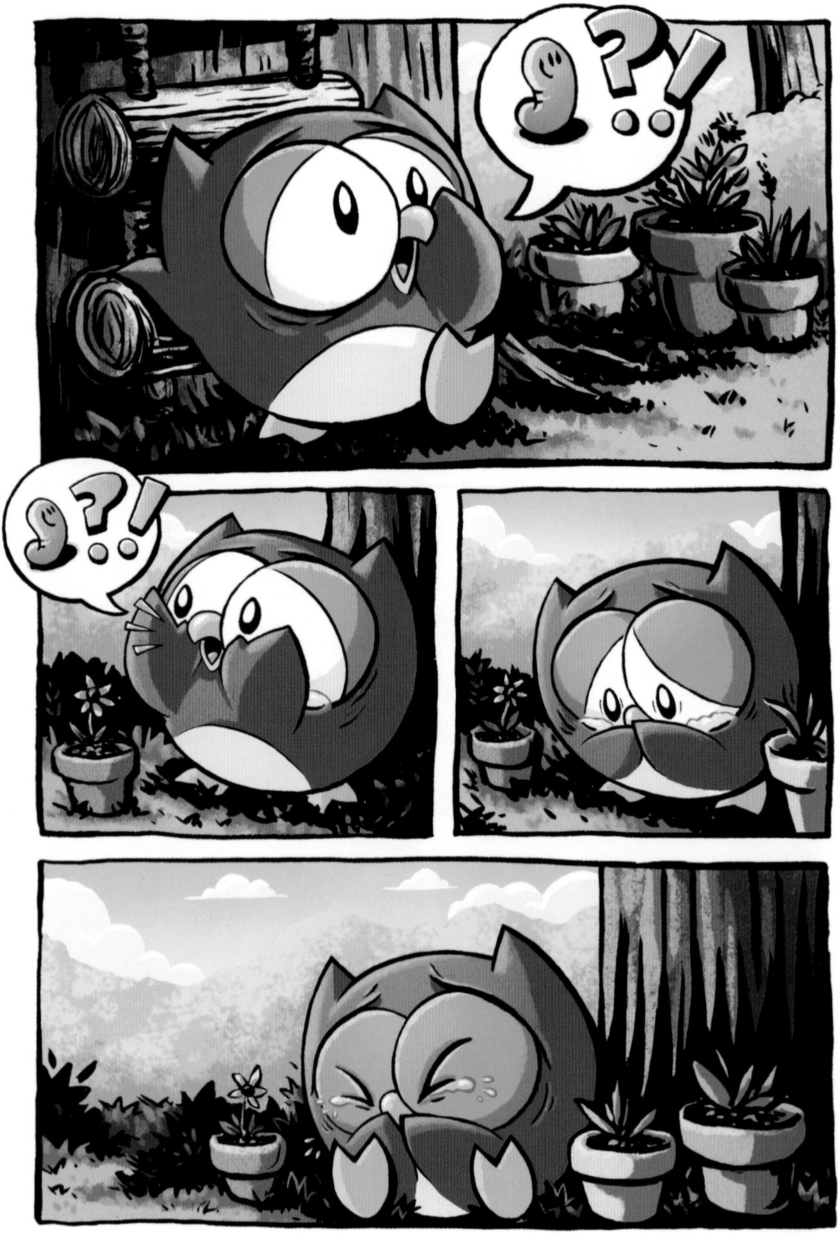

?!..
?!..

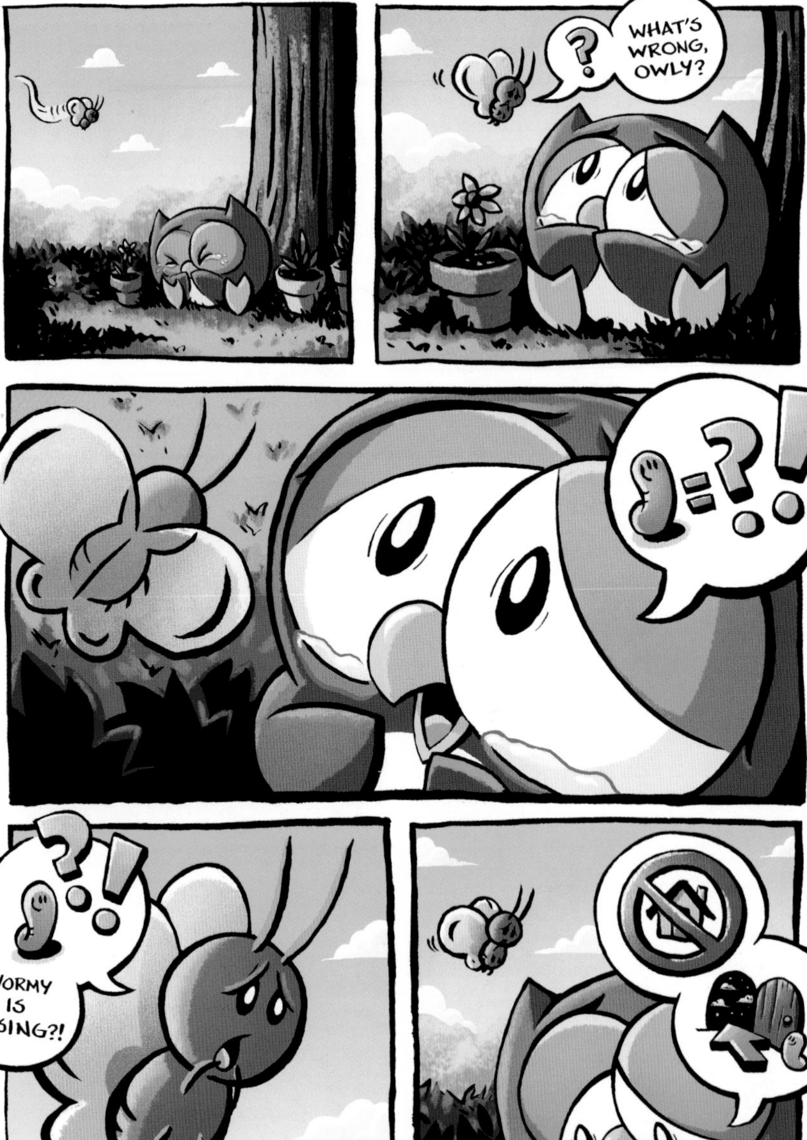
WHAT'S WRONG, OWLY?
WORMY IS MISSING?!

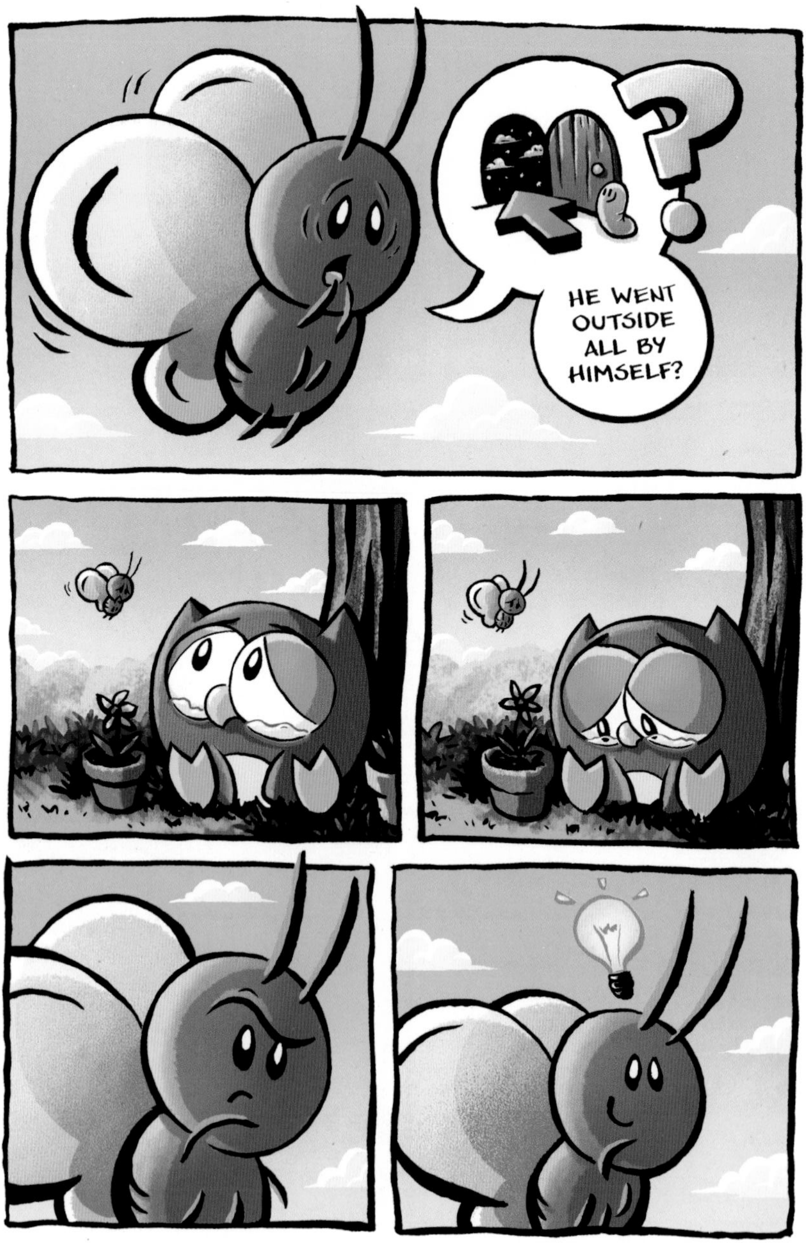
?
HE WENT OUTSIDE ALL BY HIMSELF?

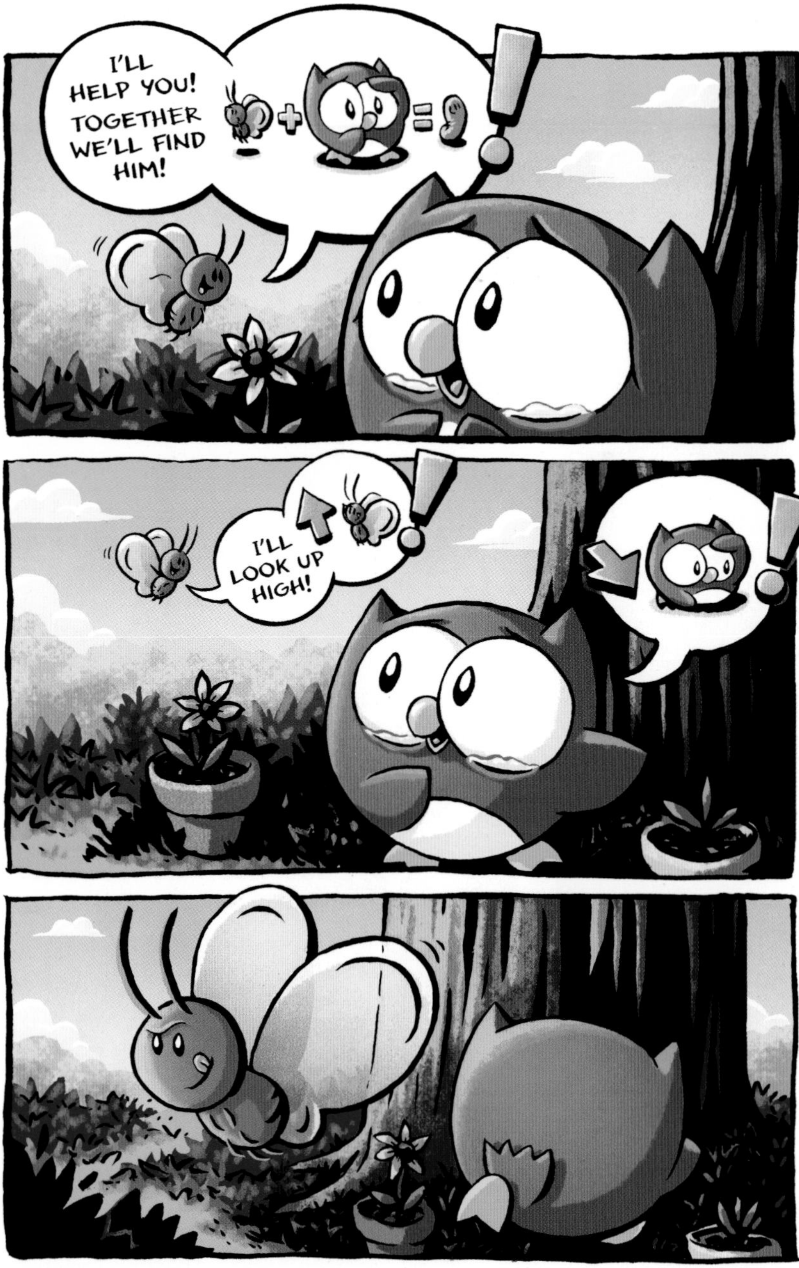
I'LL HELP YOU! TOGETHER WE'LL FIND HIM!
I'LL LOOK UP HIGH!

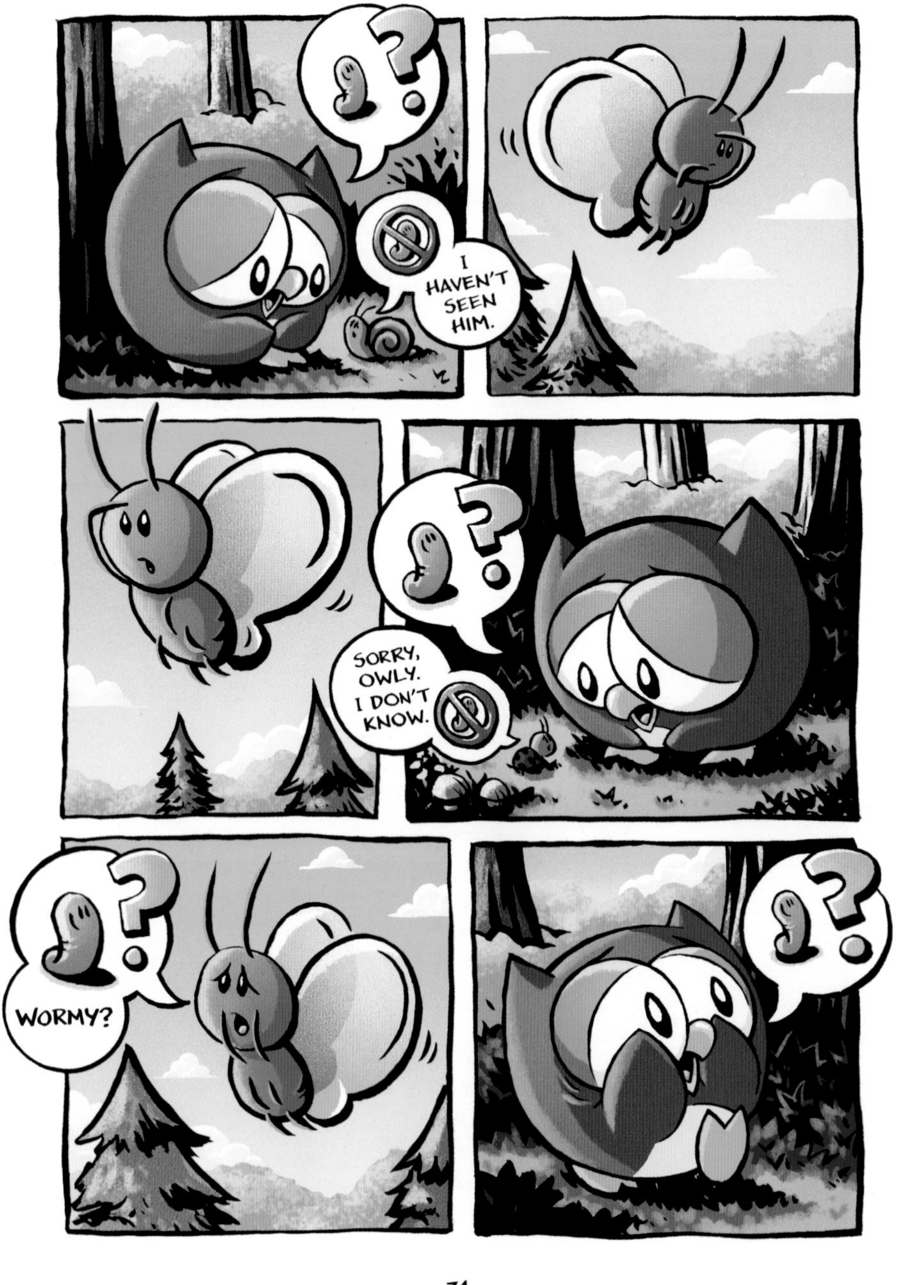
I HAVEN'T SEEN HIM.
SORRY, OWLY. I DON'T KNOW.
WORMY?

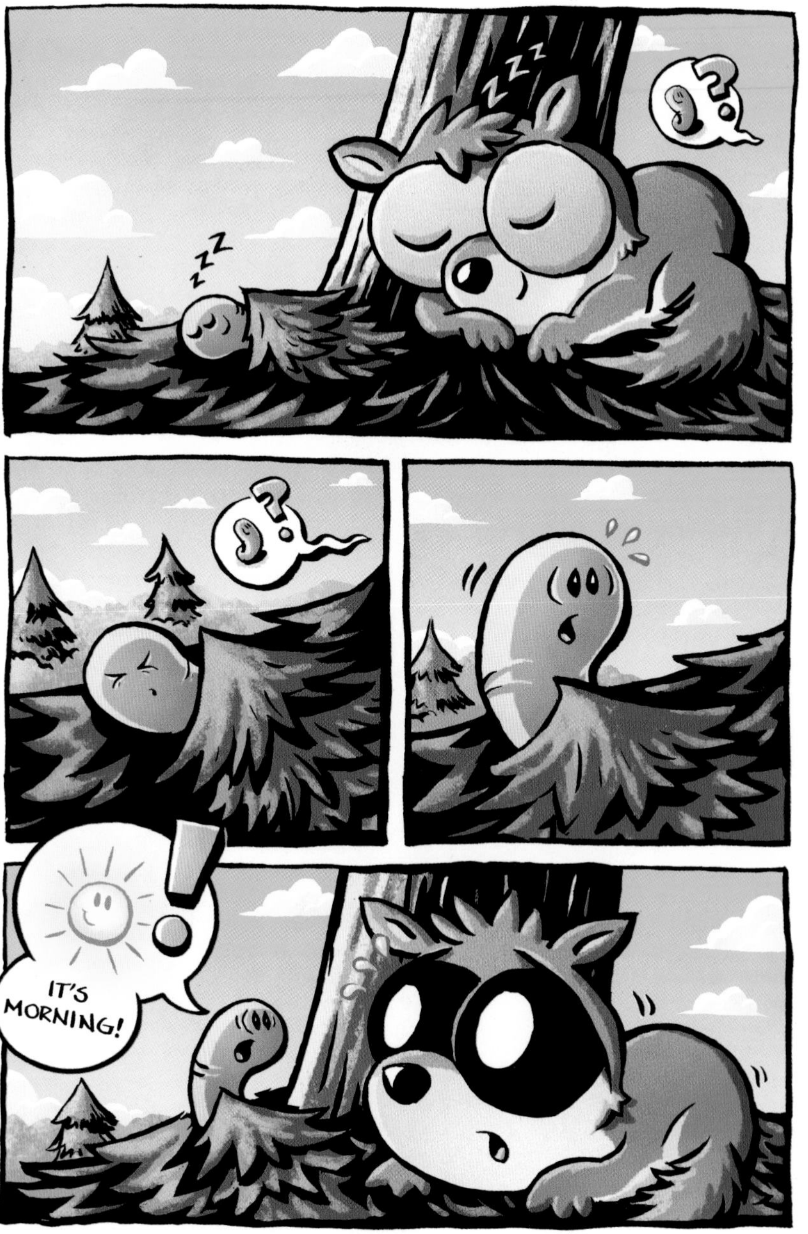
ZZZ
ZZZ
?
?
!
IT'S MORNING!

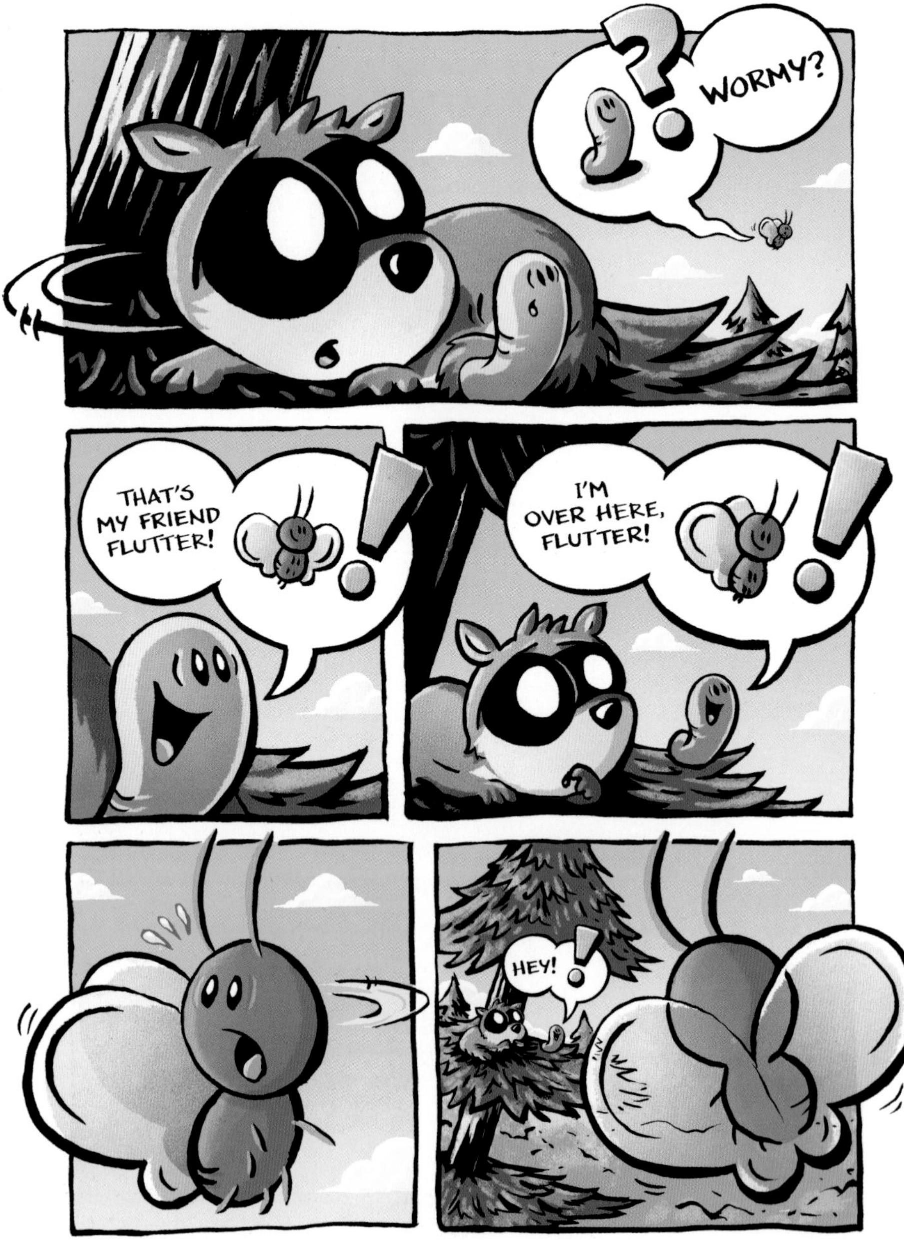
WORMY?
THAT'S MY FRIEND FLUTTER!
I'M OVER HERE, FLUTTER!
HEY!

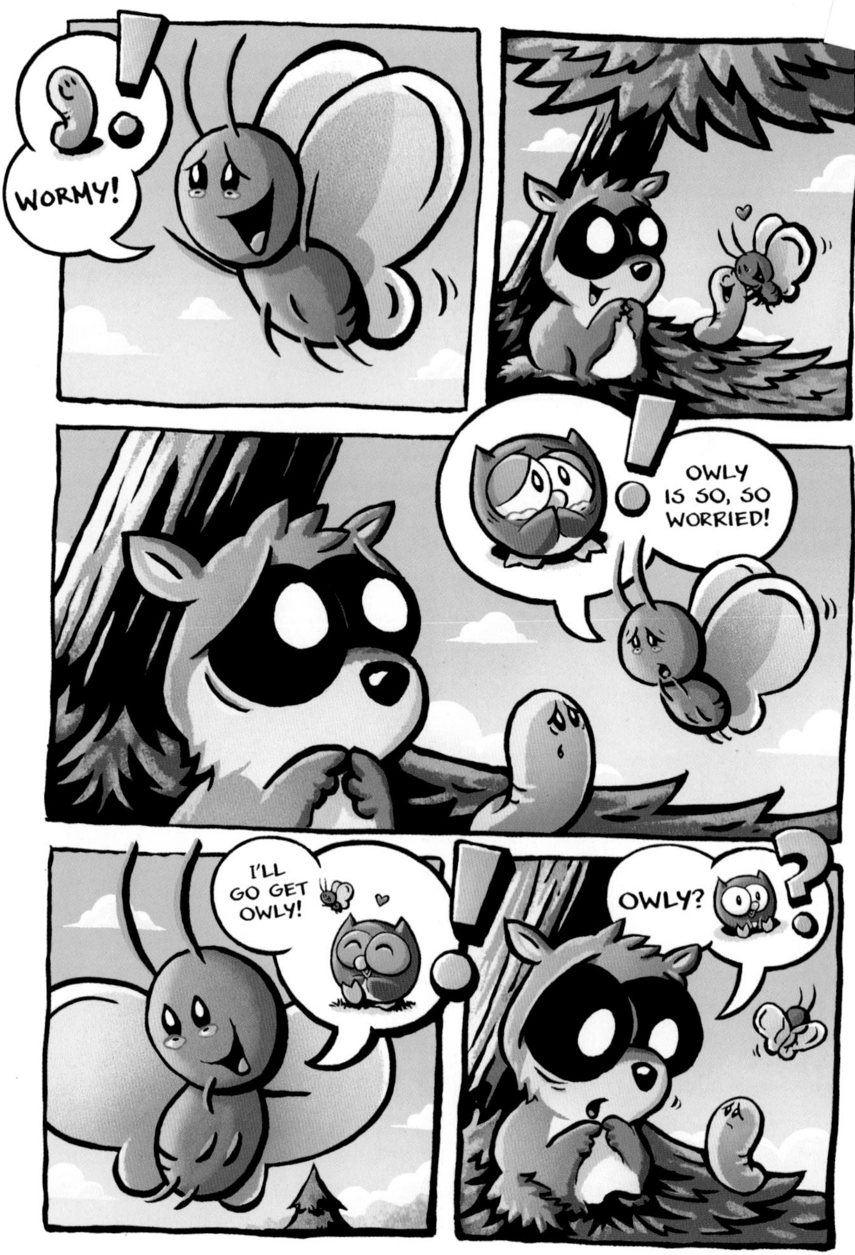
WORMY!
OWLY IS SO, SO WORRIED!
I'LL GO GET OWLY!
OWLY?

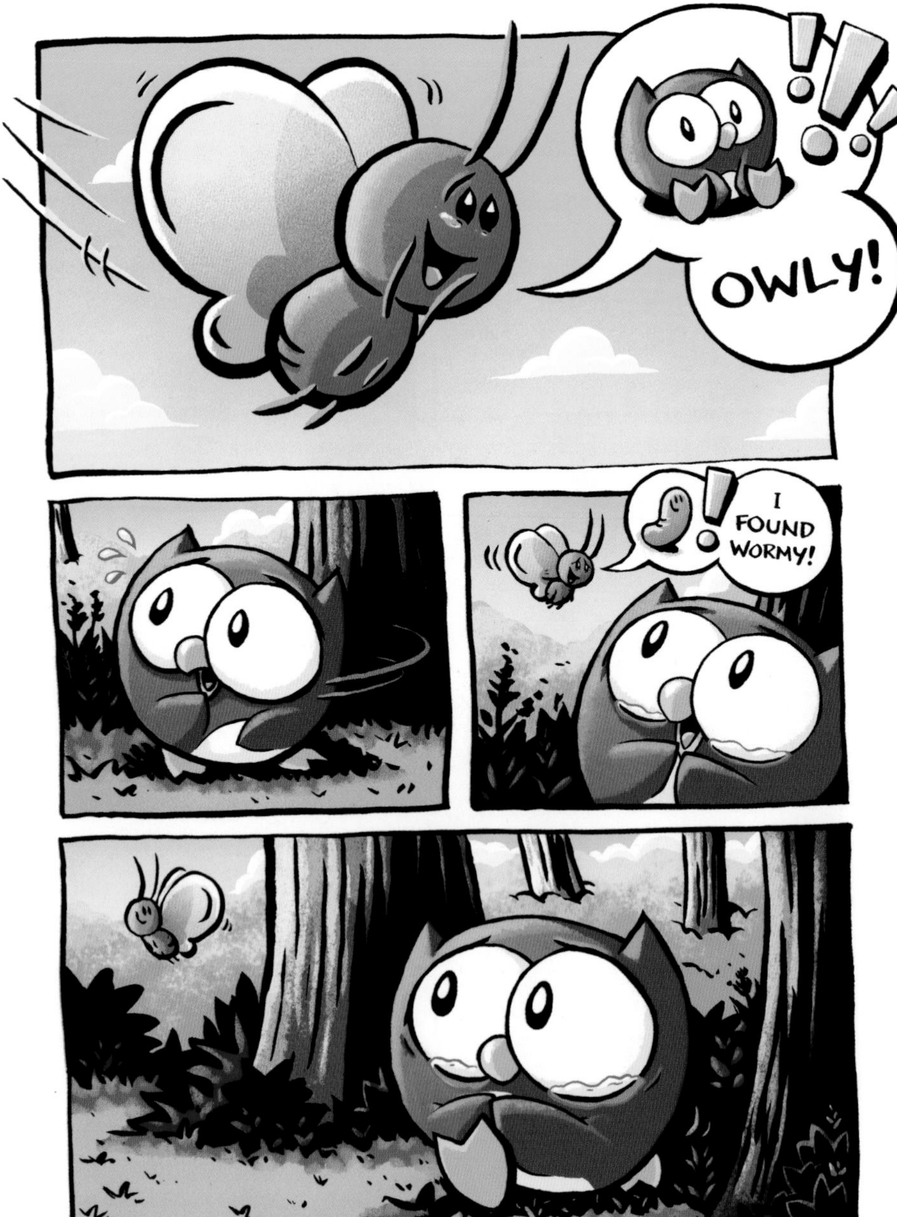
OWLY!
I FOUND WORMY!

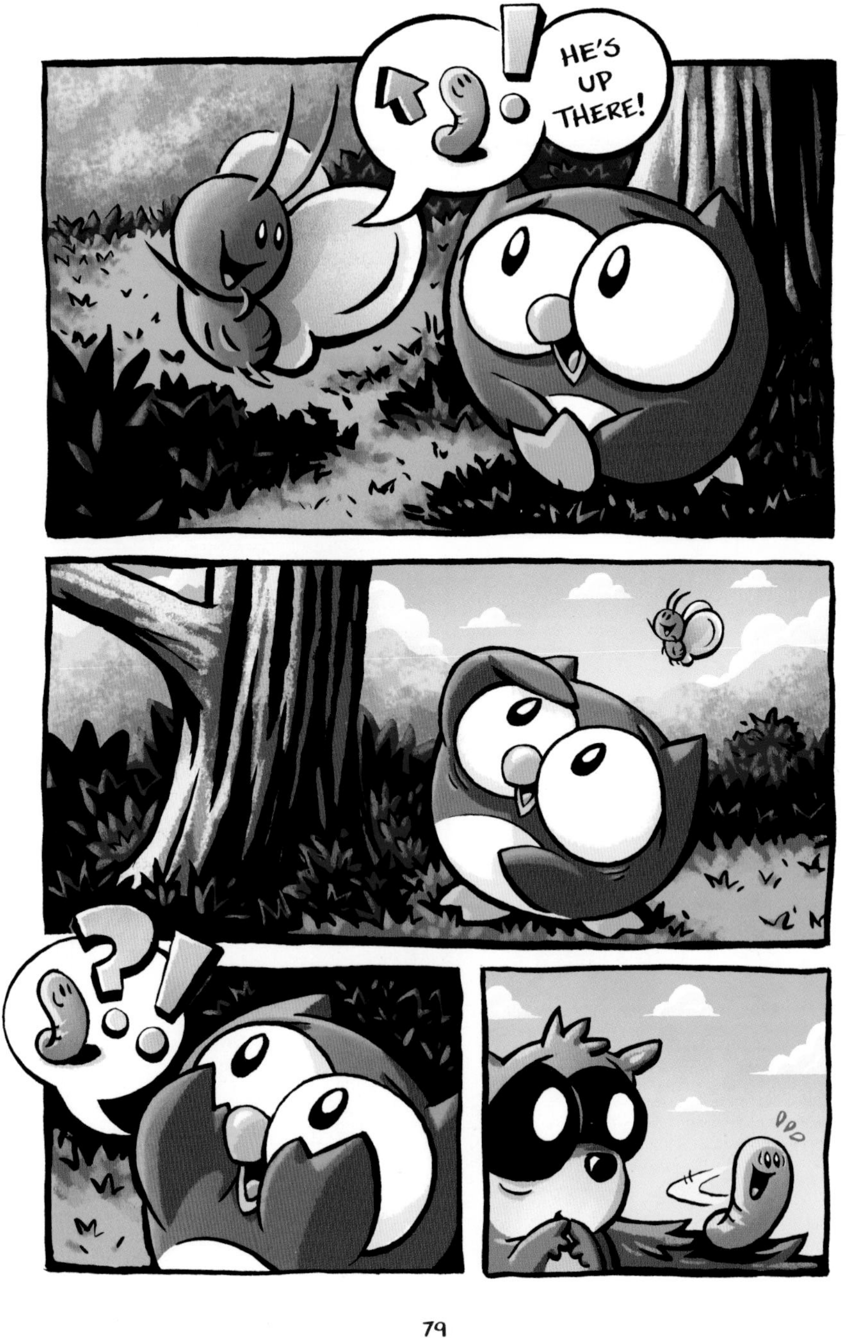
!
HE'S UP THERE!
?!

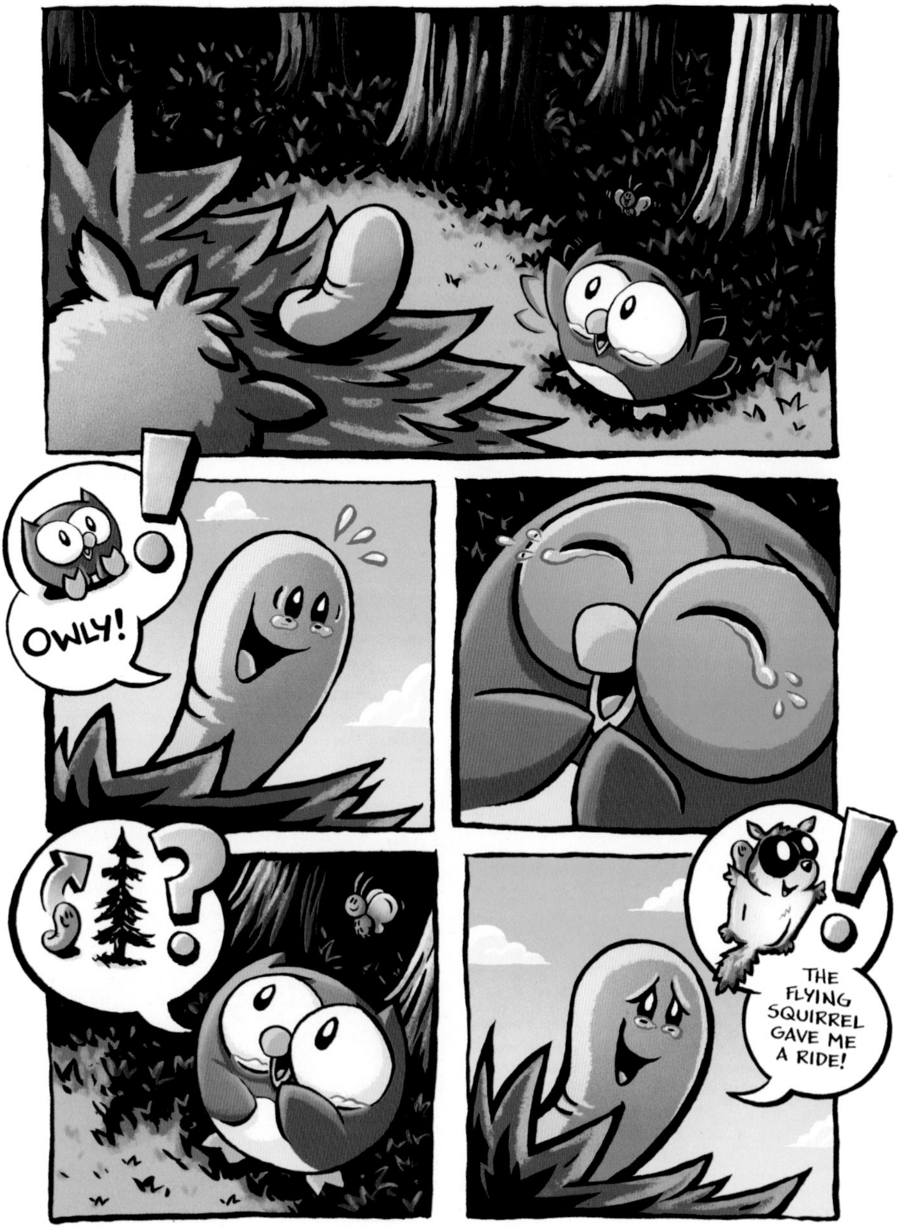
OWLY!
THE FLYING SQUIRREL GAVE ME A RIDE!

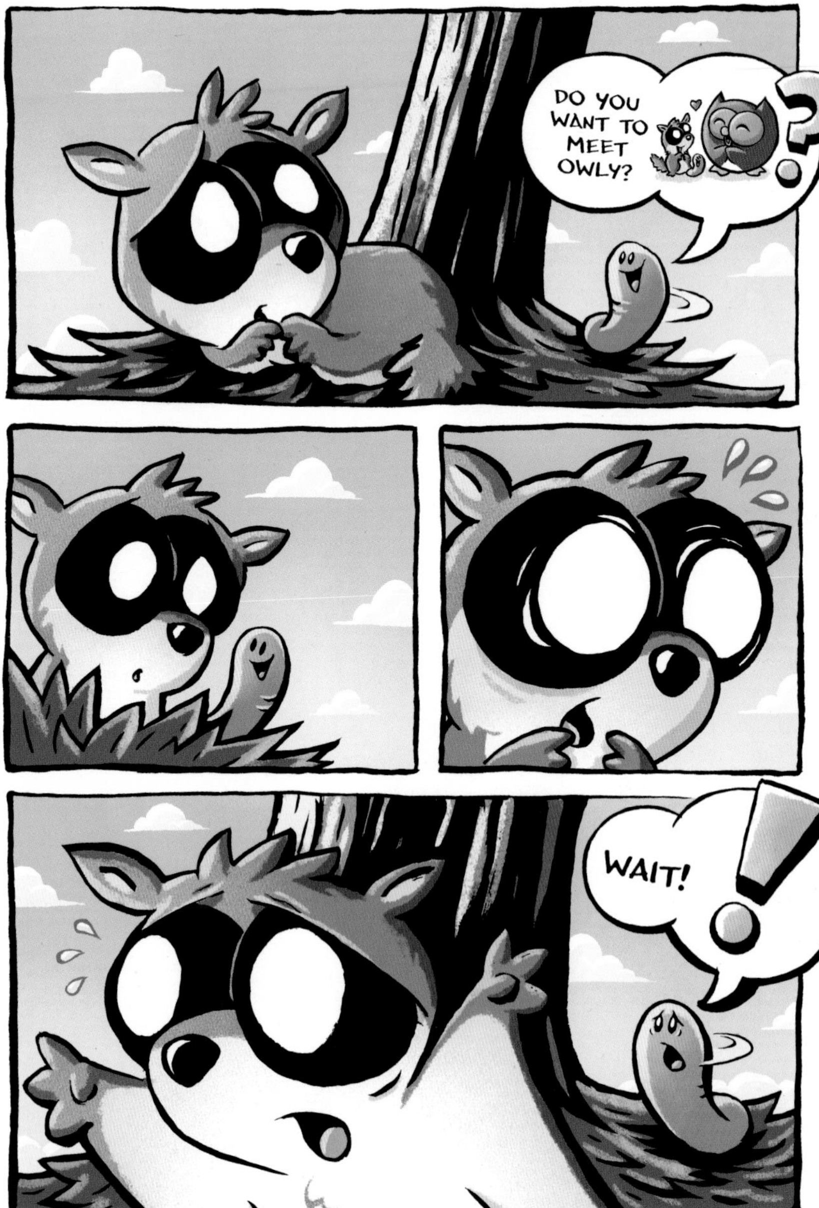
DO YOU WANT TO MEET OWLY?
?
WAIT!
!

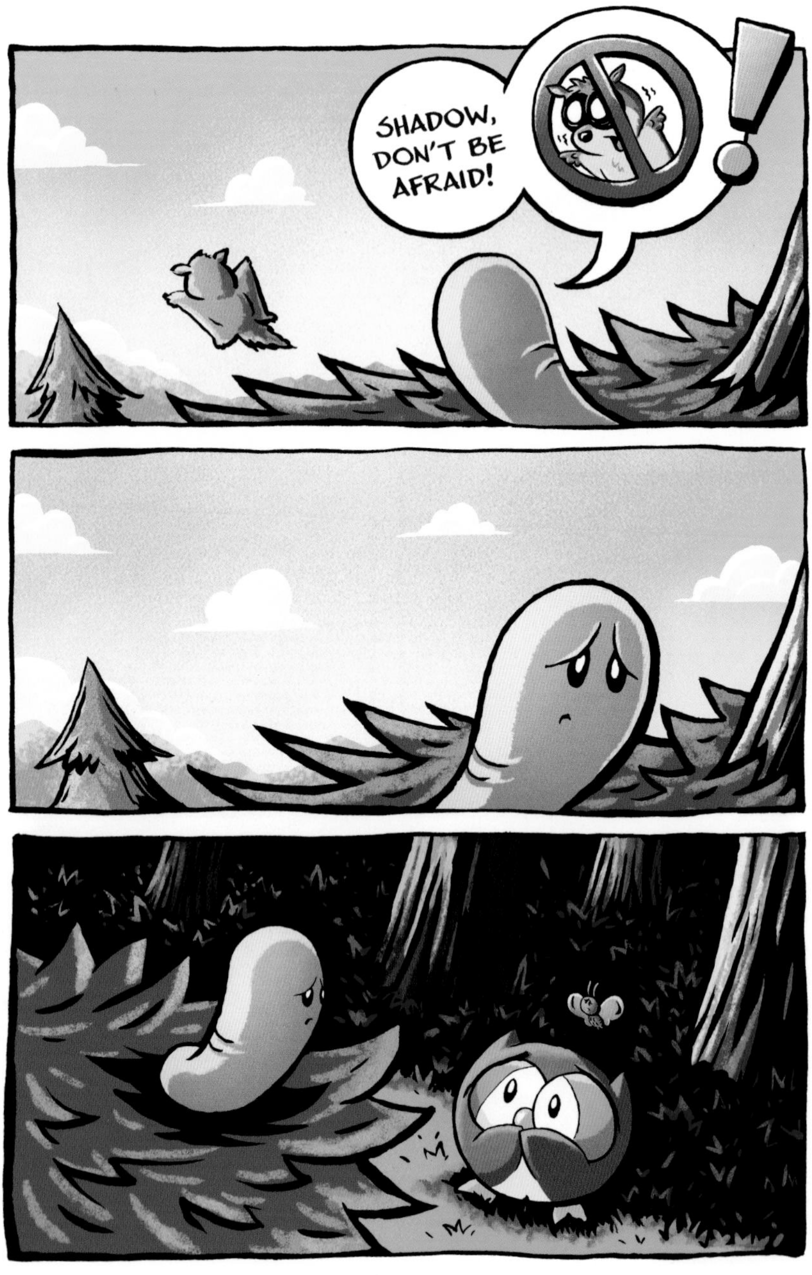
SHADOW, DON'T BE AFRAID!
!

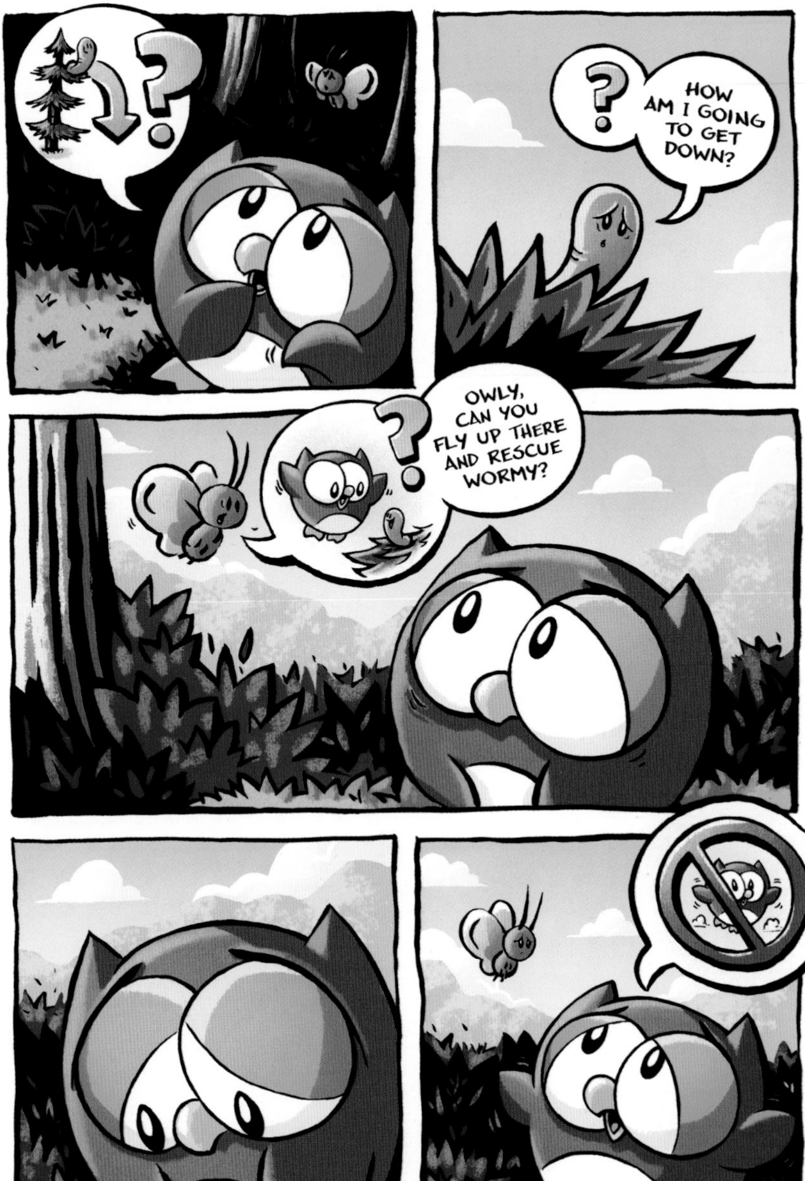
HOW AM I GOING TO GET DOWN?
OWLY, CAN YOU FLY UP THERE AND RESCUE WORMY?

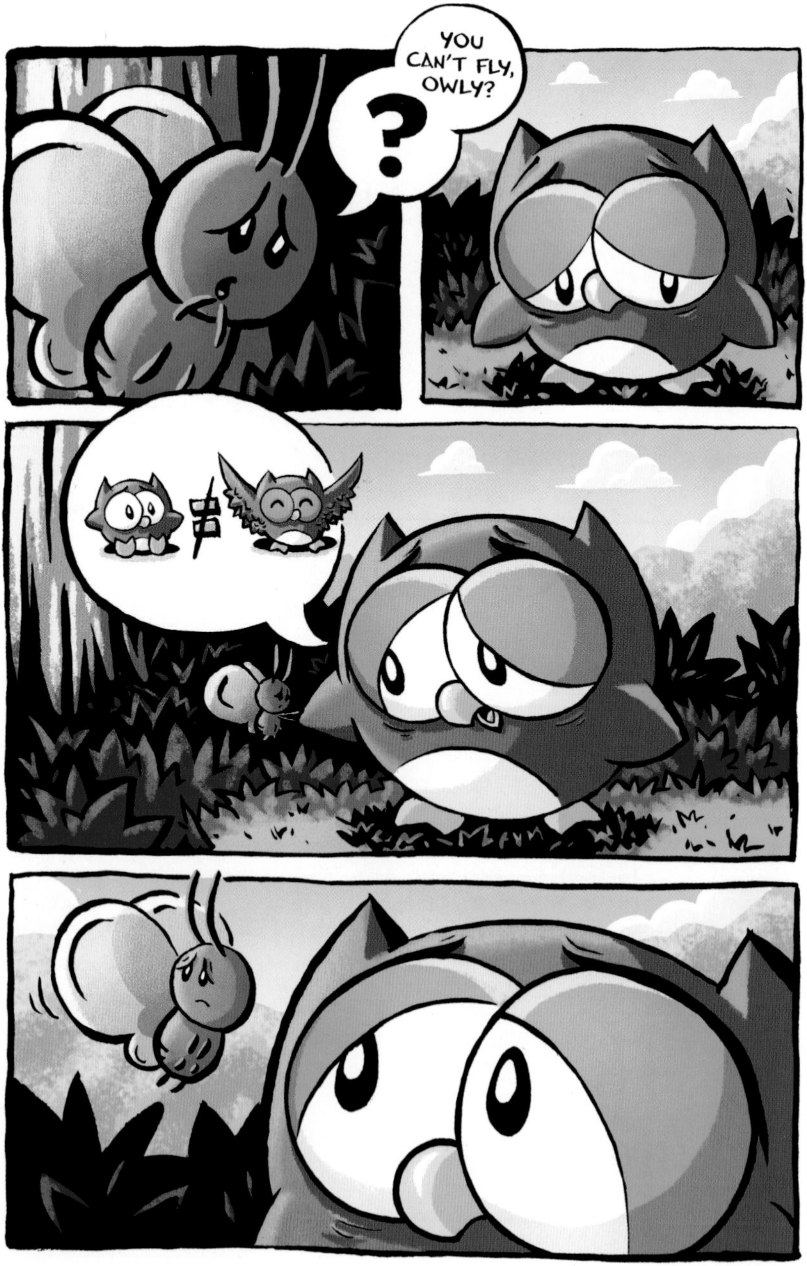
?
YOU CAN'T FLY, OWLY?

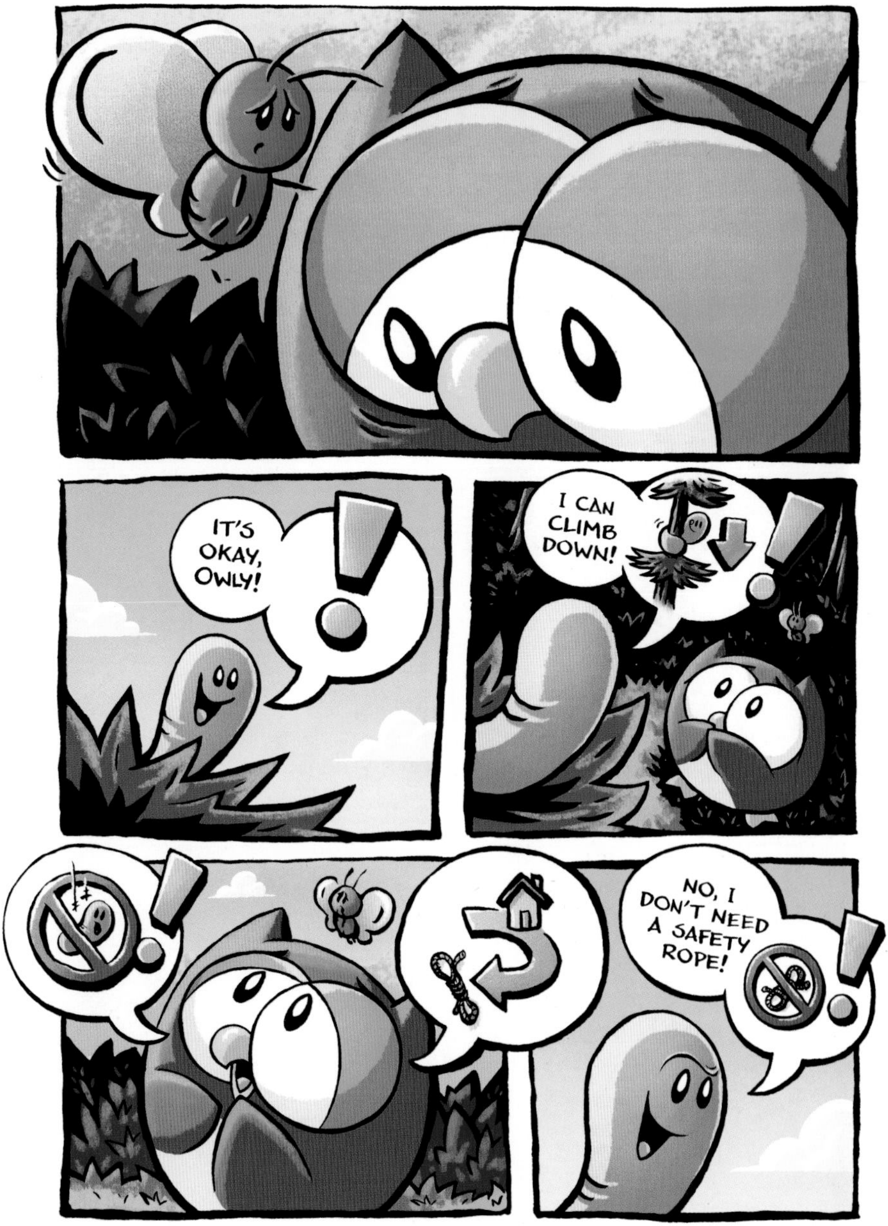
IT'S OKAY, OWLY!
I CAN CLIMB DOWN!
NO, I DON'T NEED A SAFETY ROPE!

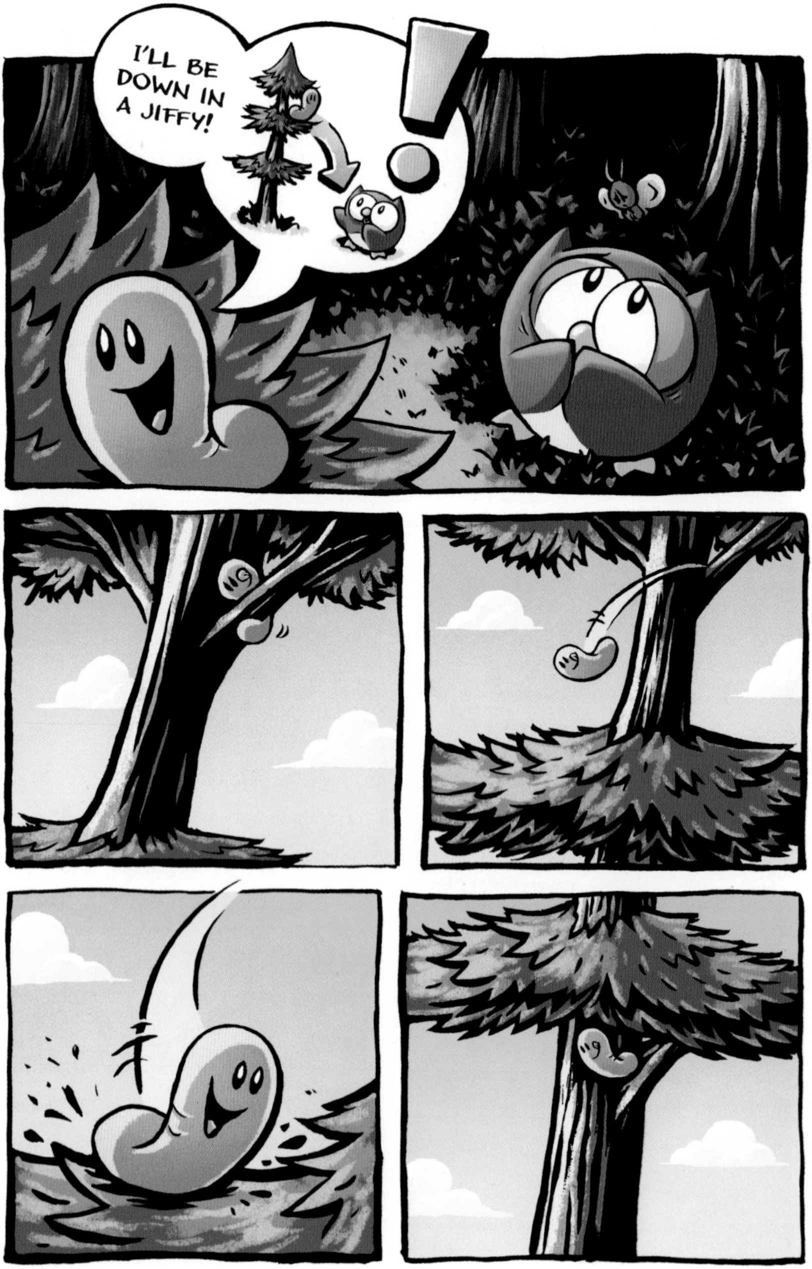
I'LL BE DOWN IN A JIFFY!
!

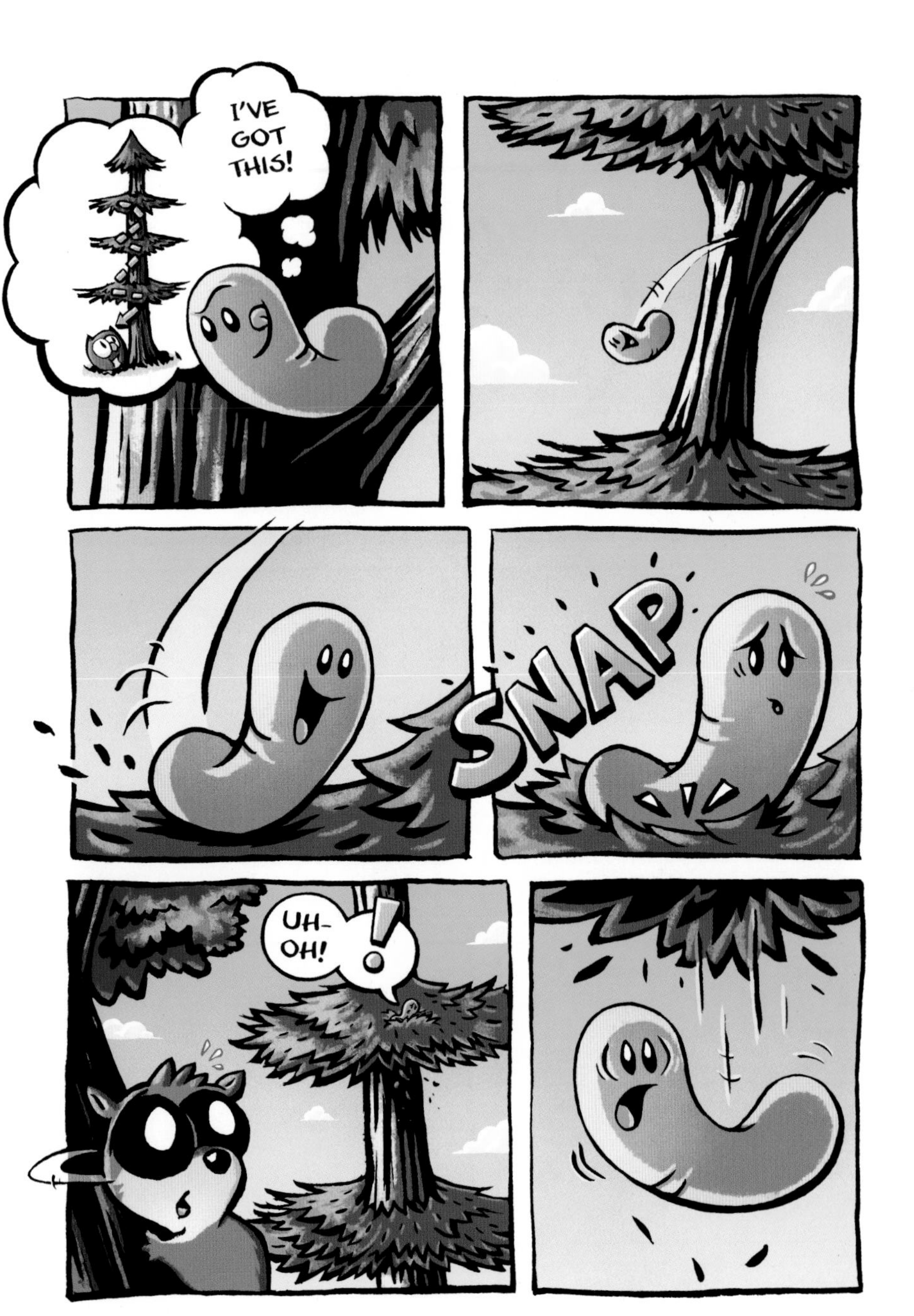
I'VE GOT THIS!
SNAP
UH-OH!
!

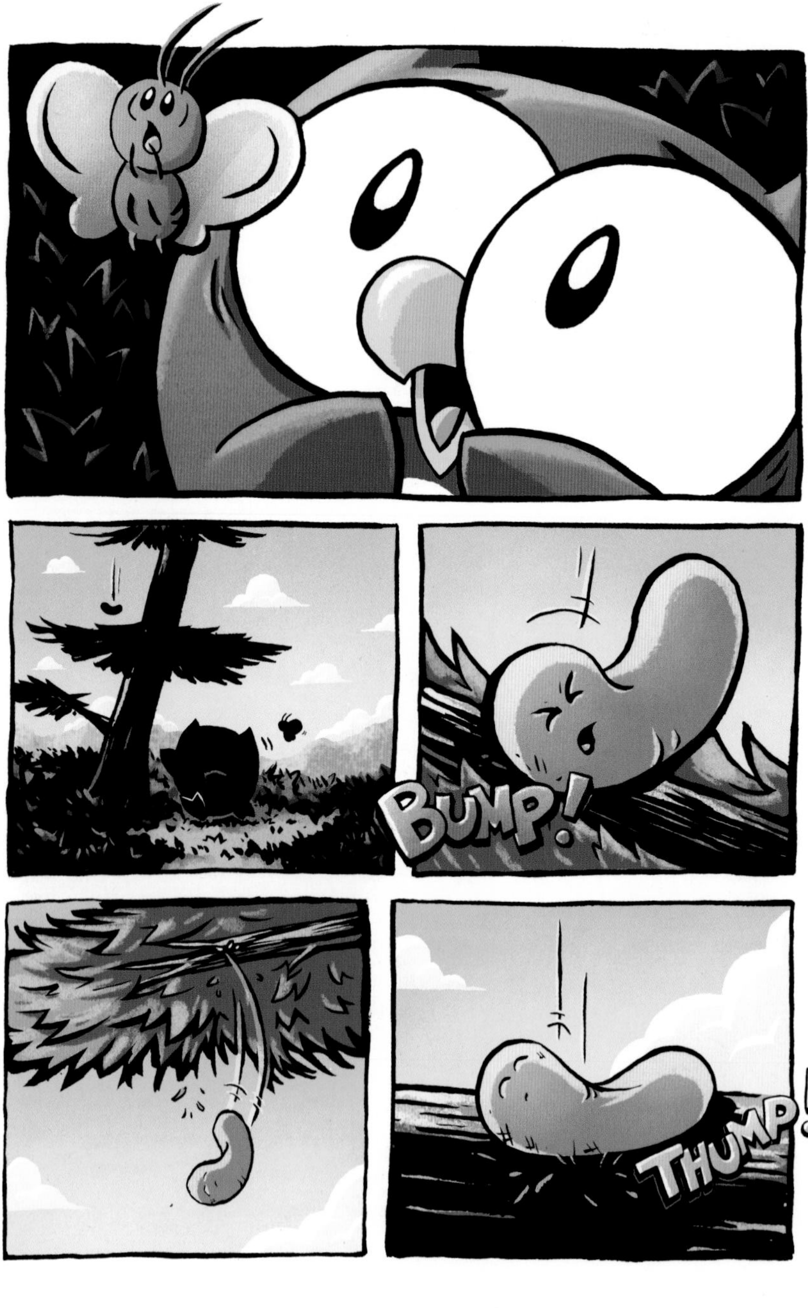
BUMP!
THUMP!

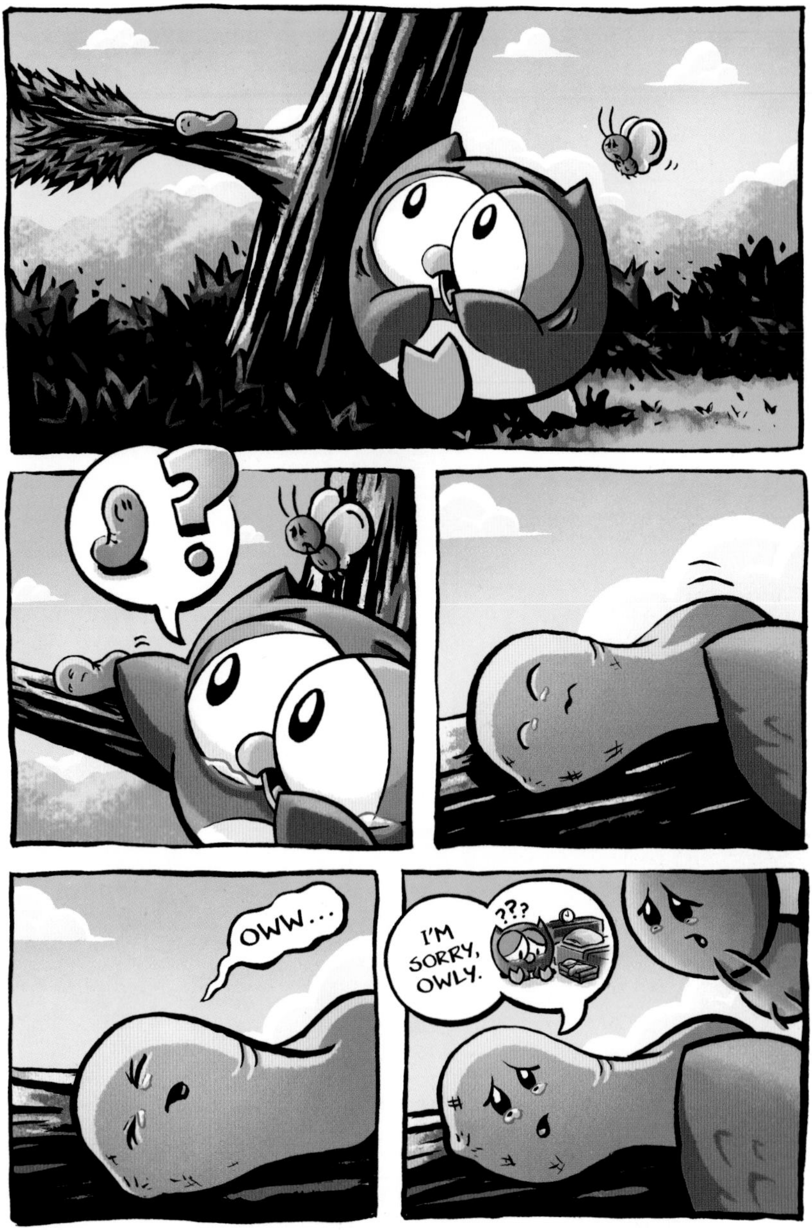

?
OWW...
I'M SORRY, OWLY.
???

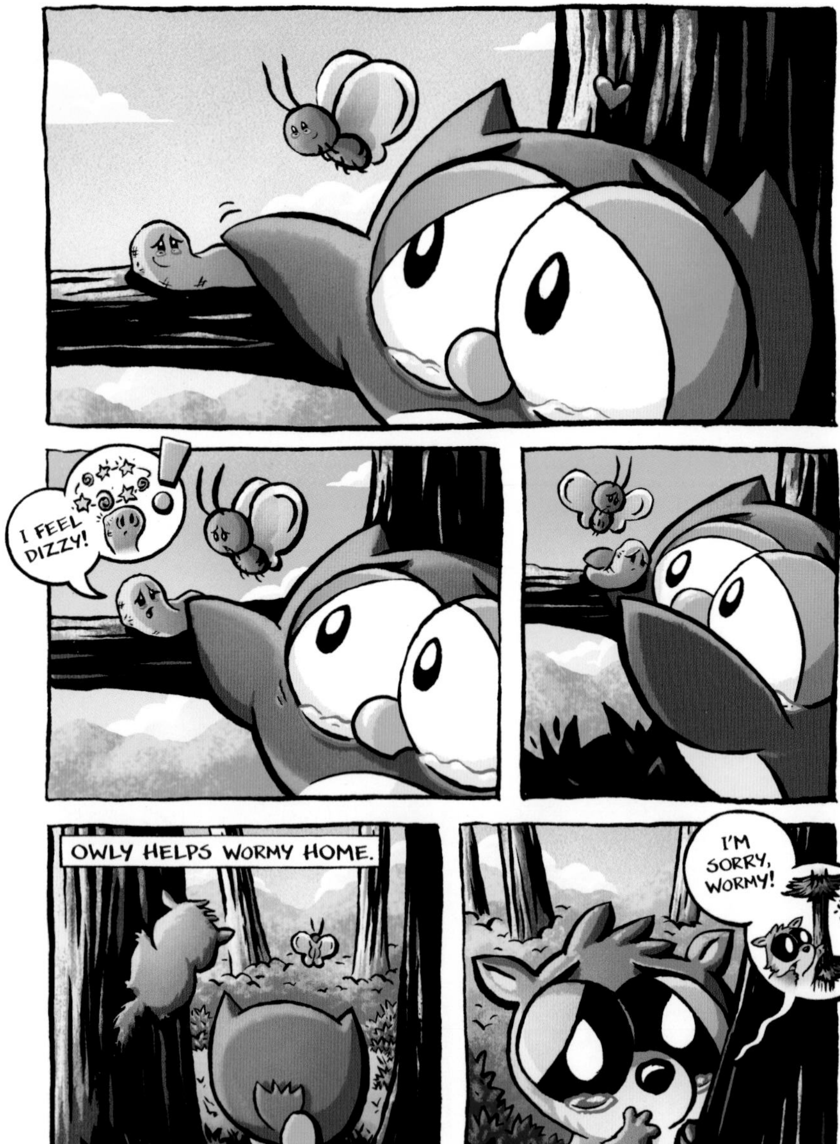
I FEEL DIZZY!
OWLY HELPS WORMY HOME.
I'M SORRY, WORMY!

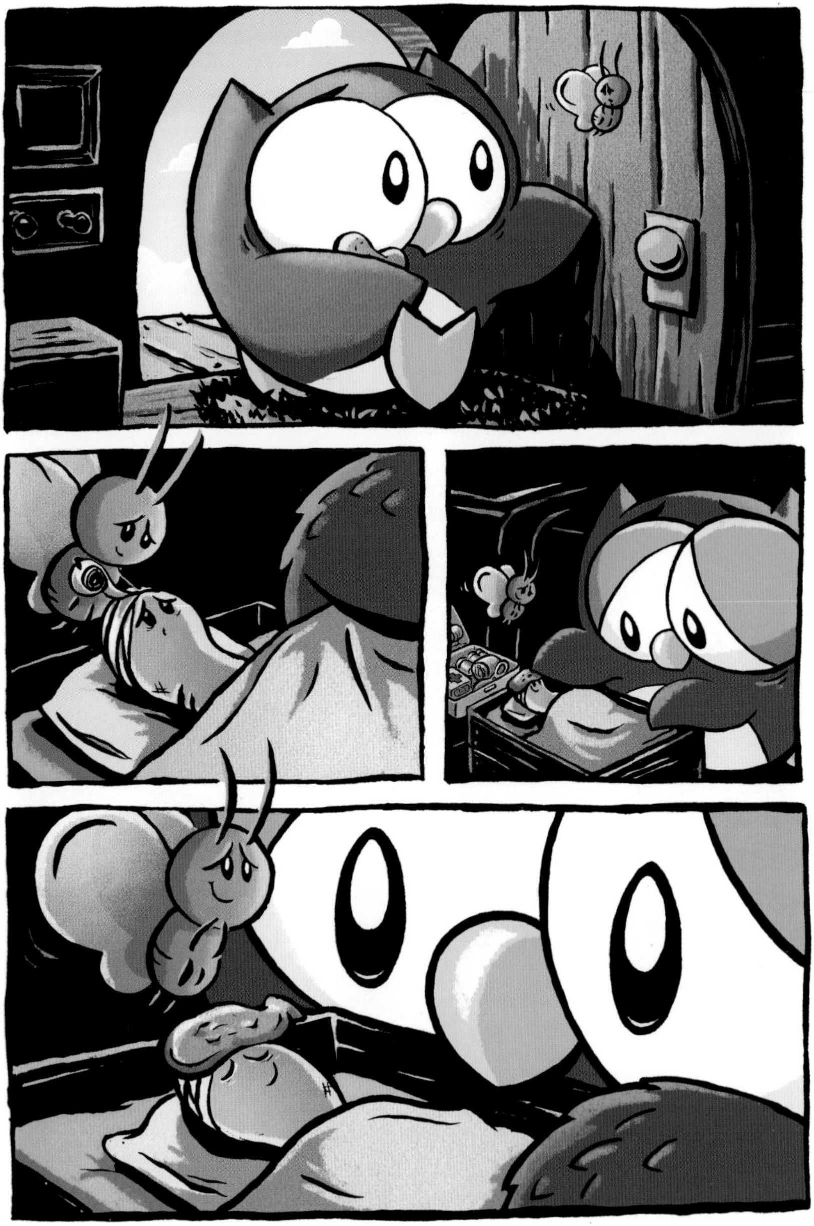

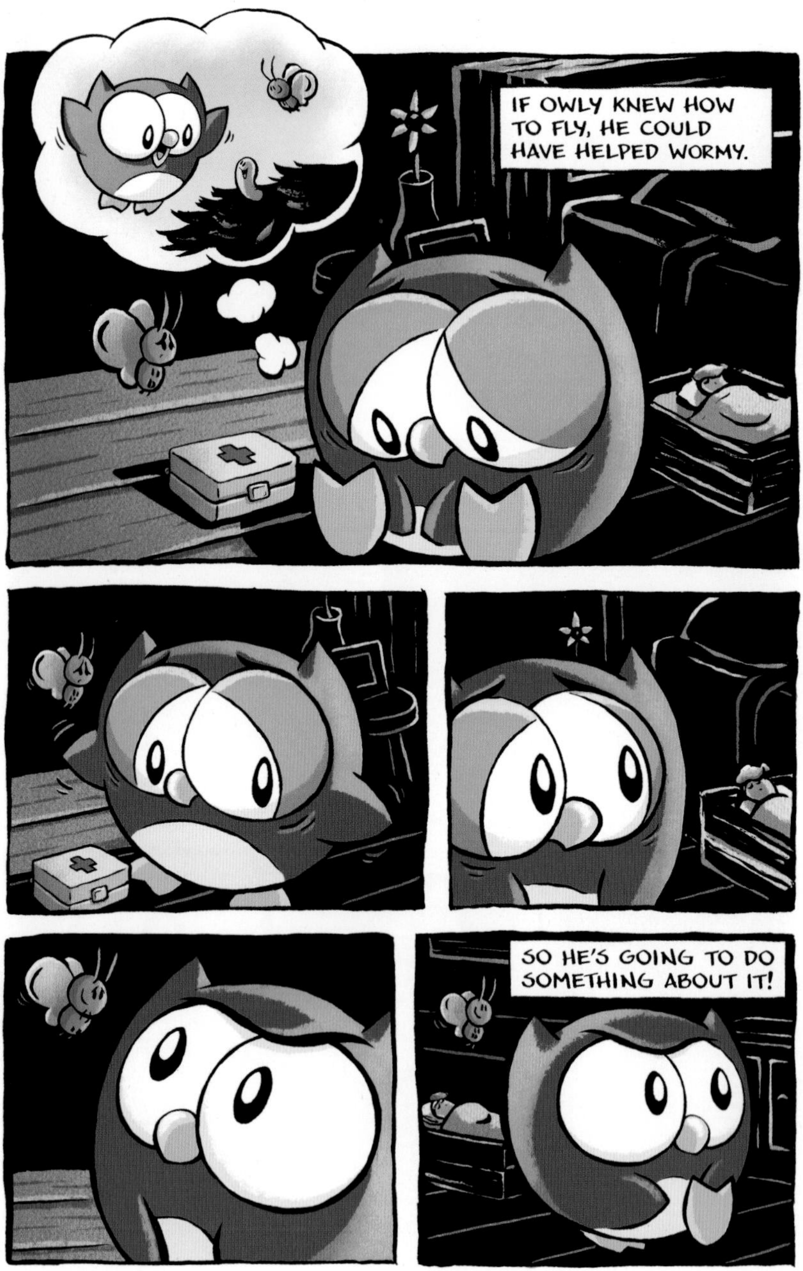
IF OWLY KNEW HOW TO FLY, HE COULD HAVE HELPED WORMY.
SO HE'S GOING TO DO SOMETHING ABOUT IT!

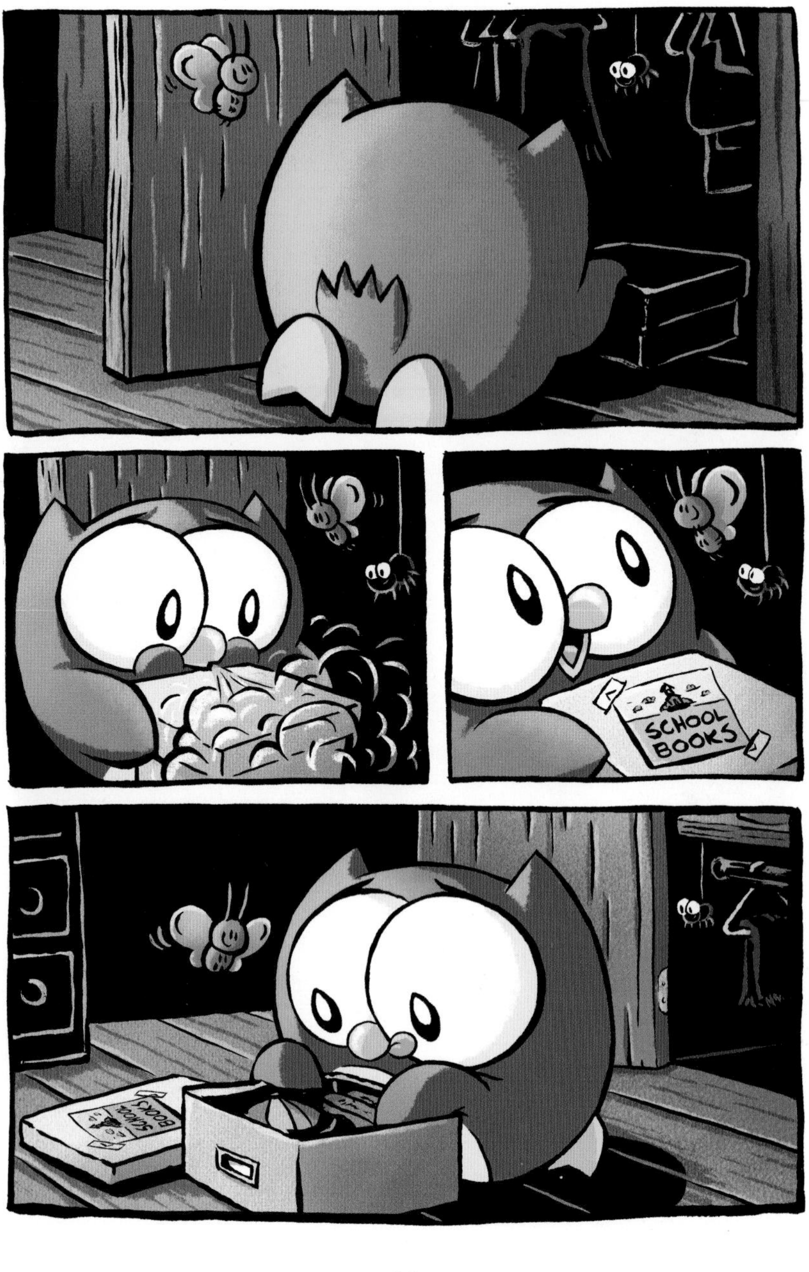
SCHOOL BOOKS

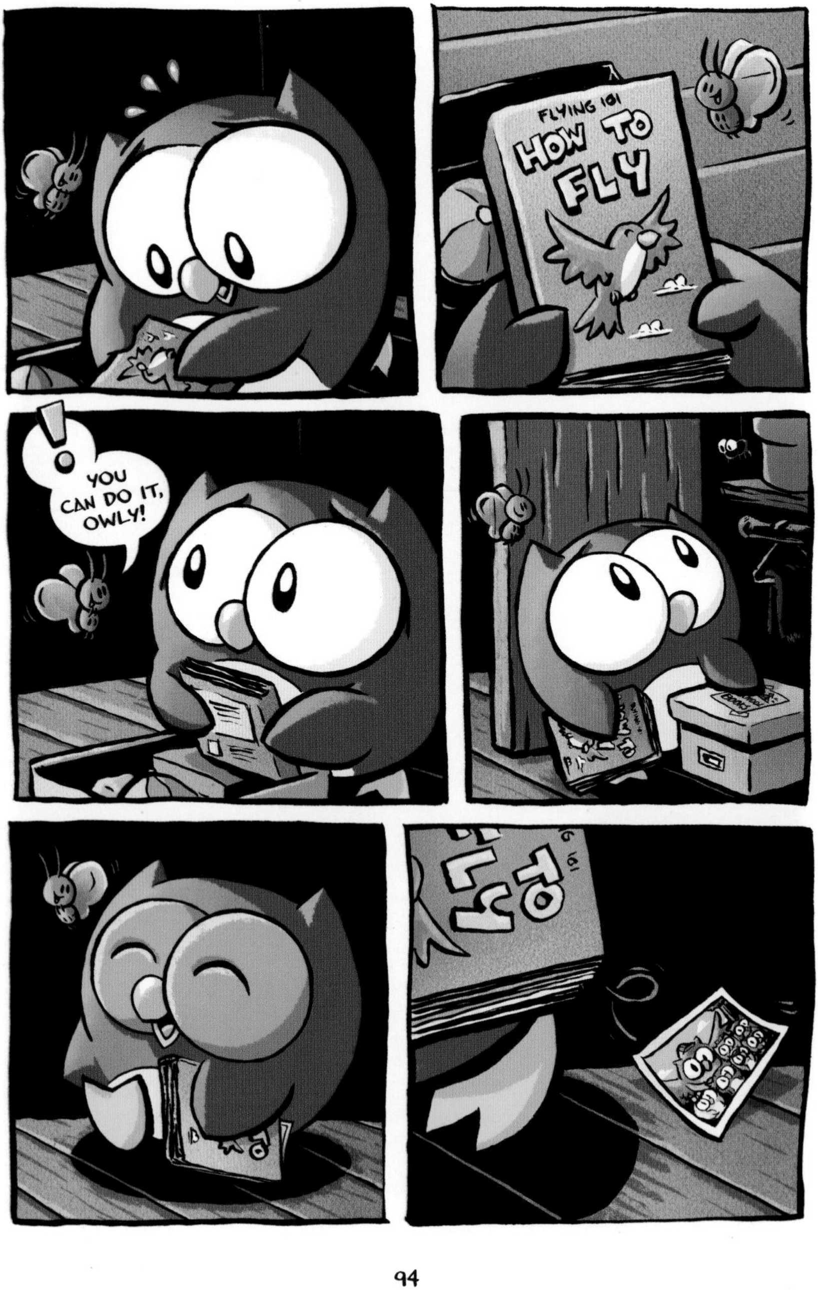
FLYING 101
HOW TO FLY
!
YOU CAN DO IT, OWLY!

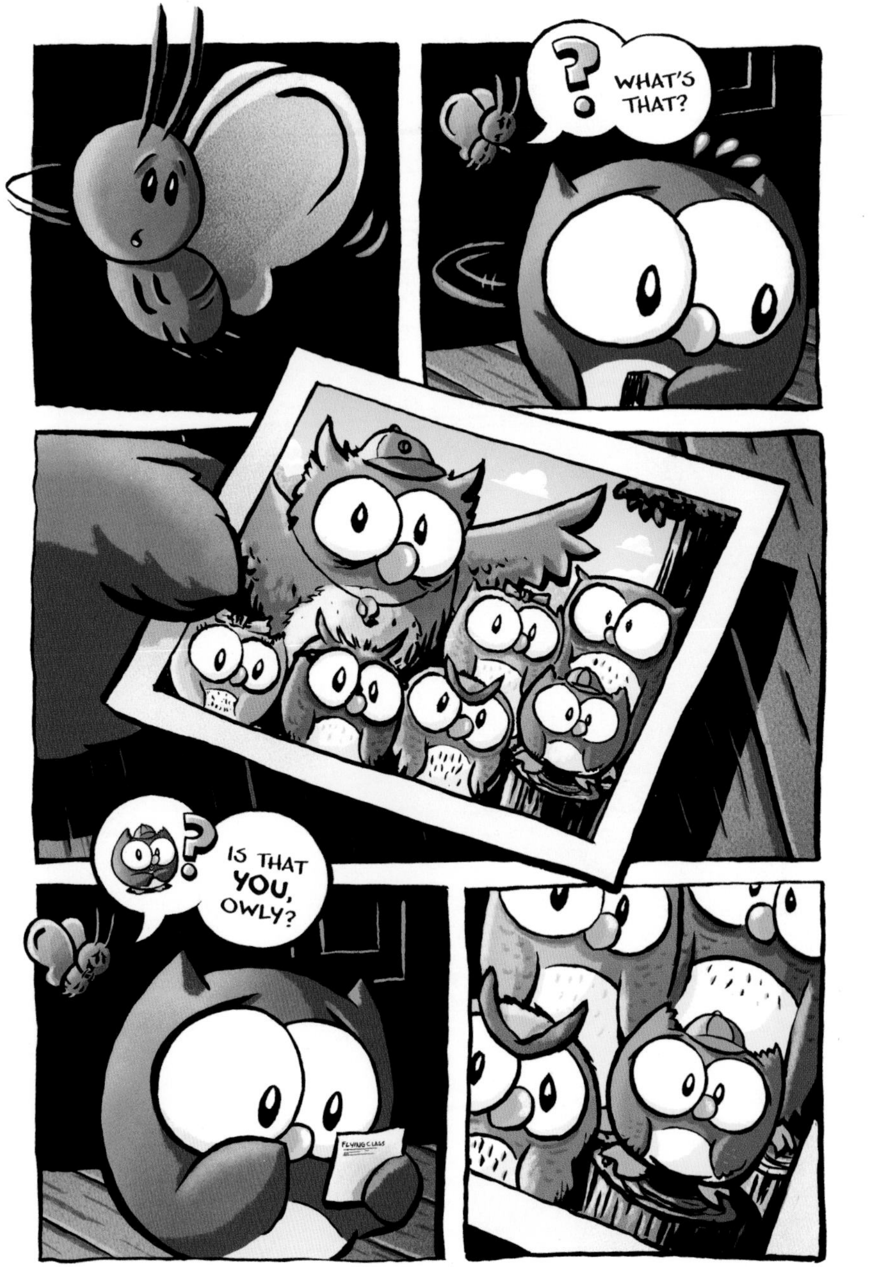

?
WHAT'S THAT?
?
IS THAT **YOU**, OWLY?
FLYING CLASS

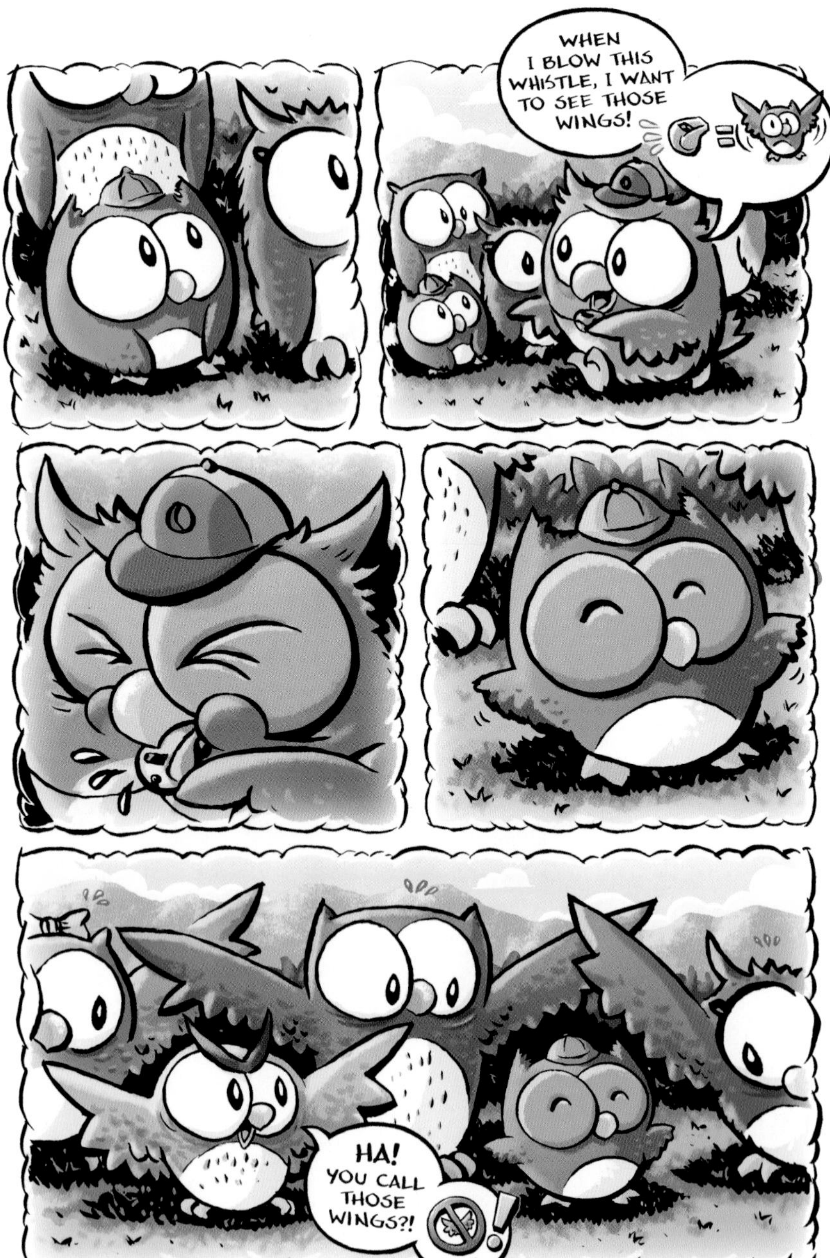
WHEN I BLOW THIS WHISTLE, I WANT TO SEE THOSE WINGS!
HA! YOU CALL THOSE WINGS?!

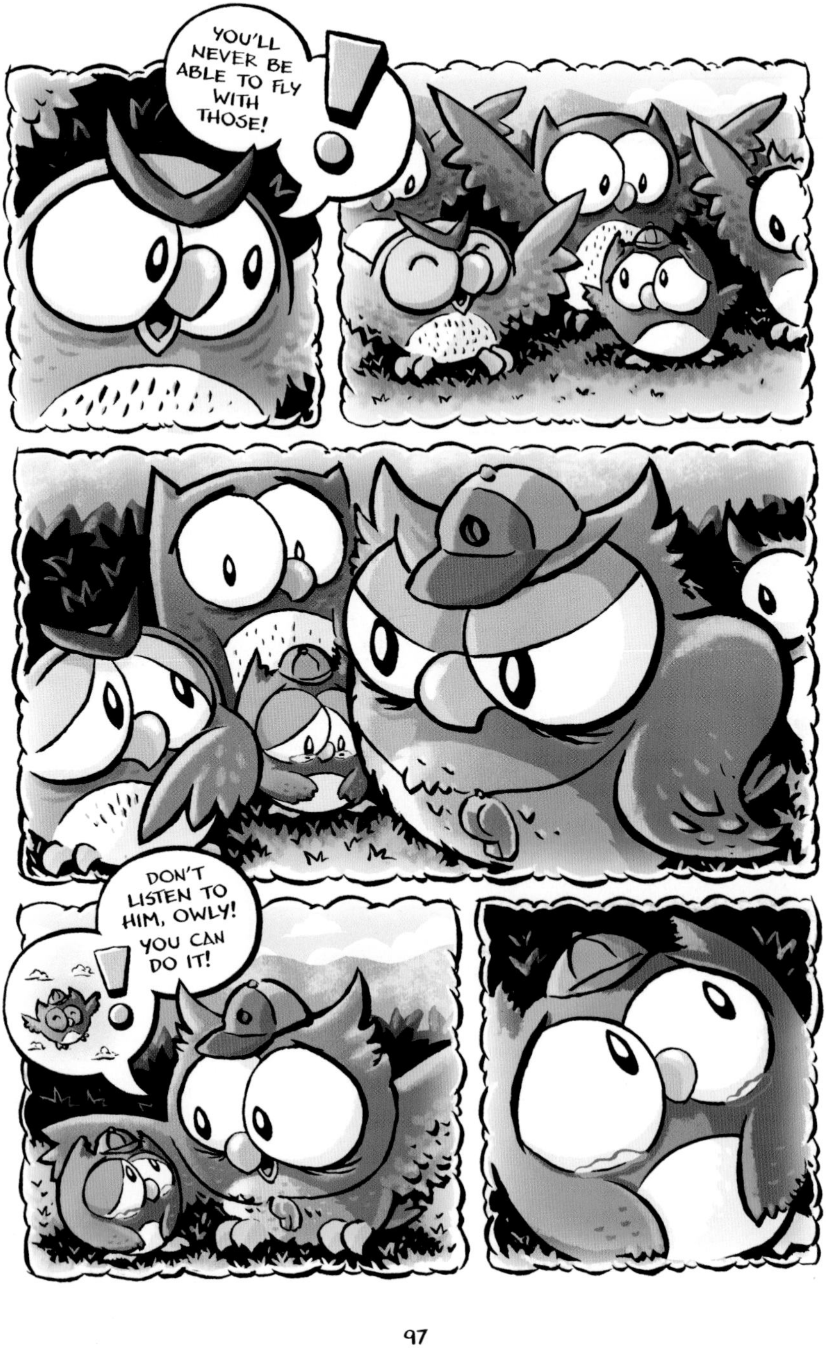
YOU'LL NEVER BE ABLE TO FLY WITH THOSE!
!
DON'T LISTEN TO HIM, OWLY! YOU CAN DO IT!
!

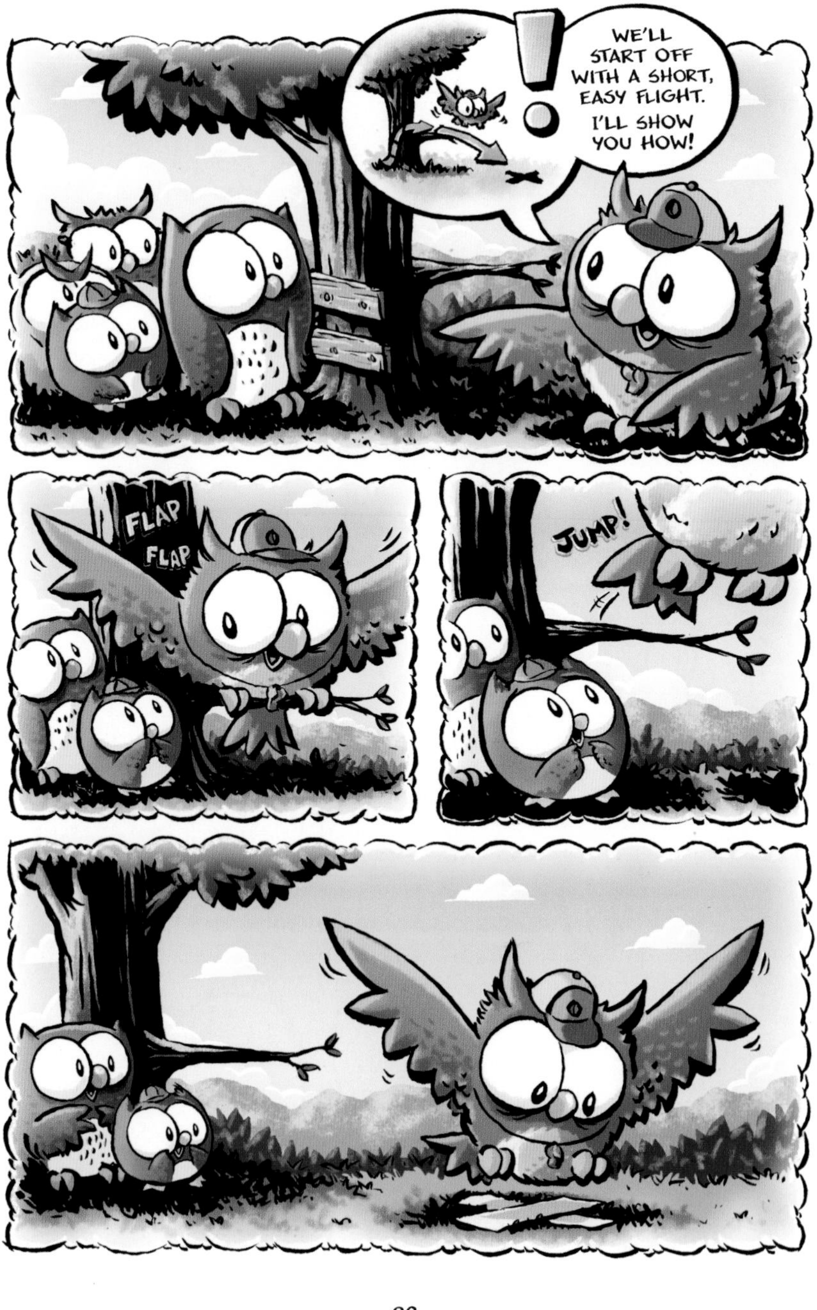
!
WE'LL START OFF WITH A SHORT, EASY FLIGHT.
I'LL SHOW YOU HOW!
FLAP
FLAP
JUMP!

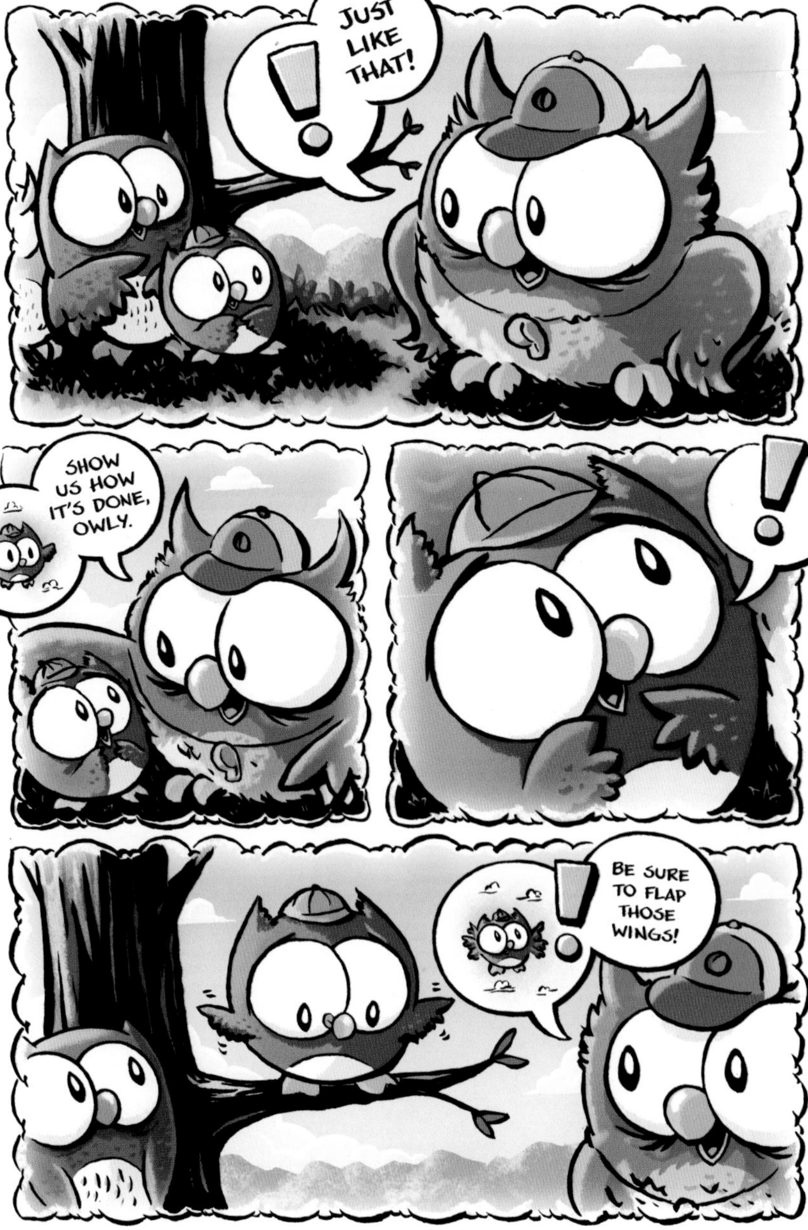
!
JUST LIKE THAT!
SHOW US HOW IT'S DONE, OWLY.
!
!
BE SURE TO FLAP THOSE WINGS!

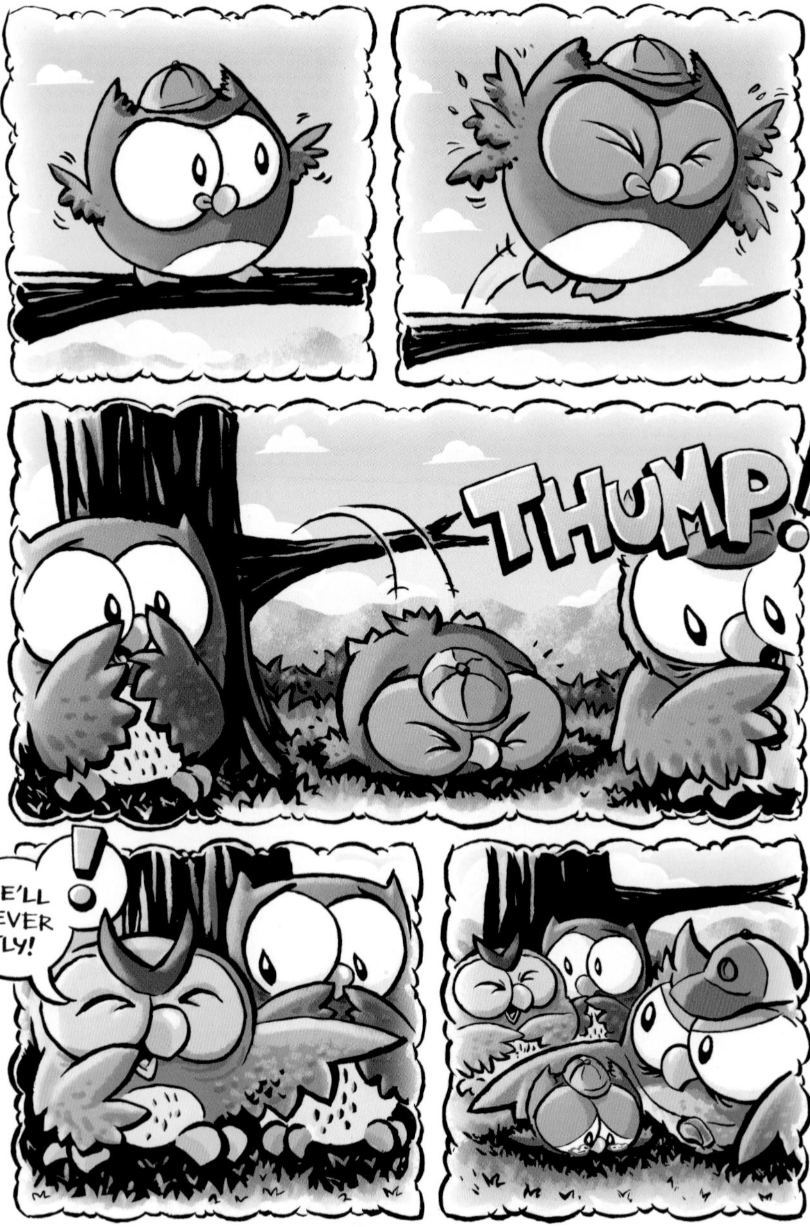
THUMP!
HE'LL NEVER FLY!

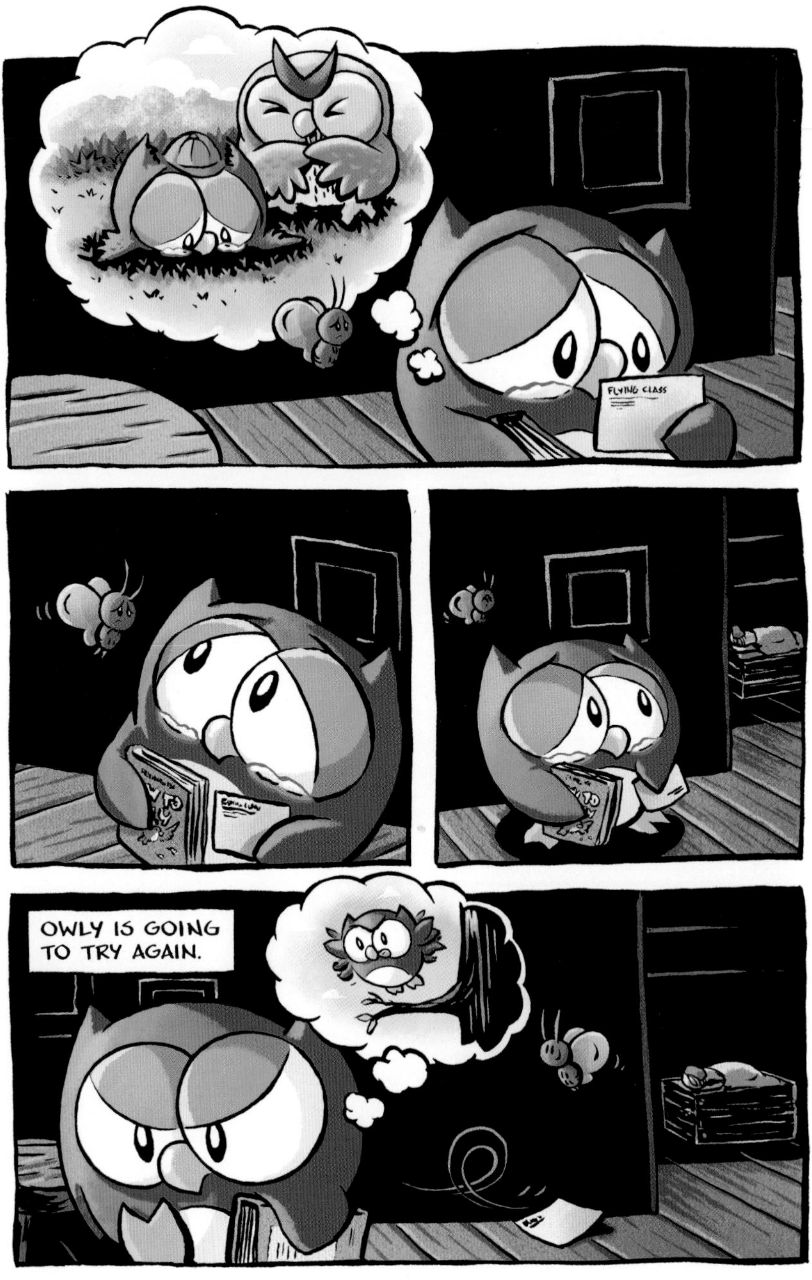
FLYING CLASS
OWLY IS GOING TO TRY AGAIN.

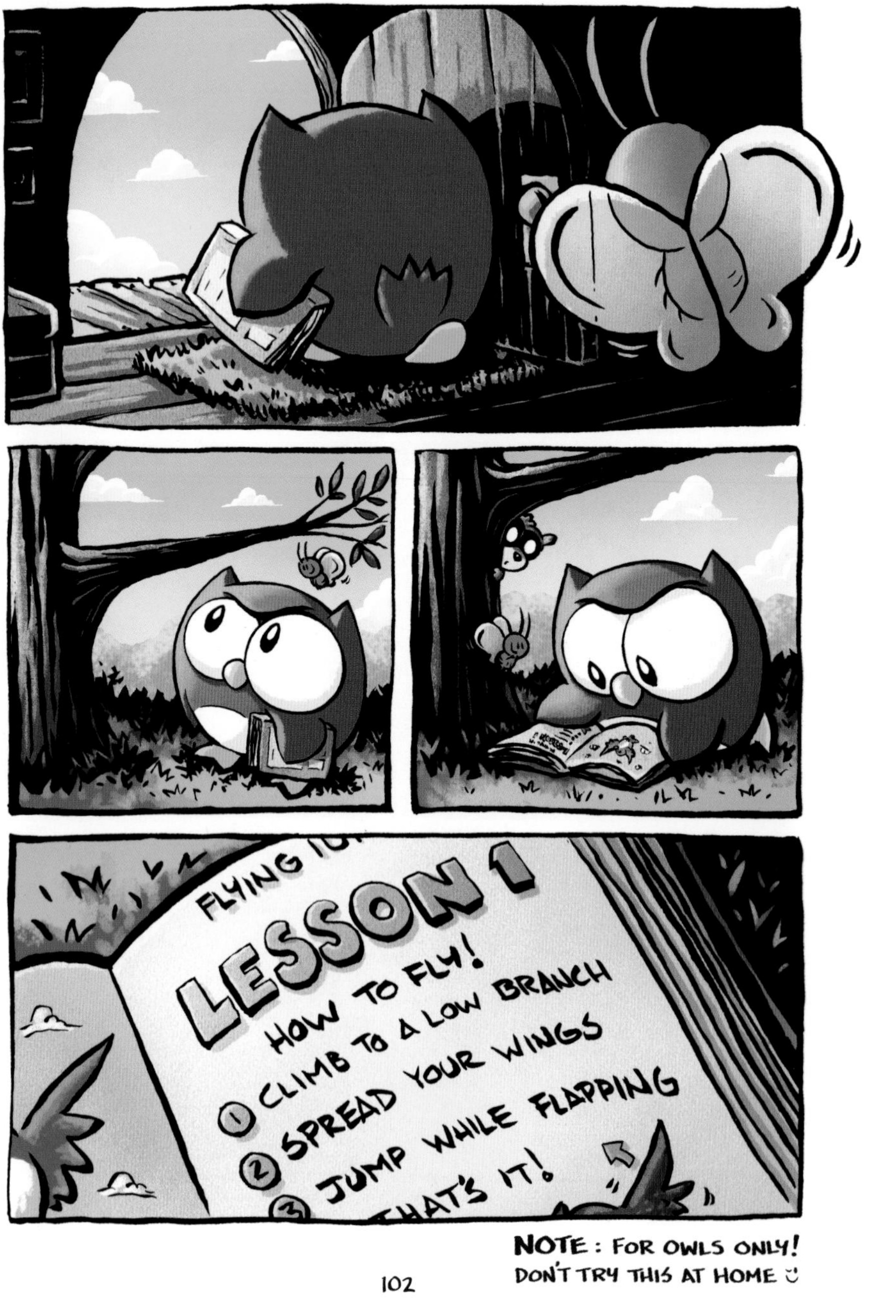
FLYING
LESSON 1
HOW TO FLY!
① CLIMB TO A LOW BRANCH
② SPREAD YOUR WINGS
③ JUMP WHILE FLAPPING
THAT'S IT!

NOTE: FOR OWLS ONLY!
DON'T TRY THIS AT HOME ◡̈

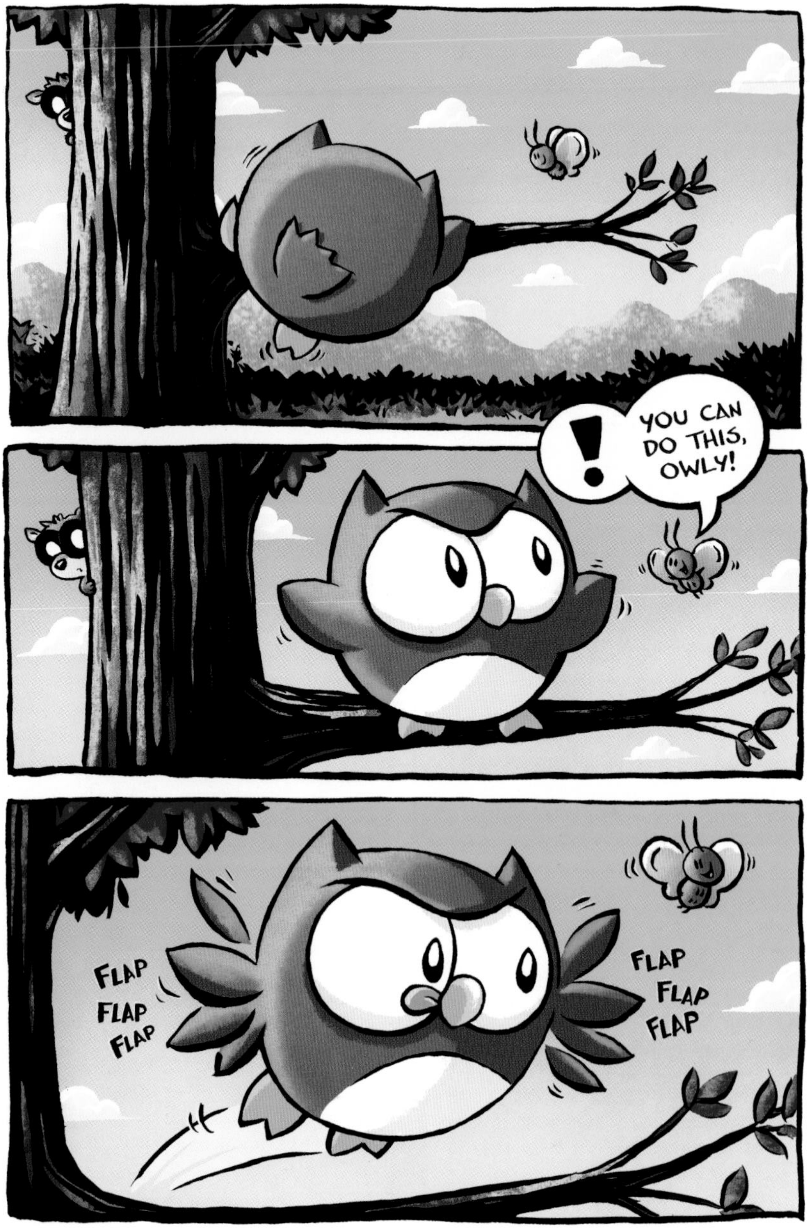
!
YOU CAN DO THIS, OWLY!
FLAP FLAP FLAP
FLAP FLAP FLAP

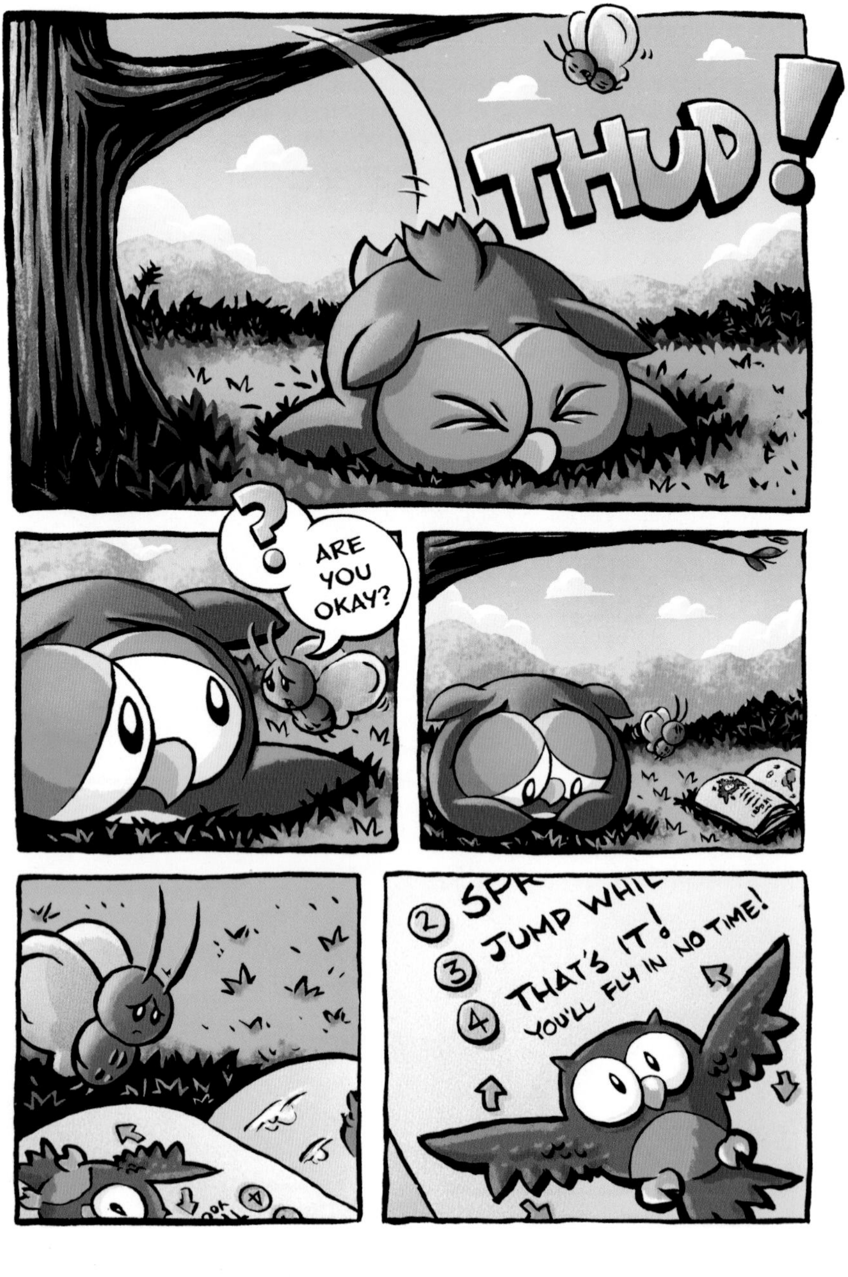
THUD!
?
ARE YOU OKAY?
2 SPR
JUMP WHIL
3 THAT'S IT!
4 YOU'LL FLY IN NO TIME!

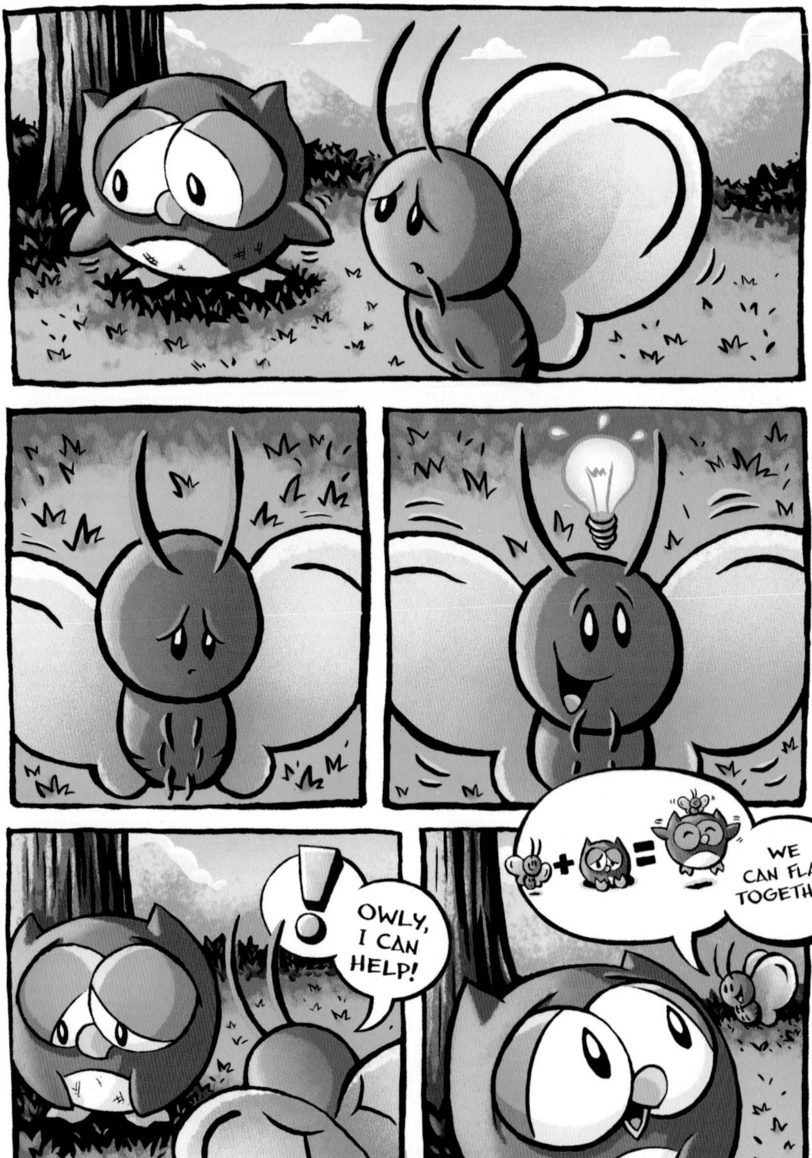

!
OWLY, I CAN HELP!
WE CAN FLAP TOGETHER!

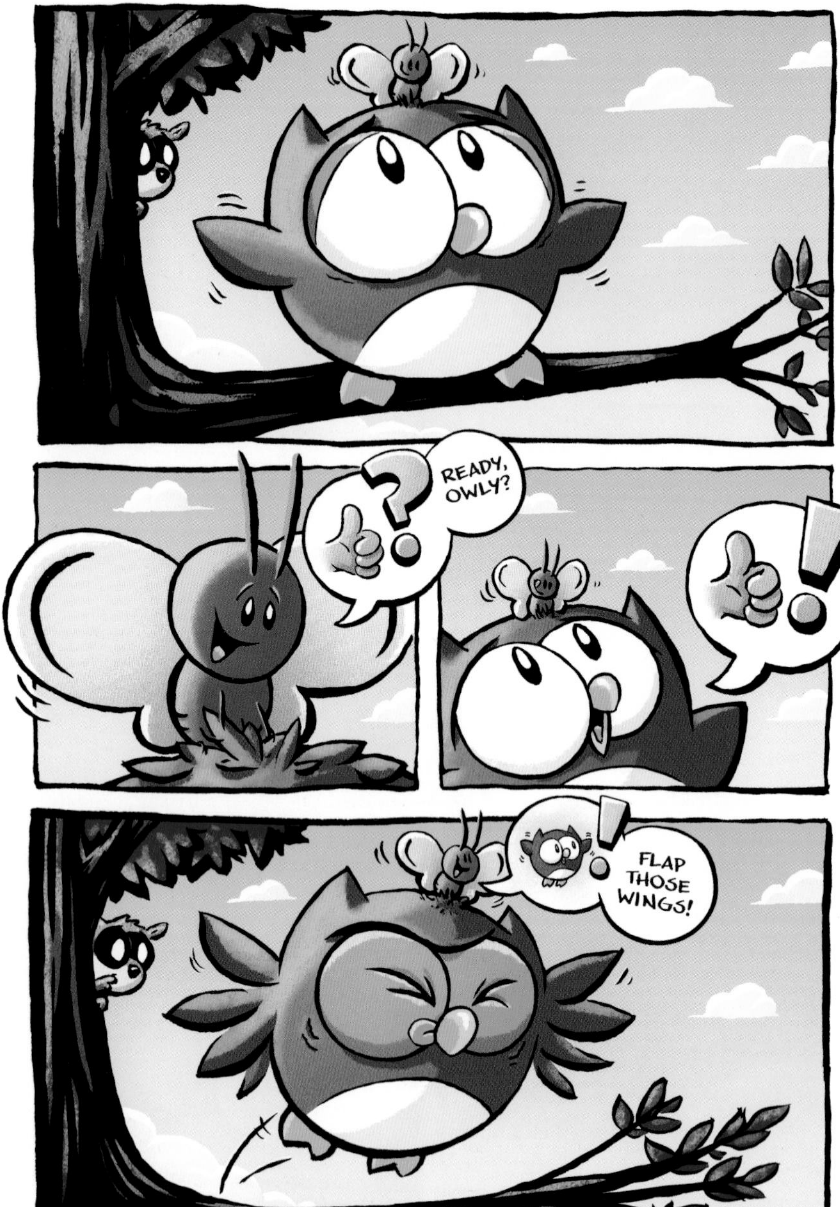
?
READY, OWLY?
!
!
FLAP THOSE WINGS!

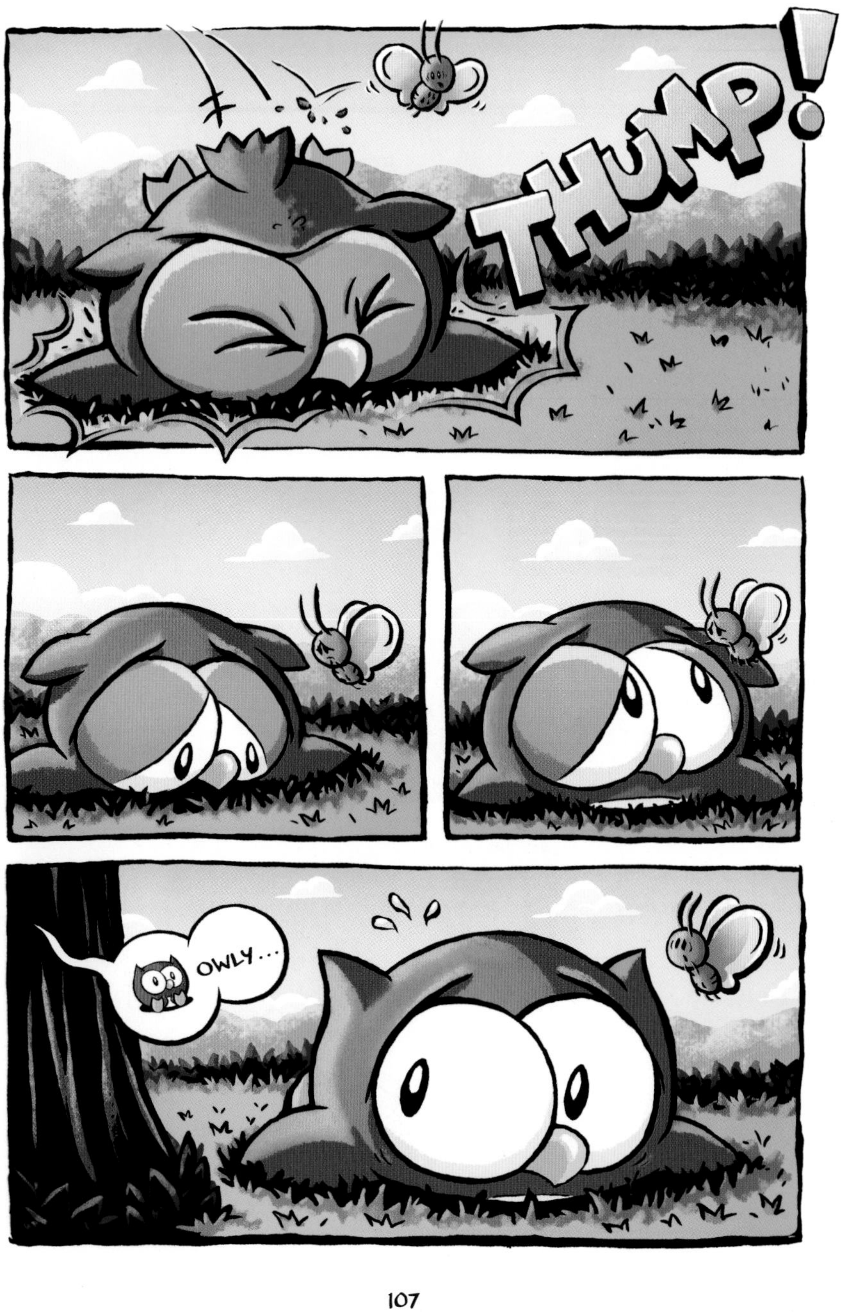
THUMP!
OWLY...

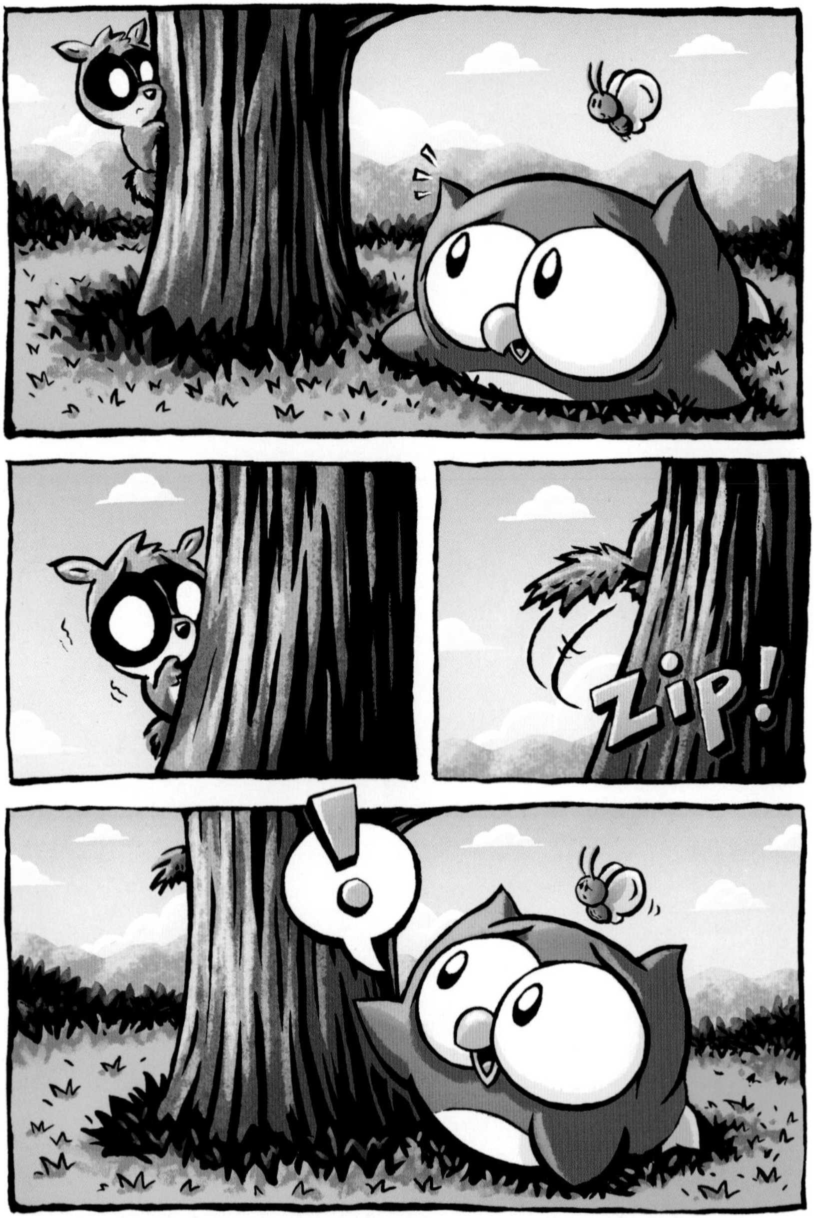
ZIP!
!

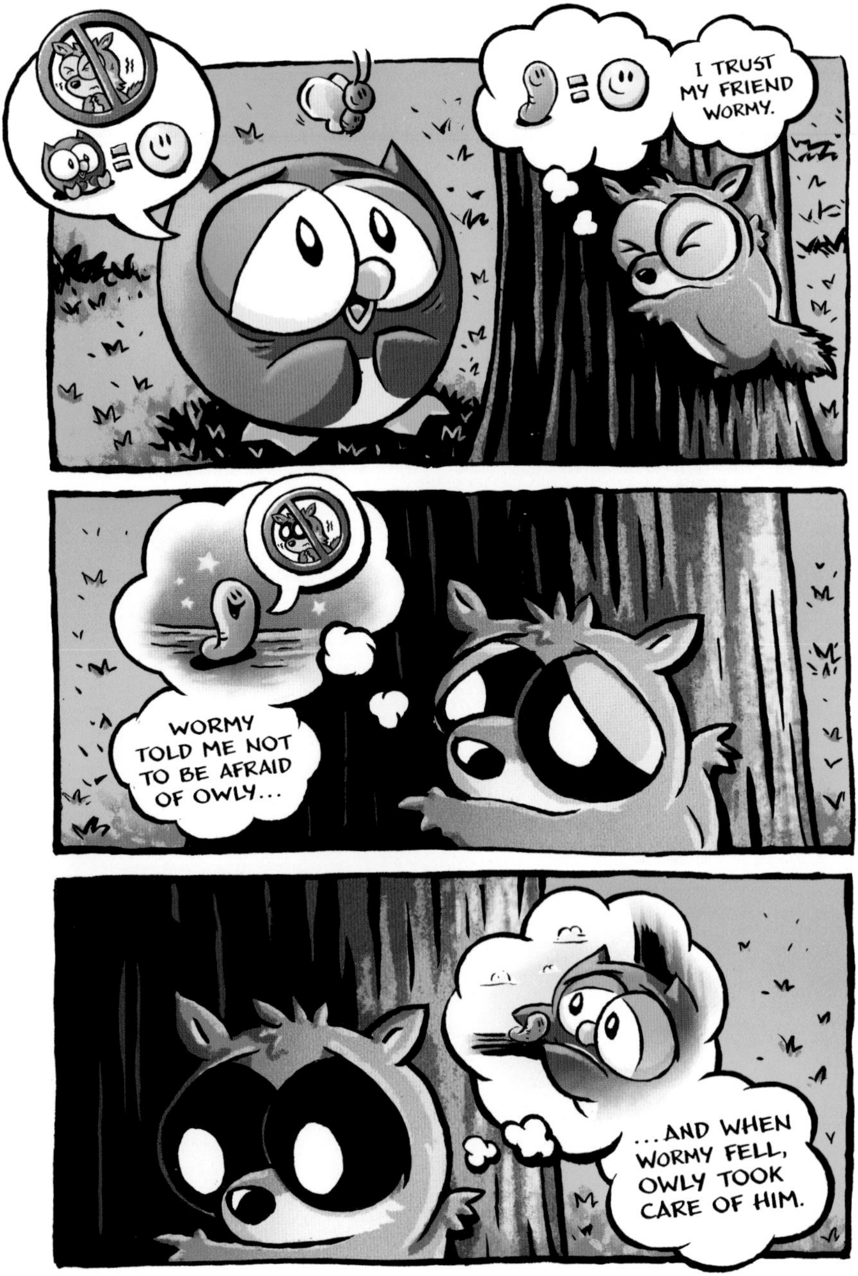
I TRUST MY FRIEND WORMY.
WORMY TOLD ME NOT TO BE AFRAID OF OWLY...
...AND WHEN WORMY FELL, OWLY TOOK CARE OF HIM.

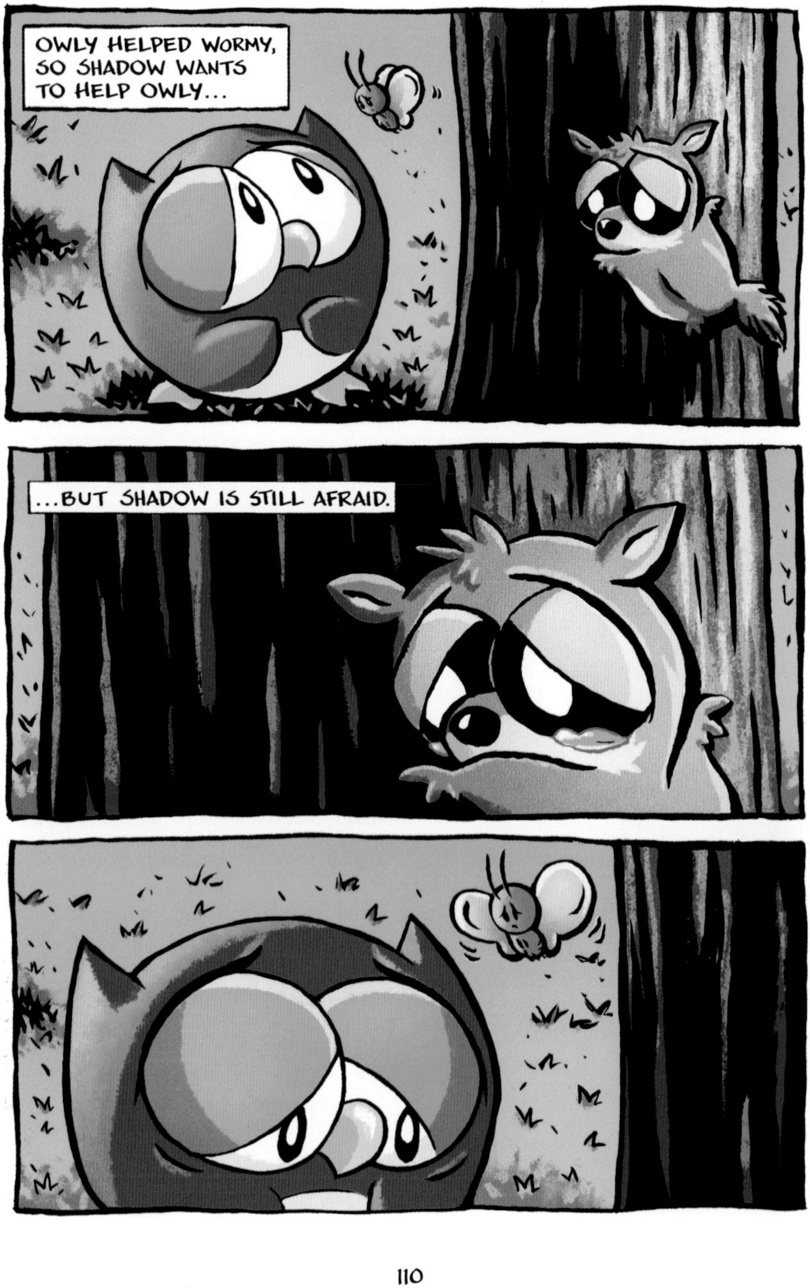
OWLY HELPED WORMY, SO SHADOW WANTS TO HELP OWLY...
...BUT SHADOW IS STILL AFRAID.

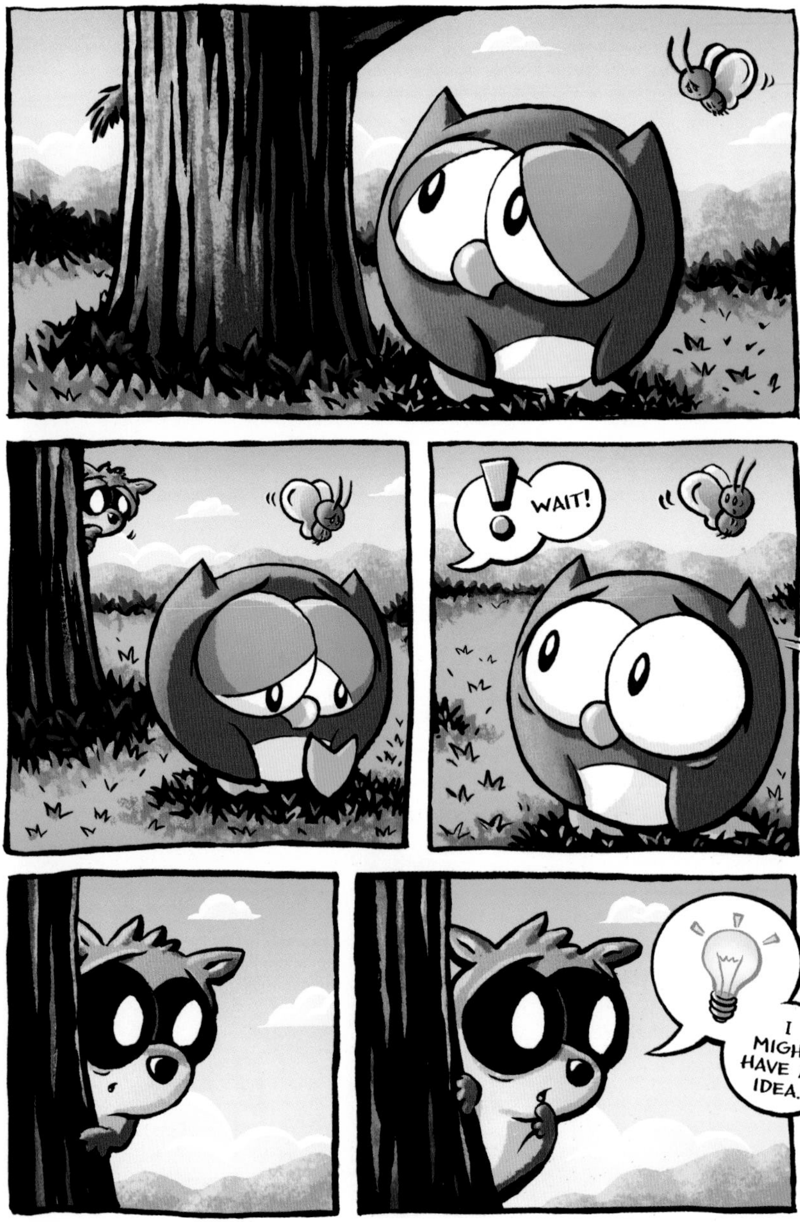
!
WAIT!
I MIGHT HAVE AN IDEA.

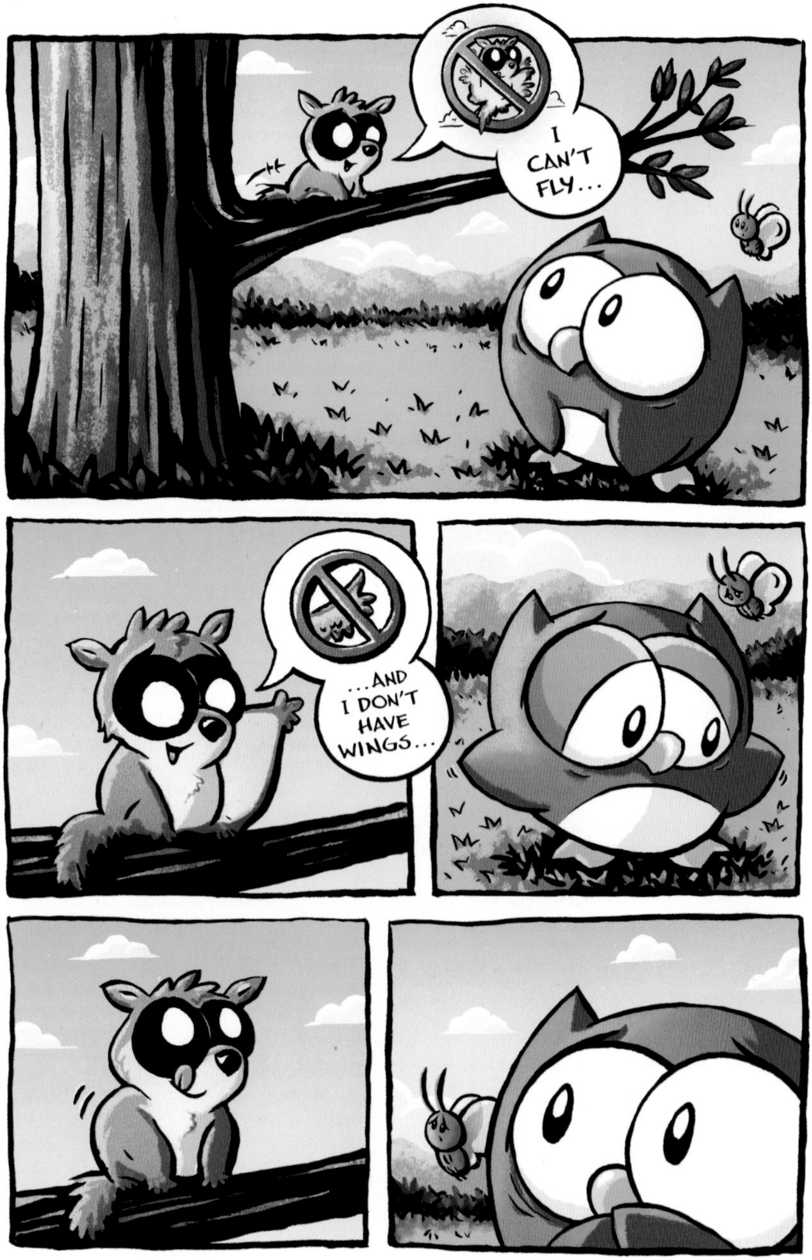
I CAN'T FLY...
...AND I DON'T HAVE WINGS...

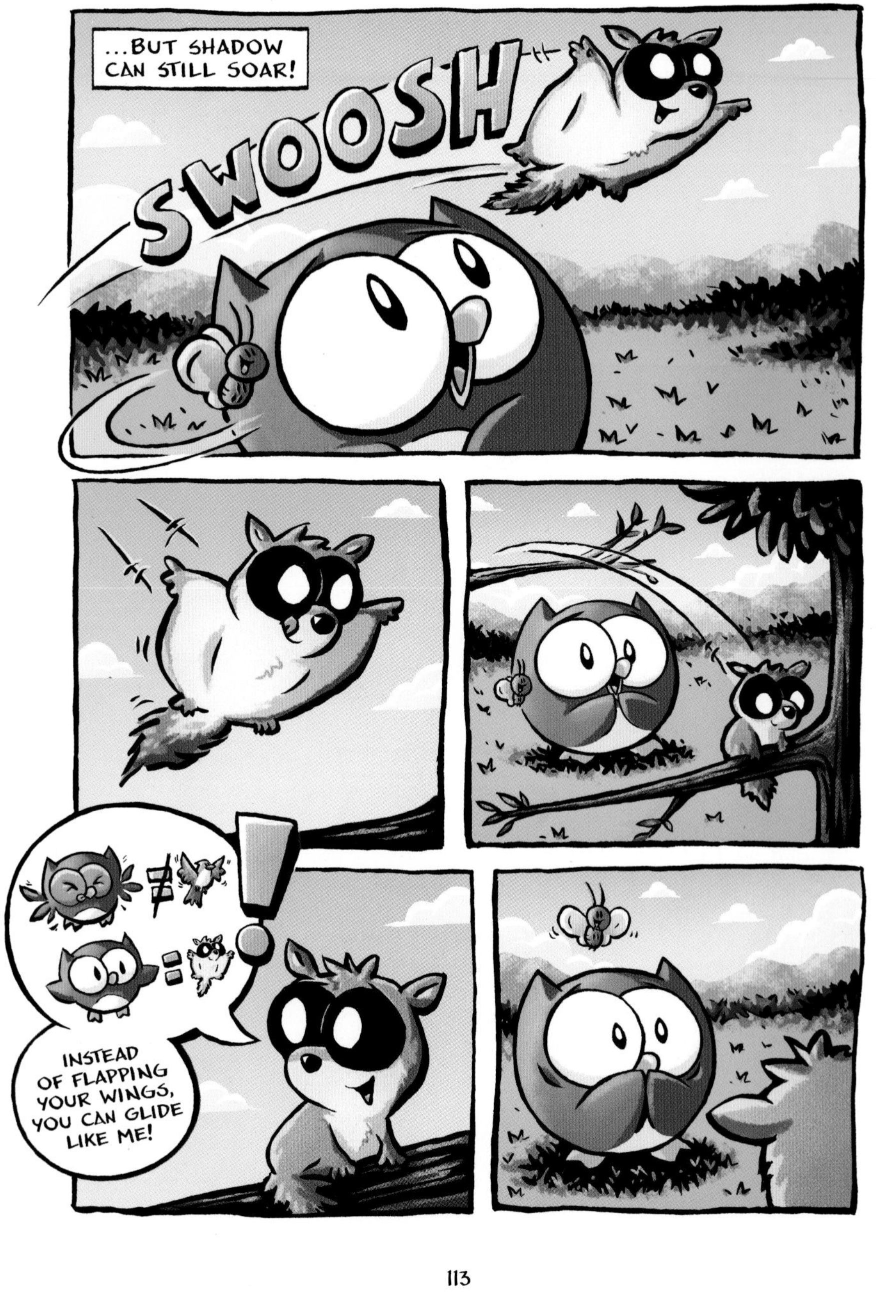
...BUT SHADOW CAN STILL SOAR!
SWOOSH
!
INSTEAD OF FLAPPING YOUR WINGS, YOU CAN GLIDE LIKE ME!

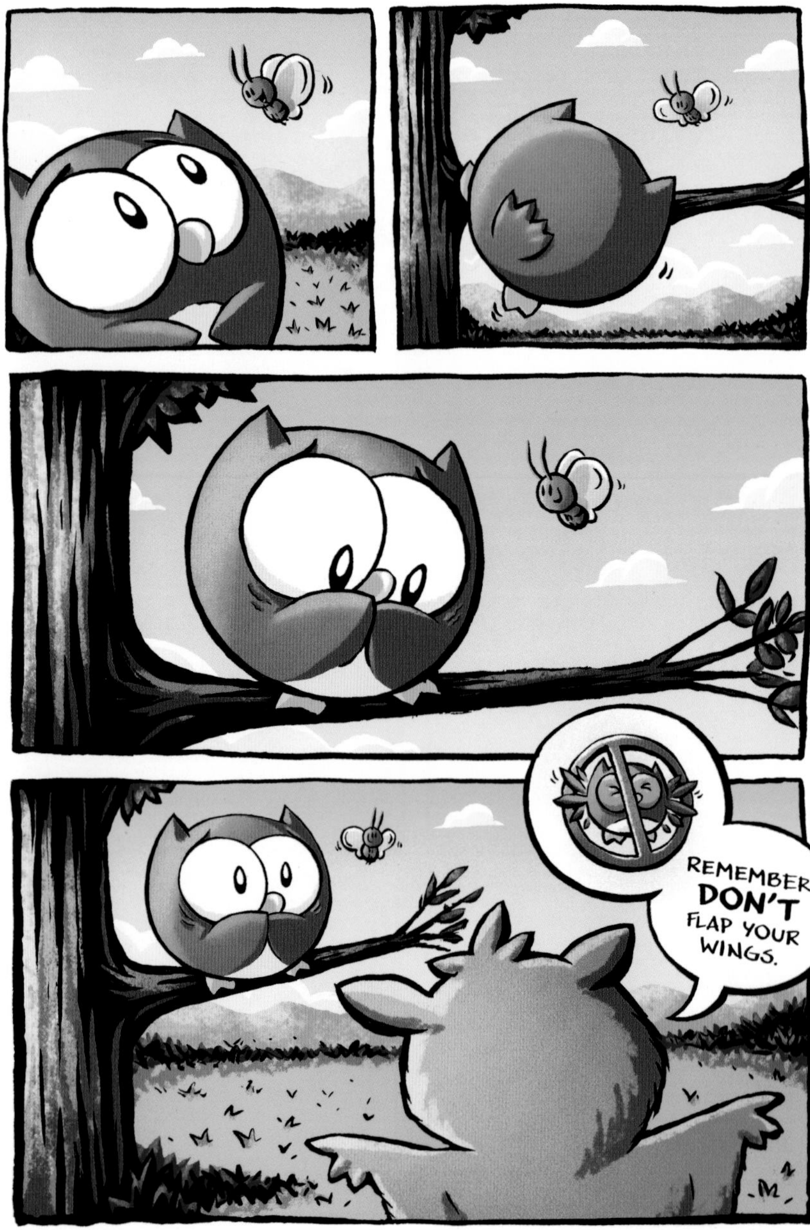
REMEMBER, DON'T FLAP YOUR WINGS.

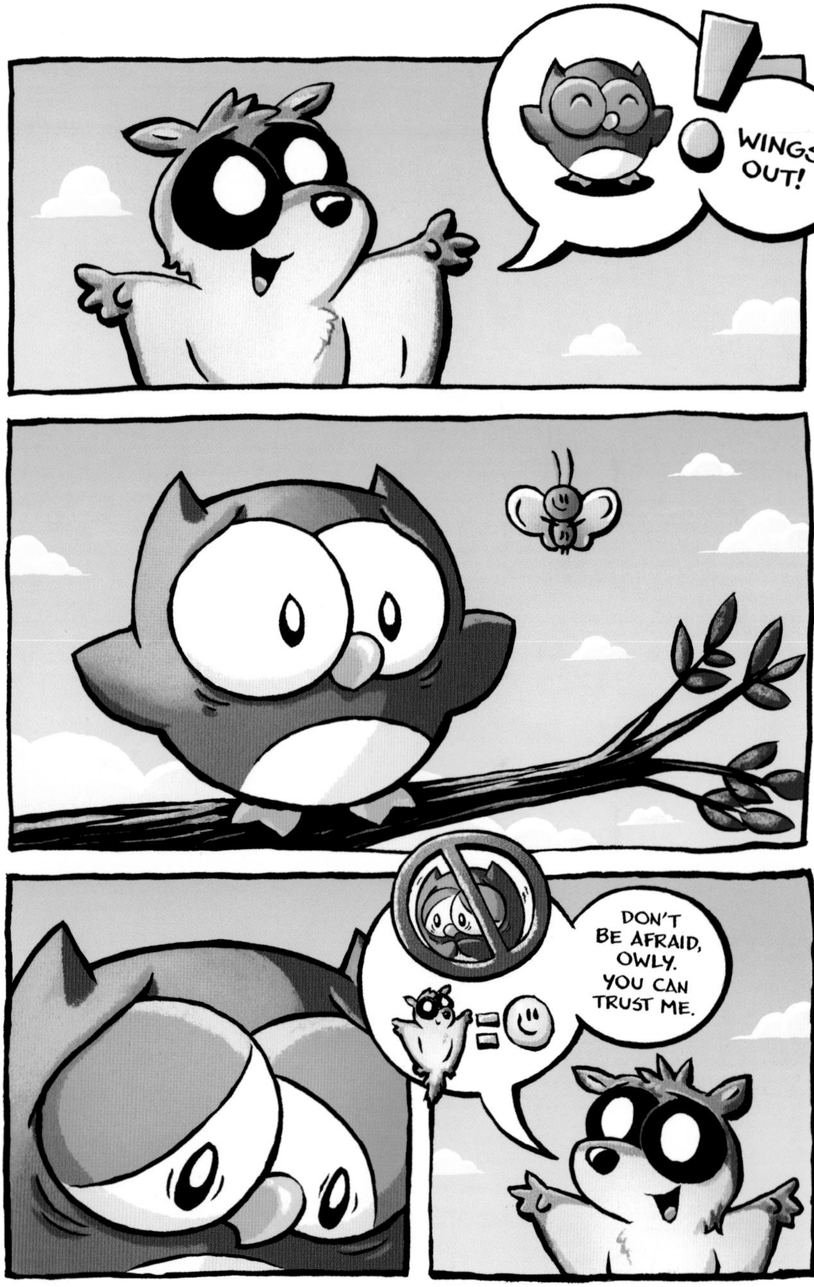
WINGS OUT!
DON'T BE AFRAID, OWLY. YOU CAN TRUST ME.

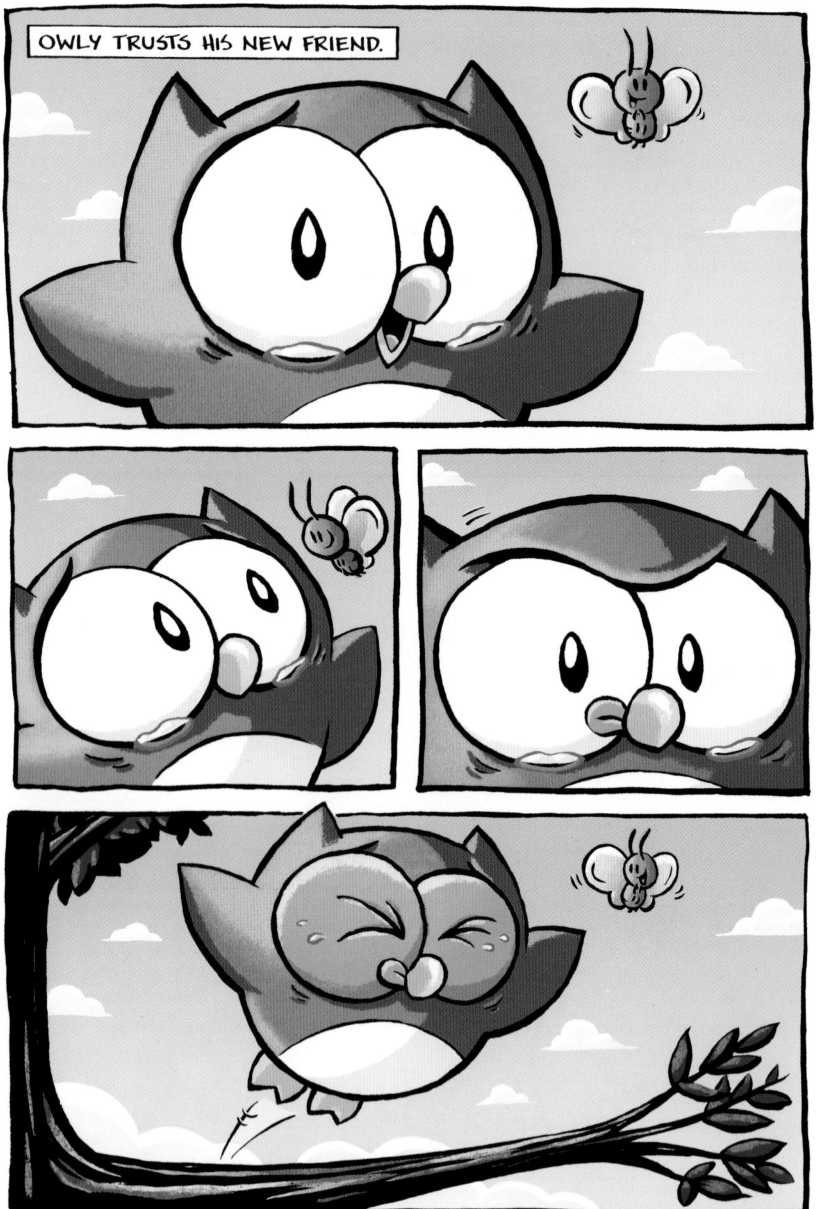
OWLY TRUSTS HIS NEW FRIEND.

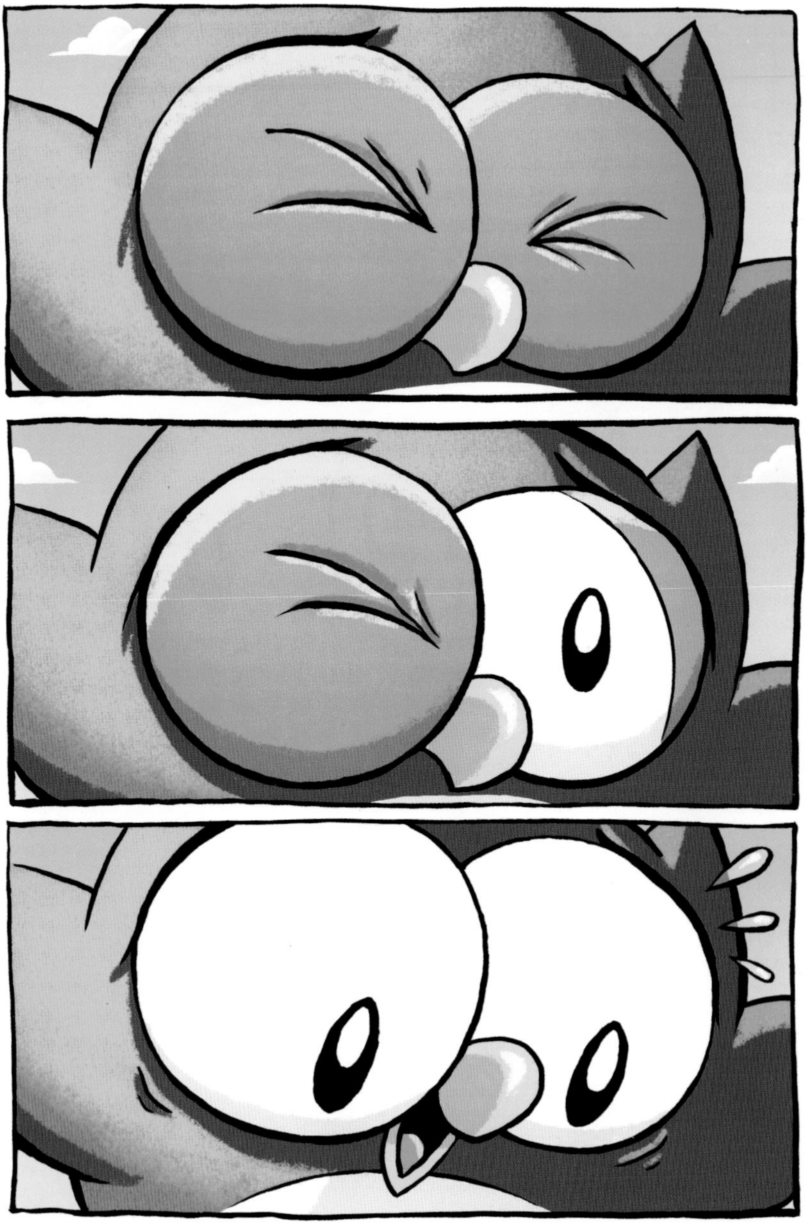

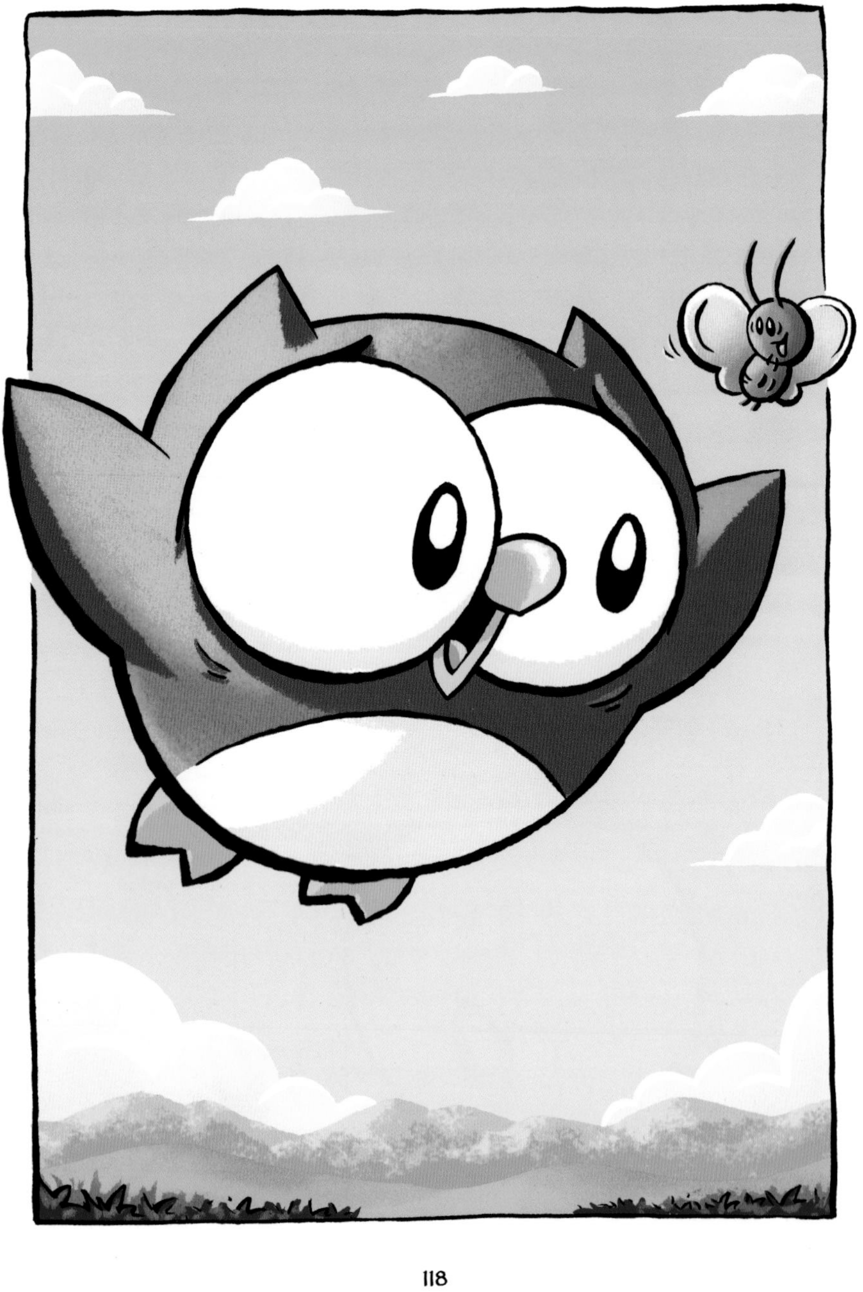

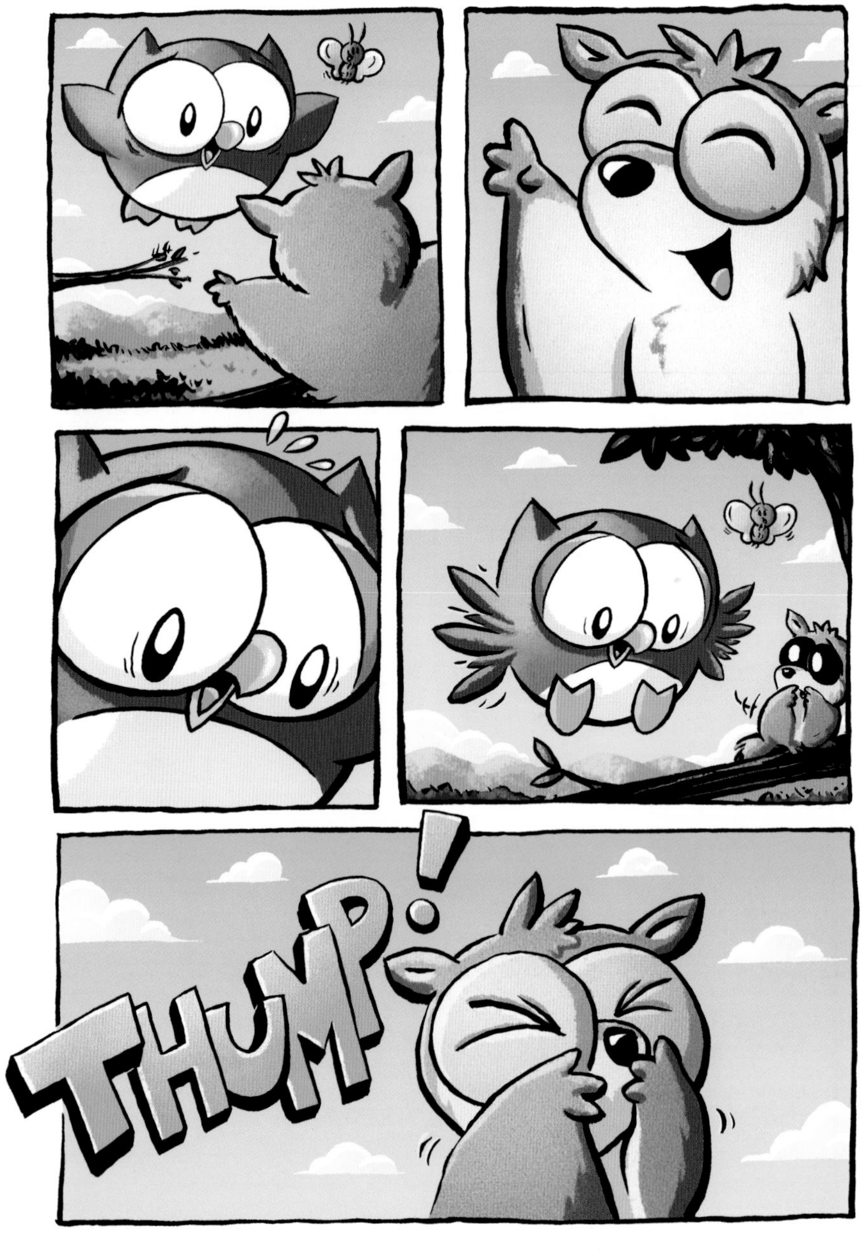
THUMP!

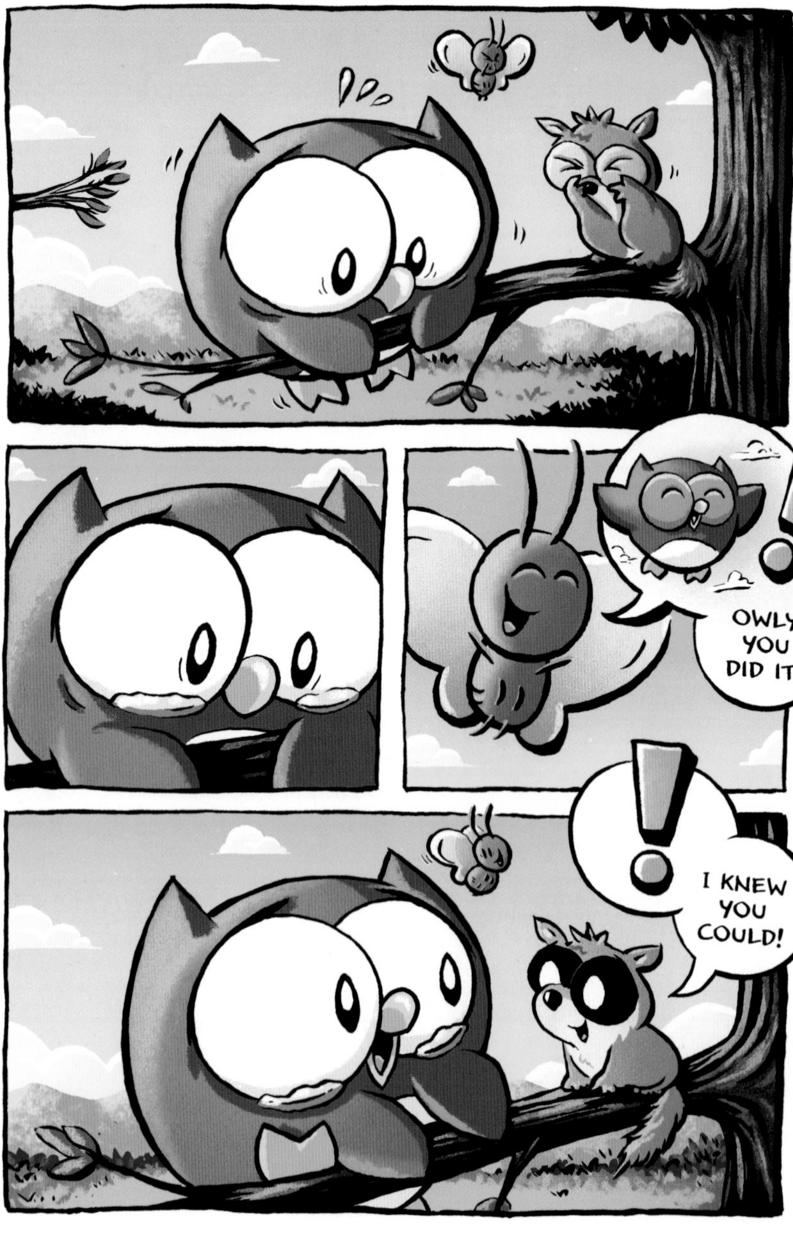
OWLY, YOU DID IT!
I KNEW YOU COULD!

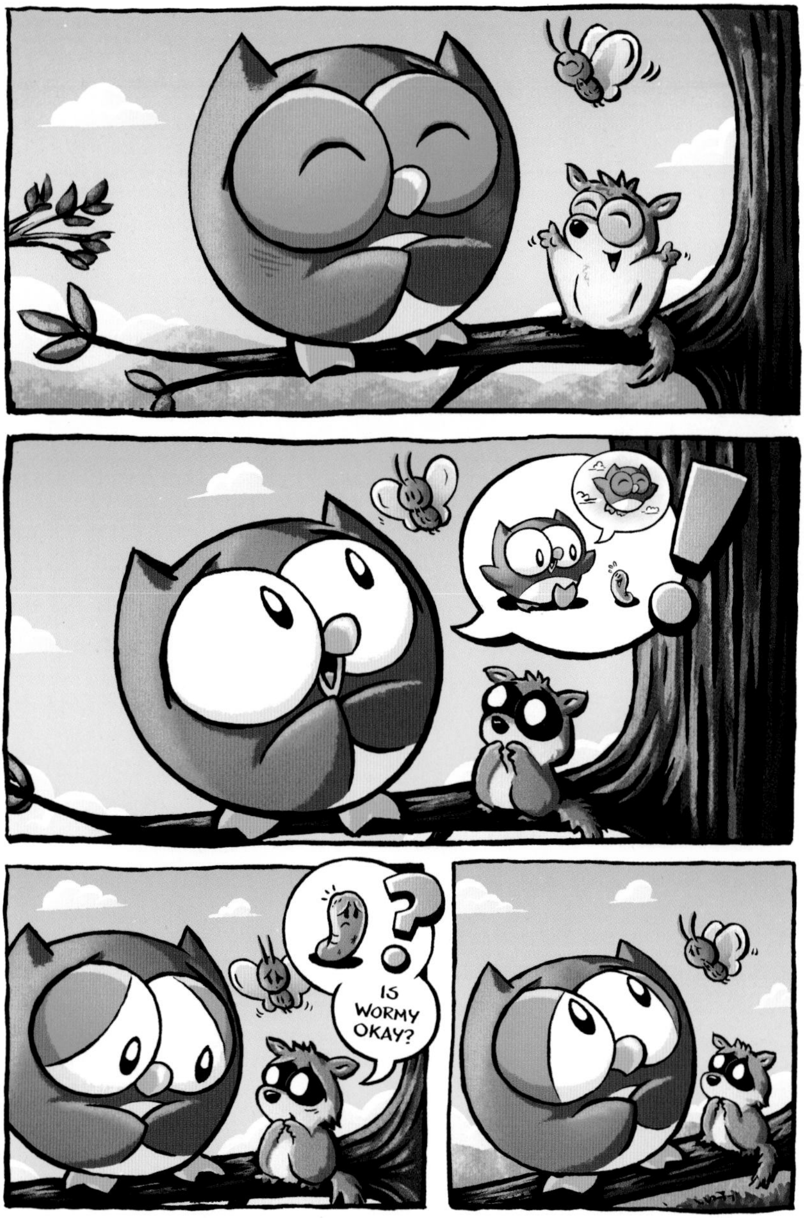
!
?
IS WORMY OKAY?

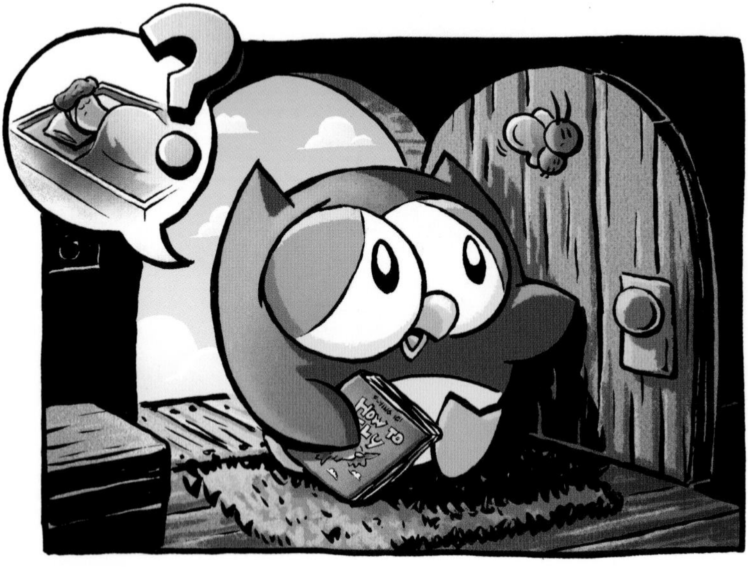
HOW TO

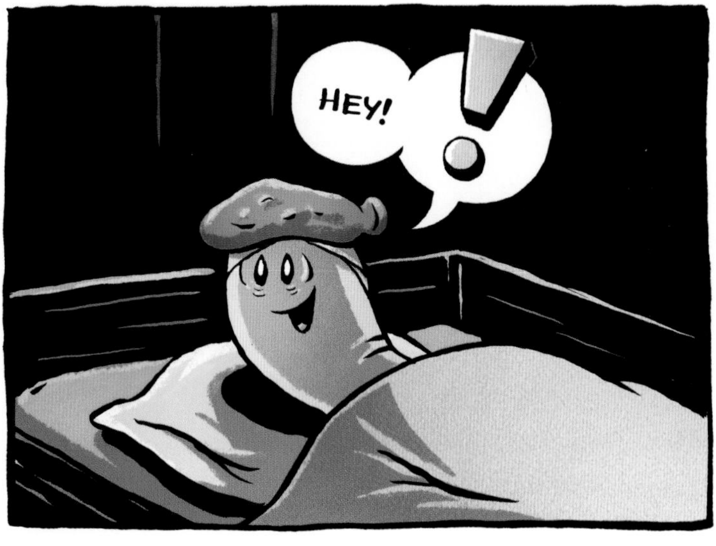
HEY!
!

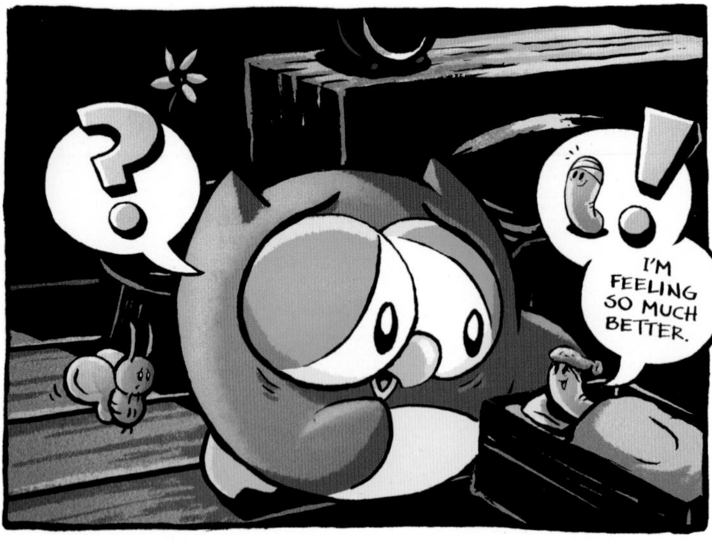
?
!
I'M FEELING SO MUCH BETTER.

?
WHAT'S GOING ON?

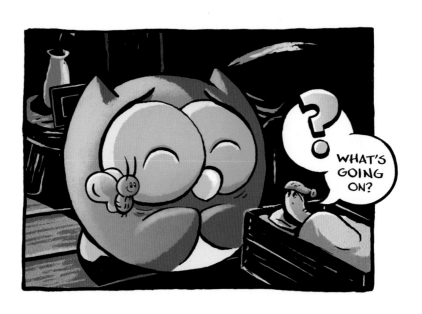

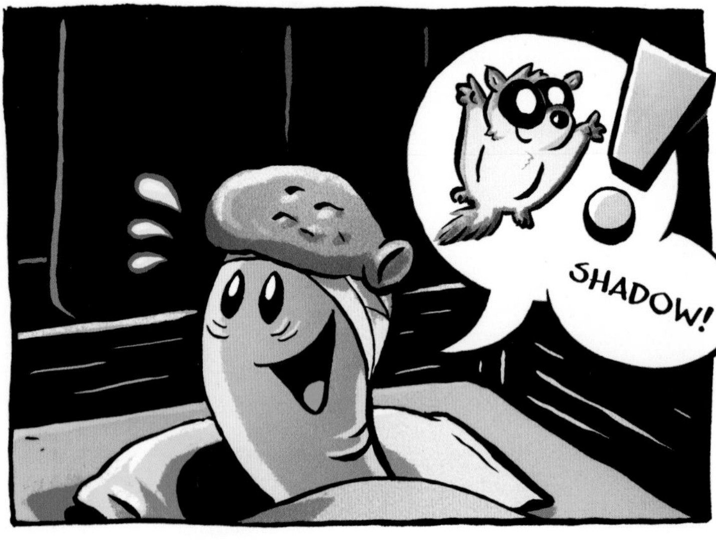
!
SHADOW!

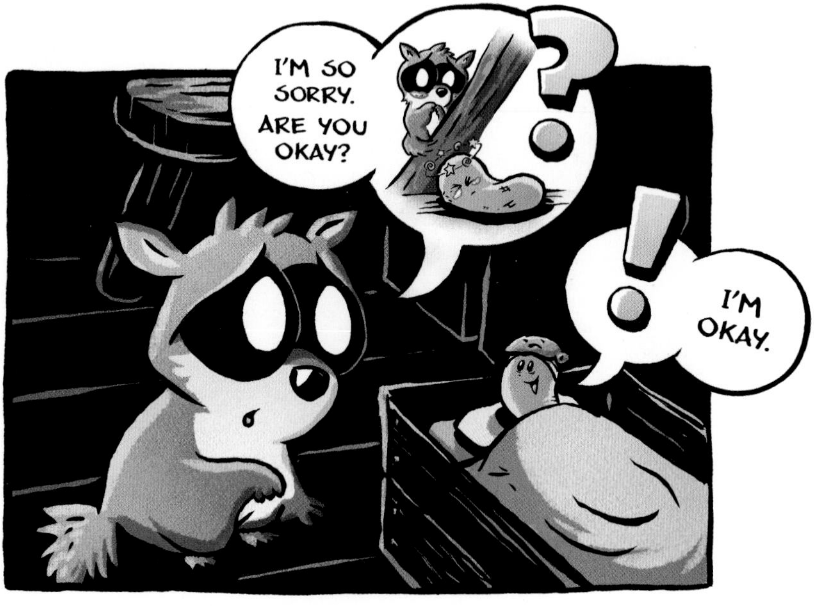
I'M SO SORRY. ARE YOU OKAY?
?
!
I'M OKAY.

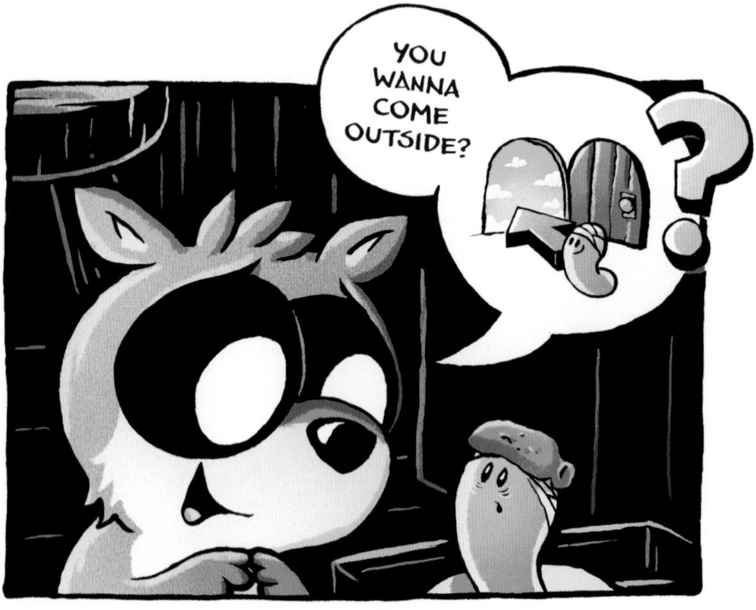
YOU WANNA COME OUTSIDE?
?

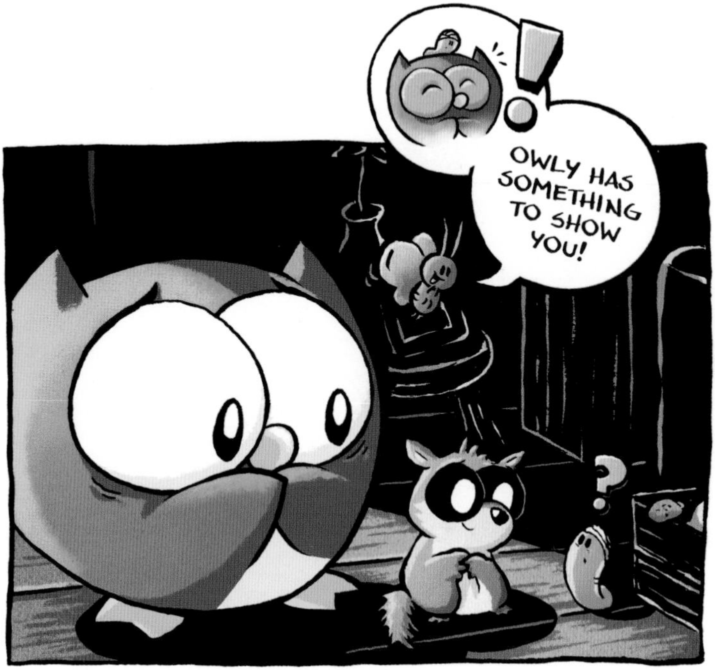
!
OWLY HAS SOMETHING TO SHOW YOU!
?

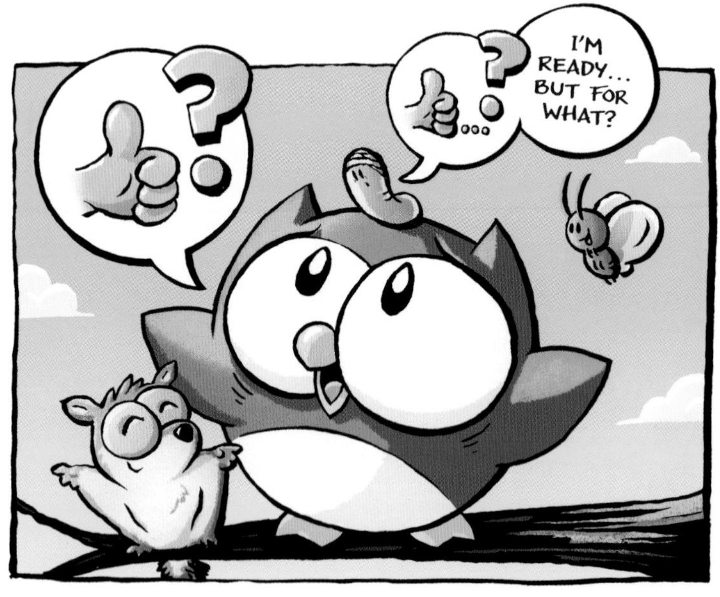
I'M READY... BUT FOR WHAT?

THE
END

Shadow and Flutter help Wormy
try on his new crash helmet.
 C"